The *Writer* and the *Engineer*

The *Writer* and the *Engineer*

A Novel

Niomi Rohn Phillips

Edited by Sharon Harris
Layout and cover design by Tarah L. Wolff

Also by Niomi Rohn Phillips

Growing Up Catholic

Table of Contents

Author's Note

This novel was inspired by the life of romance/mystery writer, Mignon Good Eberhart, and is based loosely on her writing life and her marriage from 1923 to 1948.

Despite my reading in the mystery genre for decades, I had never heard of Mignon Eberhart until my friend, June House, gifted me with a box of memorabilia and suggested the contents might "spark a story."

The box contained a framed photograph, head and shoulders side view, of a beautiful young woman with the hint of a smile, Marcelled hair, dangling earrings, pearl necklace, a sleeveless white gown with a deep V showing her bare back, signed: *Love to Carmen from Mignon;* a small, white, leather-bound 1920 commencement program from Nebraska Wesleyan University; and a novel, *While the Patient Slept,* with the inscription: *For Charles and Carmen/Remembering you with much pleasure and affection/Sincerely, Mignon/Valentine, Nebraska, June 1930.*

"Carmen was my mother," June said. "The novel was Mignon Eberhart's first. She and Mother were sorority sisters."

A cursory google search produced a spark, fired my imagination. Further research inspired a story. Mignon Eberhart's first publication was an essay in the *Engineering News Record,* a significant journal my engineer husband reads today. She divorced her engineer, Alan Eberhart, remarried him, divorced him again, married and divorced a second husband, and remarried Alan, that third marriage lasting until Alan's death in 1978.

In the years from their first marriage to the third, Mignon Eberhart wrote twenty-eight novels and earned enough money to live lavishly. Despite this publishing and financial success, she is virtually unknown to twenty-first century readers, although she published fifty-nine novels (1930-1988), numerous serials in women's magazines, short stories, plays, and movie scripts. She was referred to as "America's Agatha Christie" though she resented that appellation.

The Writer and the Engineer is fiction. It is not a factual account of Mignon Good Eberhart's life. I imagined myself in Mignon Eberhart's world, meeting the artistic icons of her time, struggling with her marriage, writing in what one editor called the "Golden Age" of publishing at a time when the relationship between writers and their editors and publishers is in sharp contrast to the writer's world today.

I have changed the names of the main characters in this story. The events and relationships in the case of factual names are fabricated. Any resemblance to actual persons, living or dead, is coincidental.

Niomi Rohn Phillips

The *Writer* and
the *Engineer*

1922-23

The Beginning

He seduced her with the dance. They moved in sync. He dipped her low to the floor, then pulled her up with one smooth move on the fading notes of "Whispering." They stepped apart and stood in comfortable silence, waiting for the next set. He held his hands out and moved her deliberately, effortlessly, into a waltz. A firm lead, easy to follow. She had never felt as graceful. She looked over his shoulder and saw her sorority sisters, Carmen and Grace, on the sidelines, smiling, pointing Mignon and Alan out to their companions.

Mignon learned later that even as a boy Alan left nothing to chance. Before he left the cornfields of Illinois for college, he had asked his mother to get him an etiquette book. Before he ventured onto Lincoln's social scene, he'd taken dancing lessons.

Between sets and the first strains of Paul Whitman's "Love in Avalon," she couldn't resist asking, "Is there an Avalon in your past?"

He squinted, looked puzzled, hesitated. Then smiled. "What do you mean? I don't know what you mean."

That might have been an omen.

1

Just weeks before that dance, Mignon had decided to tell her family that she was not going back to college. She knew it wouldn't be a pleasant conversation, but she didn't want to waste any more time in classrooms. She wanted to be a writer. And her English professors had encouraged her. They said she had potential. The Sunday dinner table after a relaxing day. That would be the time to make the announcement.

She even made an entrance. Mother and Father were already seated, the food on the table. She sat down in her usual place at the walnut dining room table across from her sister Helen, picked up the white linen napkin beside her fork, unfolded it slowly, and put it on her lap, gathering courage, though she'd been going over the speech in her head for days. But then, she just blurted it out.

"I've decided not to go back to college."

"What? What on earth, Mignon." Her mother frowned, her anger reaching her eyes. "You've nearly completed the requirements for the degree."

"I don't care about the degree."

"After all your fussing about the mathematics courses you had to take?"

"You're quitting? What am I supposed to tell my friends?" Helen interrupted.

"Your father and I left Kentucky and came to University Place because of the college. Because of the opportunities for Helen and you."

"You are dropping out? It's embarrassing." Helen again.

"You are throwing it all away." Mother went on and on.

"My sister dropped out? The girls in our set don't drop out, Mimi. They don't leave without a degree unless they flunk out." Helen's squint and frown turned to red-faced fury.

At the head of the table, Father looked from one of them to the other, his bushy eyebrows raised. Didn't try to get a word in edgewise. Bemused or angry? Mignon couldn't tell.

"The degree! I don't care about the degree. I don't want to take any more classes. I don't want to do any more required reading. I want to write and—"

Her mother cut her off. "This writing idea is frivolous."

"My professors encouraged me. Told me the novel I started had promise."

"You flatter yourself. Hemingway? Fitzgerald? Your idol, Wharton?" Helen laughed.

"No, but maybe Agatha Christie. She's earning great sums. Or Mary Roberts Rinehart. Mother, even you are subscribing to *Ladies Home Companion* to get the latest installment of her romance mysteries."

"Impulsive as always." Helen's knife and fork clattered on her plate. She slapped her napkin next to them.

"Enough." Father pushed his chair away from the table and stood up. "It's her life." He turned and left the dining room. And that was that.

Mignon moved out of the sorority house and back to her bedroom under the eaves of the two-story colonial on University Place. Back to living with her mother and father.

"The Lincoln library has an opening at the reference desk," Helen told her with more than a hint of sarcasm. "Unless you intend to live like a reclusive Emily Dickinson. They might hire you with your college English background."

They did—eight to five, Monday through Friday. More working hours than she had planned on for a writing career, but she bought a supply of the orange Rhodia notebooks Edith Wharton used, determined to sit at her desk and work on that novel she had started in Creative Writing class.

Carmen and Grace were at Wesleyan finishing their senior year, so she could still attend Kappa Alpha events, and Helen harassed her into participating in alumni activities and the University Place social scene.

"You have to stay in circulation, or you won't meet anyone," she said.

Meeting *someone* wasn't on Mignon's agenda, but dancing was, and it didn't take much of Helen's nagging for her to go the monthly dance at the Masonic Lodge.

And that was where she met Alan Edwards.

She couldn't help but notice him that evening, waiting for a valet, leaning casually against a red Pierce Arrow Coupe. Cigarette in hand. Hat pushed slightly back from his forehead. He smiled at Carmen and Mignon, fully aware of their interest and the furtive glances of other women passing by.

Mignon watched him inside the Lodge, standing amidst a group of chattering women at the edge of the ball room, attentive, glancing from one woman to another. Silent. Perhaps a bit smug. The new man in town. He looked up, broke away from his admirers, walked across the ballroom and asked her to dance.

She had to look up. He was nearly a foot taller than her 5'3"—broad-shouldered, a blond giant. He held his hand out and introduced himself. "Alan Edwards."

They made the usual small talk of first acquaintance. *What brings you to the dance? Where are you from? What do you do? What brings you to Lincoln?*

He gave intense attention to her flippant responses. Looked at her—concentrating. Serious. A serious type. Slow to smile but his blue eyes lit up when he did.

And then the dance. He took her hand and led her to the spacious, polished floor. The music began and he moved into the elegant steps of that "Whispering" fox trot. A break and then a waltz, the bunny hug, and the Charleston. He danced perfectly. The lead that made his partner look good. They both looked good, though he danced with a studied seriousness, not the laughing abandon of her usual partners.

The next day he dropped in at the library. "May I give you a ride home?" he asked. He walked her to that smashing red car and handed her in for the ride. She tucked her skirt around her legs. He shut the door. She took a silk scarf from her handbag and wrapped it around her dark waves as he backed out of the parking lot and moved onto the street. He picked up speed, and she reveled in the rush of warm autumn breeze and the falling red and gold leaves floating by. He turned to her and smiled. Pleasure shared. They didn't need to chatter. He pulled into the driveway and up to her house.

"Do you like movies?"

"I do."

"If you're free Saturday, *Robin Hood* is playing. Women seem to like Douglas Fairbanks."

"Better that than the *Headless Horseman*. Also playing now, I hear." She teased. "You probably enjoy Will Rogers, but a movie about Ichabod Crane isn't appealing."

"Dinner at Chatauqua Bar?"

They made a date for Saturday dinner and the movies.

The week dragged. The hours at the library were long and tiring, but she did retreat to her room after dinner in the evenings with good intentions. The pages of the fledgling novel were scattered on the desk she'd set up in the alcove of her spacious bedroom. But the hum of her parents' conversation on the backyard porch below distracted her, and she daydreamed. He was so good-looking. Interesting too. And intelligent. Well, how could she tell that after a dance and a drive? But she wasn't ready to meet "the person." She hadn't counted on this interruption in her plan. But a date didn't mean anything. Just fun and entertainment.

He arrived promptly at 6:00 that Saturday evening. From the front porch window, she watched him walk up the sidewalk. Long strides. He gazed at the house and turned to survey the surroundings—the wide, manicured green lawn, pruned hedges surrounding the house, Mother's cutting garden in the distance.

Their housekeeper Dorothy answered the door, but her mother appeared immediately for introductions. Alan doffed his fedora and held his hand out.

And after that prescient evening, Mignon abandoned the desk she had set up with such determination and put aside her recently assumed Edith Wharton persona, along with the Rhodia notebooks.

Alan was a moving picture buff. Saturday evenings they had dinner at the University of Nebraska's Alumni Club and went to the movies. They saw all the major moving pictures and the popular actors: Douglas Fairbanks in *Robin Hood*, Buster Keaton in *Cops* and *The Frozen North*, Lon Chaney in *Flesh and Blood* and *Phantom*.

The first time they went to the pictures, Alan called her attention to the soundtrack. "Listen to that piano." He leaned close to whisper as the opening credits appeared on the screen. Piano music in the background.

"I always wanted to play the piano. Take piano lessons," he said. "My sister took piano lessons."

"Did you ever ask your parents about piano lessons?"

"No." He paused. "I guess it didn't occur to me. Piano lessons were for girls. I played trumpet in my high school band. Considered majoring in music. My grandfather advised engineering. Engineering to earn a living. Music as an avocation."

He was quiet then. They had a comfortable silence. When the accompanying music changed from piano to orchestra, he leaned in close. Their shoulders touched, and she felt a glow of warm pleasure. "Listen to the French horn and the clarinets," he said.

She had *never* paid attention to the music in the background. She sat beside him, smiling, intrigued by this interest in classical music, fascinated by his intensity. She didn't grab his hand though she wanted to, nor utter a word of exuberance. She clenched her hands in her lap.

They danced and went to the movies, and she introduced him to what she thought of as her world. He accompanied her good-naturedly to hear William Jennings Bryan and then Carry Nation at the Lindell Hotel in Lincoln. She dragged him to the Omaha Public Library to meet the Nebraska poet laureate, John Neihardt. Later she learned that Alan had lived with his opera-loving aunt and her family in Chicago, and he admitted that he much preferred classical music and opera to theatre and literary events. Especially poetry reading.

Alan's degree from Nebraska U and his position as chief engineer of the Nebraska dam building project made him an especially acceptable suitor to her family. Helen was anxious for Mignon to settle down and join her in the Junior League and the Nebraska Wesleyan alumni associations, take her place in society. Forget the nonsense about being a writer.

Her mother smiled approvingly, beamed actually, that first time Alan came for dinner and held the chair to seat her, then waited for Dorothy to serve everyone before he picked up the proper fork. Father, usually noncommittal about her beaus, wasn't subtle about his approval. "Smart man. Great potential. He would take care of you. And you are used to the good life, Mimi," he said.

She didn't think in terms of being taken care of. She was a modern woman. She expected to take care of herself. Didn't think of herself as privileged though she supposed her father did take good care of her and her mother and Helen. His icehouse businesses were prosperous. They had a lovely home. A place in the community. Father's real love though was the horse auction house. He was a Kentucky farm boy at heart, a Nebraska city man only because, as he told it, her mother had convinced him that the Methodist community of University Place would be a good place to raise their girls. Running the horse auction house was like a hobby, and the stable and the hired boys to take care of their own horses, a bonus she took for granted.

Riding was too dirty, sweaty, and unladylike for her mother and Helen. It was also the one thing she did better than Helen, so she had her father to herself when they galloped over the Sand Hills north of Lincoln several times a week—before Alan.

Alan had never been around horses and wasn't interested in riding. He much preferred his Pierce Arrow.

"Would you like me to teach you to drive?" he asked one sunny Sunday afternoon.

Yes. Mignon didn't hesitate. Everyone seemed to be driving these days. She envisioned herself cruising down the street in that spiffy red car, the tails of her silk scarf floating behind her in the wind.

The city streets were congested and parking in Lincoln a problem, so they took her driving practice to a country road. Alan parked, got out, and opened the door for her. Then he handed her into the driver's seat, shut the door decisively, walked around the front of the Pierce Arrow, and got in the passenger side for her first lesson.

"What about those shoes?" he said. "How can you drive with those high heels? And that skirt?"

"The ribbon ties will keep my shoes on. I'll tuck the skirt under me, so it won't get in the way of the shifter," she said.

"Some basics. You have to coordinate—clutch, gas, brake," he said.

Coordinate. Right. Any of her high school gymnasium teachers would attest to her lack of coordination.

"Put your hands on the steering wheel—ten o'clock and two. Now put your left foot on the clutch. Let it out gradually and simultaneously press the accelerator.

"Gradually! Gradually!"

The car bucked, jumping forward.

"Keep your foot on the accelerator to stop the jerking. Right foot. Right foot!

"Okay. You're moving forward. Now depress the clutch again and push the lever to first gear.

"Move! Depress the clutch again and shift to second. Shift down. Down."

The car lurched like a bucking horse. Her body rammed into the steering wheel.

Alan grabbed the wheel. "It has to be simultaneous!"

He raised his voice. "You're moving forward. Accelerate a little. Put your foot on the gas."

A surge forward. She let out the breath she'd been holding.

"A little gas." And then a near shout. "Shift. Shift! Shift again! Into third gear. Down."

Finally, success! She rolled down the road with a smile—like one of those smartly dressed women in cloche and furs featured in the *Ladies Home Companion* advertisements for the new Buick—*the perfect vehicle for milady's shopping.* Though she had no desire to be one of those grocery-shopping, kid-toting ladies.

Driving a motor car was a different kind of freedom than racing across the hills and prairie on a horse. The highway stretched way ahead. "I can see the world from Nebraska," she told Alan. "And I want to see the world."

He smiled. Didn't respond. She didn't know if he shared her hunger for new places and experiences. Was he content to work in rural Nebraska?

She did know that he was a patient man. Gentle. Always calm. He never went off on a tangent. Thought before he spoke, considered all the options before he acted, always in control, unlike her impulsive self. He was never flippant. Complimented her often, always in a serious tone. "You look nice." "I like that dress." "You have a good head."

He's a good listener. He's interested in my opinions. Unlike most men I know. College boys. He grounds me. And he's dependable. She thought about all that and about his chaste kisses. Tried to ignore what was missing. Her romantic ideas about passion were probably idealistic, the figments of an overactive imagination and too many romance magazines. *Passion will grow,* she thought. She comforted herself with *He is just being respectful.* Her friends envied her his impeccable manners. Such a gentleman.

The weeks went by. Alan Edwards and Mignon Starks became an item.

She and Carmen laid on her bed with the windows open, cigarette smoke hovering as they practiced exhaling smoke rings. "Don't let him get away," Carmen said.

She didn't want him to get away. Didn't know what she wanted.

"Have you told him about the hysterectomy?"

"The hysterectomy? The hysterectomy isn't even on my mind."

"Well, it should be," Carmen said. "He's serious about you. He has a right to know."

If she didn't talk about it, it would go away. *You're like an ostrich about anything unpleasant,* her mother had told her more than once.

Sophomore year at Wesleyan, Mother had taken Mignon to a doctor for the stomach cramps and profuse bleeding that put her in bed a couple days a month. Mother and Helen were of the opinion that horseback riding contributed to the problem. Mignon's "discomfort," as Helen insisted on referring to the debilitating stomach cramps, was simply "the curse" at its worst. And she was a whiner. But Mother did take it seriously.

A nurse at the clinic took her to a small, curtained, closet-sized room. She told Mignon to undress. Then handed her a blue cotton gown, and tied it in the back around her waist and neck. The nurse then led her, shivering, across the hall to a sterile room furnished with a lone high, narrow table. There she helped Mignon step up from a stool and lie on her back. Then she spread Mignon's legs, strapped her feet in metal stirrups, and stepped aside for the doctor.

A stern, officious, white-coated man Father's age swept into the room followed by a cadre of minions. Mignon shivered. She, of course, had never had a pelvic examination. The nurse stood by as the doctor inserted a cold, metal funnel. "A speculum," he informed her, in a voice as cold as the funnel. The pain made her eyes water.

"There is nothing amiss here," the doctor said. "Sometimes women who are overly sensitive or very nervous have chronic pelvic pain," he said, as he spread the speculum open. She squeezed her eyes shut with embarrassment and pain. He withdrew the thing, stepped back. and the nurse helped Mignon get down from the table.

Dressed and sitting with Mother in the doctor's office, she listened dumbfounded when he said, "You're a very sensitive, emotional young woman. I believe I will simply prescribe Laudanum to calm you and relieve your anxiety."

"Laudanum? Her painful menstruation is due to hysteria? To emotionalism? I understood that correlation was discounted years ago," Mother said. "Laudanum? There must be some other solution." She stood up, put her gloves on and walked to the door, motioning Mignon to follow.

"Well, you certainly can be an emotional woman, but that man has archaic ideas. We need to find another doctor," she said as she hurried Mignon down the hall and out the door.

Then a friend of her mother's recommended Dr. Taylor, the chief of staff at St. Elizabeth Hospital in Lincoln. He first surmised that Mignon had an ovarian cyst, but then ruled that out.

"You have massive fibroid tumors in your uterus," he told them after further examination. "I have to recommend a hysterectomy."

He used words like "nulliparous uteri" she didn't understand, and she suspected even her mother didn't, although Mother didn't ask any questions about the surgery itself. It was something about a more complex procedure to remove the tumors for a woman who had never given birth.

"I *am* reluctant to perform the surgery on someone so young," Dr. Taylor said, "but these tumors can become cancerous."

"She won't be able to have children! Are you certain hysterectomy is the only solution? She is only nineteen years old. It's a life sentence," Mother said. "There must be something else you could do."

"Cancer *is* a sentence, Mother. I can't stand the cramps and the hassle of the week-long confinement anymore. I miss class because of it, and I can't even study. And I don't care about children. Housewife with kids is not my dream. I want to be a writer."

Mignon couldn't imagine Alan's reaction to that story and how embarrassing it would be to talk about the details. Despite the disdain Mother and her friends had for Mignon's generation and what the older women called "unbridled freedom," they didn't talk about their bodies. They might expose their legs with short, revealing dresses and abandon themselves in the Charleston, but only loose women flaunted their sexuality or discussed their bodily parts.

And there was no reason to bring up the subject to Alan. She didn't even want to introduce that kind of seriousness into their winter content of music and movies.

Then, the Saturday before Christmas Alan invited her to dinner at the Lindell Hotel, a lovely surprise because the Lindell was the place to be seen in Lincoln, and Alan often had a perverse resistance to that kind of society's expectations. He knew by now though that, unlike him, she loved swanky places.

The maître d' led them to a quiet, sheltered corner of the elegant dining room. The teardrops of the crystal chandeliers reflected soft light onto the silver flatware and crystal wine and water goblets on the white linen tablecloth. She couldn't stop smiling. The maître d' seated her, lit the candles on the table, and stepped away.

Alan realigned the knife and spoon beside his dinner plate. Very quiet. Then he reached across the table and grabbed her hand. "I'm being transferred to Chicago, Mimi. An underground tunnel project . . . a challenging opportunity."

Her dismay was naked. Father always said he enjoyed playing poker with her because her face betrayed her. She didn't know what to say. What Alan expected her to say.

"We've had fun these past months. We have a lot in common. We'd make a good team. I love you, Mimi. Come with me."

His impulsiveness took her by surprise. Not an "I want to ask your father for your hand in marriage" comment or even on bended knee with a little white box from Tiffany's. She obviously got those ideas from romance novels.

Years later she puzzled over that uncharacteristic impulsiveness.

At the time, her mind was a muddle. Marriage. They hadn't even uttered the love word before this night. She hadn't uttered the love word. Marriage. Now she did have to tell him about the hysterectomy. Maybe that would end it. What to say? *Life with me may not be what you envision, Alan . . . We've never talked about having a family, Alan . . . Do you like children, Alan?*

She finally blurted it out. "I should have told you before . . . I'm sorry. . . I need to tell you . . . because of some female trouble, I had an operation when I was in college . . . I can never have children."

He listened intently, elbows on the table, head resting on his hand. Those serious deep blue eyes didn't even blink. Then he leaned across the table and put his big, soft hand on the side of her face. "It's okay," he said. "I love you. It doesn't matter."

It didn't matter then.

They were married at Wesley United Methodist on April 13. Meadowlarks sang. The heady perfume of white and purple lilacs on either side of the church steps sweetened the air. Green of every shade was emerging everywhere—a heart-lilting spring day.

Mignon wore a V-neck, floor-length, white silk dress that hugged her hips and fell to the floor in soft pleats to a swishy train. White satin over-the-elbow gloves and a white fur stole. Her mother's pearl and crystal necklace and a silk headband with crystals completed the ensemble.

She stood with her father at the back of the church and listened with a nervous smile to the first notes of Wagner's "Wedding March". . . Carmen, then Helen, in a procession of measured steps down the white-carpeted aisle, every pew marked with a large white bow. She and Father paused at the double doors. The congregation stood.

"Pretend all these people are naked," Father whispered in her ear, tucking her shaking hand under his arm. She clutched the bouquet of white tulips as they paced the rehearsed, measured steps down the aisle.

Alan, resplendent in striped trousers and a long gray morning coat, met them at the altar.

After the ceremony, they went to the University Club where the receiving line snaked around the room and onto the wide, pillared front porch of the Club. Mignon's mother and father had lived in University Place for thirty years. Her father had businesses in the community, and they both belonged to every town and gown organization. The guests, in suit coat and tails and lovely spring pastel gowns, chatted as they waited their turn in the receiving line to congratulate Mignon and Alan.

They hugged, cheek-kissed, and shook hands for hours, it seemed. Then, the sit-down dinner with speeches and toasts. Like a last act, Mignon left the dining room to change from the wedding dress to her pink going-away suit with Carmen's help. They returned to the ballroom, she threw the bouquet into the waiting hands of her sorority sisters, and she and Alan escaped. Wedding night in the Lindell before leaving on the morning train for Chicago.

She went to the bathroom, changed from her pink suit to the sleeveless, white, long and clingy, diaphanous silk nightgown Helen had given her for her trousseau.

She had anticipated *the* wedding night with trepidation . . . desire . . . anxiety . . . excitement. Carmen and she had once found her mother's college textbook from an anatomy class, and they read with horror and fascination about what happens to a man's genitals. So, she knew what was supposed to happen but not how. No one talked about sex, even her married friends.

Mother's only reference to marriage had been off-hand comments about a "woman's duty and obligation."

In the college sorority house, girls had sat around the bridge table in the alcove-like room they called the smoking room next to the entry, slapping bridge cards down, making bids and commenting *sotto voce* about the girl who came in the front door with tumbled hair and whisker-red face. "She's going to get herself in trouble." Or the girl who slid in the door minutes before curfew. "She sleeps around."

Her married friends had slipped little jokes about their sex lives and about the wedding night into conversations, but they didn't share anything but a secretive grin and banal comments, such as, "you'll find out for yourself."

Alan smiled when she came out of the bathroom. Embarrassed and self-conscious, she slipped into the feather bed. He undressed, and methodically put his suit coat on a wooden hanger, folded his trousers onto another hanger, and hung both in the closet.

His body was beautiful—broad shoulders, flat belly. He got into bed beside her, kissed her forehead and hugged her tenderly. He moved closer. His naked body next to hers. She was stirred with pleasure. He put his tongue between her lips in a deep kiss. She tingled— from lips to groin. And then . . . nothing more.

"A long day," he groaned and moved away.

"I'm sorry. I'm sorry." She brushed embarrassed tears. Was there something she needed to do? What was she supposed to do? Had she done something wrong?

What was a woman supposed to do? She cursed her naïveté.

He got out of bed, avoiding her eyes, and stepped into navy-blue silk pajama pants, then put the jacket on and buttoned it slowly, one button at a time. Back in bed, they cuddled, like spoons in a silver chest, and fell asleep. And that became their nightly ritual.

1923-25

Chicago

Chicago was a mecca for the girl from Nebraska. Mignon and Alan rented a two-story frame house in Oak Park with a lawn that swept from a curving driveway to a double-doored front entrance and majestic, mature oak trees in the side and deep back yards.

Alan's Aunt Nelle and Uncle Oscar lived nearby.

"I'm so pleased to meet you," Aunt Nelle said when Alan first introduced Mignon. "I thought Alan was never going to settle down and get married. We were beginning to accept him as a pedantic bachelor. No girl ever suited him." She clasped Mignon's hands in hers. "You must be something special. We are so happy to welcome you into the family."

Mignon was impressed and enamored. Aunt Nelle composed opera and art songs, the first woman librettist to have her work performed at the Metropolitan Opera. Alan's cousin Constance taught voice and performed as a mezzo-soprano in the Chicago Civic Opera.

Mignon embraced all of it—from the opera to the speakeasies.

"Meet me and my wife at the Red Ivy restaurant," a work colleague of Alan's told him, on one of their first weekends in the city. Ted and Irene greeted them in the entrance of the Red Ivy and took the lead. The maître d' smiled and nodded as they strode by him. Some of the diners looked up from their plates squinting with questions, mouths pursed in what Mignon assumed was disapproval, as they threaded their way around tables and chattering patrons in the spacious dining room to what looked like a padded door. A leather-faced door, at the back of the room.

Ted heaved it open, and they followed him inside. White-coated waiters carried trays of drinks. Booths surrounded a dance floor. Music. Laughter. Mignon tried for nonchalance.

They settled into a velvet booth, Ted motioned for a waiter, and Irene pulled the heavy, velvet privacy curtains to show Mignon how they worked.

"Al Capone comes here," Ted said. "Rumor has it that there are secret doors and tunnels so he can escape in case of a raid by the police or a rival gang."

"You might get a glimpse of him," Irene said. "Isn't it exciting? Keep your eyes on the booth around the corner. He usually sits in the same place."

"His bodyguards will be conspicuous thugs in black suits," Ted added. "The anticipation is in the air like the cigarette smoke." He laughed. "Is he here tonight?"

The waiter brought their drinks, Mignon's bourbon in a china teacup. She lit a Lucky Strike and determined to get a cigarette holder like the ivory and silver one Irene held and waved for emphasis. Mignon sipped the decadence. Felt the excitement down to her toes. Louis Armstrong was on the stage. She couldn't stop smiling. Alan grinned.

He got up and held out his hand. And they danced.

There was no end of entertainment in Chicago. The Aragon ballroom. The Green Mill Jazz Club. Dancing every weekend. And then The Uptown Theatre opened. People called it a "picture palace."

"Six storied pillars to a dome," Alan read to her from *The Chicago Tribune.* "I wonder what makes it laterally stable? If the dome is supported by those pillars, it has to be laterally supported or the pillars would buckle."

Just what Mignon was thinking . . . not about the Spanish Renaissance style or the fact that it seated five thousand people, but how those columns were supported. Whatever that meant.

Alan was anxious to see the place and bought tickets for the opening of Cecil B. DeMille's much lauded *The Ten Commandments.* But his curiosity about the pillars was only mildly satisfied when they entered the cavernous lobby; he continued to natter on about it as they settled into the red velvet cushioned theatre seats.

He leaned forward in his seat for most of the movie, intent on the organ soundtrack, a Gaylord Carter composition. Mignon wept with the hymn-like music at the end.

"I want to see California," she told Alan after the exodus scenes shot in the sand dunes at Seal Beach and in San Francisco.

"I thought you were happy here," he said.

She was. She was very happy. It was an exciting place. She didn't miss Lincoln. She did miss Carmen.

Wished she could share all this with her.

> June 30, 1923
>
> Dear Mignon,
>
> I am missing you, but I'm sure Lincoln and University Place are far from your thoughts. You finally got away!
>
> I will, no doubt, be spending life in Lincoln. Do you remember Charles Hornsby? We met him at an English Department gathering. He was a new faculty member our junior year at Wesleyan.
>
> I kept running into him at writers' events and the theatre and art exhibits on campus. You know how the same small group of people seems to attend these things. It wasn't love at first sight—more like love evolution! He reads poetry, and we are both reading *Gatsby*, so we can discuss it!
>
> We're planning a late summer wedding, just before Charlie begins the fall semester at Wesleyan and my job at Jackson High begins. I know it's a long drive to Lincoln, but I'm counting on your being my maid of honor.
>
> Oak Park—isn't that the fashionable suburb Ernest Hemingway calls home—when he is at home? The tabloids report that he is in Paris now hobnobbing with his friends the Fitzgeralds and spending time with the other ex-pats at Rue 7 with Gertrude and her Alice. No doubt you will meet them all when you launch your writing career!
>
> I imagine *The Ten Commandments* will eventually reach the hinterlands. I have heard that the music is spectacular. Charlie and I are looking forward to seeing it.

I ran into your sister at an alumni sorority meeting last week. She has taken on the responsibility for the Homecoming activities and looked fabulous as usual.

Call when you get to Lincoln. Keep in touch.

Love, Carmen

Mignon actually enjoyed living five hundred miles from her sister. Helen was one of those women who felt compelled to dominate every conversation. You could hear her piercing voice telling stories with embarrassing dramatic flourishes the moment you entered a room. Everything was "fabulous," "marvelous," "amazing," as she waved her arms and hands in demonstration.

In Lincoln, their social circle was small. They were thrown together, bound to each other, constantly. Helen played Sister Superior. She couldn't resist giving Mignon advice and orders. Never let Mignon forget that she gave up on college and didn't graduate from Nebraska Wesleyan. Now though, Helen crowed that Mignon had married well. Marrying well was important to Helen. She fulfilled their mother's quiet ambition for prominence and recognition in University Place social circles and the town and gown events. Followed Mother's footsteps in PEO, the Junior League, and the Eastern Star. The Alpha Kappa alumnae too. None of that interested Mignon.

Aunt Nelle's social circle did. Like a fairy godmother, she took Alan and Mignon under her wing and included them with her musicians and writers.

Mignon would always remember the Sunday afternoon Aunt Nelle invited them to meet Chicago Civic Opera soprano, Mary Garden, and hear her sing "At Dawning," one of the songs composed by Charles Cadman with Aunt Nelle's lyrics.

Nelle had had a spacious corner drawing room added to their home in Oak Park especially for those musical affairs. Floor to ceiling windows on three sides of the room faced an English garden. The maroon velvet drapes were tied back for the afternoon. Light snow dusted the hedges and the dormant coneflowers and alliums, Russian sage and hydrangeas, a black and white palette in the perennial flower gardens. Sunlight on the sweeping lawn and curving pathways brought bright, snowy light into the room like a background painting for the occasion.

Chairs with maroon velvet upholstered seats were set up for twenty guests, all prominent people in the Chicago music world—the Civic Opera, the Chicago symphony.

Alan had spent time with Aunt Nelle and Uncle Oscar and their entourage all his life, but Mignon was star-struck. Found it difficult to contain her childlike excitement.

Constance sat down at the Steinway concert grand piano in the corner. Mary Garden made an entrance through the double doors from the hallway into the drawing room. She swished into the room wearing a full-length, deep rose-colored gown with lace bodice and cap sleeves, three long strands of pearls around her neck and pearls in her ears. The women's dresses in the room were all beautiful, but hers was a step up.

Mignon's indecision about what to wear to the event had amused Alan that morning. He stood in the doorway to their bedroom smiling, while she tried on one dress after another, tossing the discards into a heap on the bed, finally deciding on a below-the-knee, sleeveless, black-beaded silk.

"You make quite a mess," he said. "Why do you worry? You always look great." He had no idea how important clothes were to women. How they scrutinized each other. Made judgments about all sorts of things based on clothes.

Mignon had never seen Mary Garden off stage. She had never seen her without stage makeup and in costume. The tabloids didn't lie—Garden was stunningly beautiful. Her dark auburn hair was waved in Marcel style, one side pulled back with a diamond clasp. She had full lips; white, perfectly shaped teeth; and big eyes beneath dark, plucked-to-perfection arched eyebrows.

She smiled, nodded at Constance seated at the piano, tilted her head up and turned to face her audience. She opened her mouth, and that lyrical voice filled the room to shivering:

When the dawn flames in the sky I love you
When the birds wake and cry I love you
When the swaying blades of corn
Whisper soft at breaking morn,
Love anew to me is born,

I love you. I love you.

Dawn and dew proclaim my dream, I love you
Chant the birds one thrilling theme, I love you
All the sounds of morning meet,
Break in yearning at your feet.
Come and answer, come, my sweet,
I love you. I love you.

Mignon moved closer to Alan, her bare shoulder against his. She could feel the warmth of his arm through the sleeve of his cashmere suit coat. She grabbed his hand. Overwhelmed with the music. With the day. With joy. With love and longing. *He* was focused—listening, she supposed, to every note and nuance, every tone and undertone, critiquing song and singer. Oblivious to her. Unmoved by her emotion. Her touch simply a tactile gesture, conveying nothing— certainly not stimulating any physical desire. *How long can we go on like this?*

"That was wonderful," Alan said when they got into the car after the performance. She simmered and then burst like a storm.

"How long can we go on like this, Alan? Don't you realize how strange this is? Do you care about me at all? Married people have a physical relationship. Married people have sex." She couldn't control her cracking, shaky voice. "What *is* wrong? Is there something about me you find unattractive? What will change this? What do you want me to do?"

"It has nothing to do with you, Mimi. You aren't doing anything wrong. It's not your fault. Why can't you be content?" He kept his eyes on the road, hands clutching the steering wheel. He wouldn't turn to look at her.

Did only loose women enjoy sex? How was she supposed to know? Osmosis? No one talked about it. She had been content. Sleeping close to him. Legs and feet touching. Waking next to him. It had been new and enough. But now it wasn't.

Music pacified her and soothed their lives. They met Aunt Nelle's friend, composer Charles Wakefield Cadman, who lived with the Omaha and Winnebago Indian tribes in Nebraska to learn their music and had become an expert. He traveled the U.S. and the world lecturing on American Indian music. He'd become famous with his "From the Land of Sky-blue Water" which they heard constantly on the radio. Aunt Nelle had written the lyrics for that melody.

The third Sunday of every month that summer—the fun of Ravinia. "Take the train to Highland Park," Constance said, the first time they went. "We'll meet you there. Bring your bourbon. I'll take care of the rest."

Alan carried the basket with their flask and a bottle of wine as they walked from the train station to the park that first sunny, Sunday afternoon. He grabbed her hand, and they weaved in and out of the chattering throng of laughing men and women.

Constance, Aunt Nelle, and Uncle Oscar met them at the gates which opened onto gentle green slopes.

Groups of picknickers in their Sunday best and holiday moods gathered around tables, sat in lawn chairs, or lounged on blankets facing a large pavilion.

They found an open spot and spread their blanket. Oscar set up a small table, Constance slapped a white tablecloth on it, and like a magician performing for Mignon's delight, produced china plates, silver flatware, and crystal wine goblets from her basket. Then fried chicken and potato salad. Mignon noticed that the foursome nearby had candelabra on their table. What a way to enjoy an afternoon of opera!

Harmony in their life but nagging discord in their marriage. They were newlyweds, but he didn't want sex. *What is wrong with him?* Mignon thought. *With me? Should a woman care this much? Have these feelings?* She tried to comfort herself with the fact that Alan didn't show interest in other women beyond his usual chivalry and courtesy. And life in Chicago was interesting and fun.

One summer Sunday, Alan's engineering friends and their wives invited them to swim at Oak Street Beach, apparently the summer place to see and be seen. The occasion called for a trip to Marshall Field's. Mignon was not quite daring enough to wear the new two-piece bathing suits shown in the fashion pages. Mother always admonished about looking cheap, but she bought matching one-piece suits—also in style—white for her, black for Alan.

"You're more than a little vain, Mimi. You expect me to wear that?" He laughed when she pulled the suits out of her shopping bag. But he wore it. Maybe a little vain himself.

As they strolled the lake front, women walked by and then turned to glance back at him and smile. He was handsome. They made a handsome couple.

Then the lake. Alan jumped in. "C'mon in, Mimi."

She hesitated. Tempted. But a lifetime in Lincoln, the nearest lake miles away, didn't lend itself to comfort in water.

"I can't swim," she said.

"I'll teach you. Jump in."

This was one new experience she hadn't the courage to try. She wouldn't embarrass herself. He finally gave up in frustration and joined his friends for a raucous game of volleyball. They screamed and laughed. Taunted and challenged each other. Mignon watched, envious of the fun. The camaraderie.

She strolled the sandy beach. Then spread a towel and basked in the sun, throwing her sunhat aside with guilt, mindful of her mother's admonitions—"Don't ruin your skin. Ladies don't have tans."

Those Sundays at the lake with Alan's engineer friends and wives or girlfriends became a summer habit. Alan swam and played in the water. She walked the shore. The lake, big as an ocean, was sometimes calm, sometimes angry. White capped waves rhythmically roared ashore. Mirrored her moods. Drowning any other sound.

In the winter they had opera. Alan loved opera. Mignon learned to enjoy it. Their first winter season, they saw Mary Garden in *Salome, Carmen, Manon,*

Cleopatra, and *Tosca.* They also saw her frequently at Aunt Nelle's.

"Don't be surprised by the menu," Nelle said the time she invited them to a small dinner party that included Mary Garden. "She eats only soup, fish or meat, unadorned, and a simple vegetable. Oh yes, two glasses of champagne, exactly two, and fruit for dessert. She's adamant about her diet. No variation. I'll serve the Caesar dressing and the Hollandaise sauce for the rest of us on the side."

When they arrived, Nelle directed them to seats next to Mary at the dinner table. Alan sat down and methodically unfolded his napkin and arranged it on his lap before he turned to her. She watched him, smiling, looked amused.

He held out his hand. "I'm Nelle's nephew," he said when he had finally situated himself. "We met here when you sang Aunt Nelle's 'At Dawning.' And Mimi and I have been going to the opera frequently."

Mary nodded.

"Your voice rivals Lucrezia Bori's." His eyes lit with his rare smile. His solemnity could be charming when it suited him.

"Why, thank you. You know Bori? Where did you hear her?" She beamed. Mary enjoyed the attention of men and was not without her own charm. "Nelle's nephew . . . yes, I remember. You are from Nebraska . . . Tell me. What are you doing in Chicago?"

He launched into an account of the underground tunnel project. Mignon cringed at the excessive, boring detail. Mary listened attentively, her eyes never leaving his, and when he took a breath, she laughed, looked at Mignon, and said, "My father is an engineer."

After that dinner party, she often invited Alan and Mignon to join her in her dressing room on opening nights. She enjoyed discussing her performance with Alan.

"Don't be so flattered or naïve," Mignon told him. "She has legions of admirers and a host of lovers. She probably finds you a unique specimen, the man from the middle of nowhere who knows opera. And you remind her of her father."

He ignored the taunt.

Mary Garden was not only a flamboyant archetypal diva of the Chicago Civic Opera, but also the director—she preferred "Directa." She sang all the modern operas that winter—many of them world premieres: *Pellea et Mélisande, Louise, Salome,* and Massenet's *Aphrodite and Camille.* People commented that her dramatic flair and flamboyance made the new works come alive.

"I only go to the opera when Mary's there because, you know," one of Alan's friends remarked, laughing, "she really is good to gaze upon."

And she enjoyed scandal and sensation. Mignon wasn't the only one who had gasped when John the Baptist's head was brought in on a platter with trumpets blaring in Garden's *Salome.* After the performance Mary said, "I think the audience liked me better though in *Thais.* I wore fewer clothes."

Mignon and Alan saw nearly every Saturday opening performance, and the Sunday reviews were their morning entertainment. Mignon perked and poured coffee, and they settled into easy chairs in the sunroom, leisurely sharing the sections of *The Chicago Tribune.* Alan liked to read to her, things like an anonymous letter: "After many years of study and thought, I have learned why they give grand opera in foreign languages. It is so they may present Massenet's *Cleopatra* without danger of police interference. Compared to it, her *Salome* was demure."

Then, Mary's *Saphro,* later described by a critic as an orgy, proved providential. After the performance, Aunt Nelle and baritone William Beck, who sang the male lead, joined Mignon and Alan for cocktails at the Green Mill. They understood that William planned to meet Mary at her apartment later.

When the phone rang before dawn the next morning, Mignon answered with trepidation. Late night and early morning calls never boded well.

"I need Alan," Mary said when Mignon picked it up. "I need Alan to come. Something terrible has happened. William is dead. The police are here. They think he was poisoned."

That was the beginning of frequent calls for Alan's advice. Threatening notes were taped to the mirror in Mary's dressing room. A revolver was left in her dressing room. She found a knife at her dressing table. A box of bullets was delivered with one missing and a note explaining that the missing bullet was for her. Alan comforted her.

Then she quit performing at intimate soirees. Mignon and Alan saw her less. She quit calling Alan.

She hired a bodyguard. The Chicago worlds of Al Capone and Mary Garden entwined.

In March Mignon's mother and father spent two weeks with them. Her mother had always enjoyed shopping in Chicago. They shopped and lunched in the Crystal Room, enjoyed hours in Marshall Field's trying on clothes. Clothes shopping was the one thing they had always enjoyed doing together. Mother tolerated the short skirts and flares and flounces Mignon wanted for her speakeasy evenings, but frowned with distaste at Coco Chanel's new chemise which was touted as "perfect freedom of movement for dancing." She did approve of the ankle-length and gossamer fabrics of Mignon's choices for the opera.

Her father endured the city for her mother's sake. Mignon and Alan were anxious to show off their city. Took them to all their favorite places including the speakeasies. Mother dropped her haughty reserve and inhibitions and seemed to enjoy this foray into Chicago life. Father had always enjoyed his bourbon, a challenge in Lincoln with Prohibition. He was all smiles and jokes with the dark side of Chicago, amused with Mother's drinking bourbon from a teacup, and the ease of filling his glass. "How dry does a fellow have to get?" he muttered frequently at the Green Mill.

Mignon had hoped Alan's six-month evaluation for this job would guarantee his employment in Chicago for more than a couple years. His supervisor wrote that he was not a flashy engineer, but very conscientious, a detail person.

Not flashy—what an understatement.

However, the Union Station project was completed in record time. Alan applied and accepted a position as chief county and state engineer in Valentine, Nebraska.

Valentine. Back to Nebraska. Not even Lincoln. The Sand Hills. Hundreds of miles from Lincoln.

What would they do in Nebraska? They had music here. And theatre. Friends. Aunt Nelle and Constance. They enjoyed Chicago. They had fun and good conversation and even some contentment.

The frantic social life had compensated, helped her evade the problem in their marriage. Her groin ached. She wasn't bold enough to force the issue, and her tentative, gentle movements to elicit some physical response from Alan were met with warm hugs.

They slept together like they had the first night.

Niomi Rohn Phillips

1925-30

Valentine, Nebraska

Mignon missed everything about Chicago. She wanted to get dressed up on Friday night and go to the opera. Dance and drink bourbon at the Green Mill. There were, of course, no such things in Valentine, Nebraska. Her silks and furs were crammed into the back of a minuscule closet in one of the nicest homes in town, according to the Realtor. The only suitable house available. A two-story clapboard with front and side porches four blocks from Main Street. It wasn't anything like her lovely, spacious Oak Park house.

But Alan embraced it all. The small town. The Sand Hills. The Niobrara River and the challenge ahead for him in building a dam and bridges across it. "This is hunting country," he'd said with a boyish lilt of delight when they first drove the miles and miles and hours and hours across the state from Lincoln to Valentine.

"Just look." His left arm resting on the open window, fingers lightly on the steering wheel, he turned to her, sweeping his right hand across the windshield to call her attention to the treeless emptiness.

"I'm going to need a dog. Can't hunt without a dog. I grew up with a dog," he said. "And I miss having a dog around the house." That afterthought for her benefit. They'd never discussed having a dog.

Surprised by his emotion, Mignon had argued, but half-heartedly. His strong feelings were unusual, infrequent. "I've never had a dog. We didn't have dogs or cats at home. Mother wouldn't tolerate house pets," she said.

"You loved your horses though," Alan had countered. "Dogs are more affectionate than horses. And a dog would be company for you when I have to stay at the bridge sites."

She hadn't agreed, aloud anyway, but the place was like a foreign country and her acquaintances limited to say the least, so when Alan walked into the kitchen a few days later with the puppy in his arms, she was intrigued if nothing else. An English setter, a good hunting dog, a people dog, Alan said. They named him Jericho.

The most active women's organization in the town was the Homemakers' Club. Homemakers. The bank president's wife was the chairman, the school principal's wife the treasurer. Mignon's husband had a responsible position in the community. She must join. They insisted she join. Meet other women. She could learn to sew. Sew!

They also found her a hired girl. A hired girl— housekeeper or maid in other places. That too was an expectation for a prominent man's wife. Rita Rose came to clean and cook and do the laundry with their highest recommendations.

And Mignon had never been so bored in her life. She tried to escape from the place with the books she brought from Chicago and with women's magazines.

"Do you really need all those magazines?" Alan nodded at the clutter of *Ladies' Home Journal* and *McCall's* and *Good Housekeeping* on every table in the living room.

"I *need* to keep in touch with what's happening in the world no matter living in this god-forsaken place. I can at least ask the hired girl to try some of the new recipes. And *Vanity Fair* . . . I don't want to be embarrassed and my clothes out-of-date when I get to the city."

"Your vanity is showing . . . And the *Saturday Evening Post?*"

"They're publishing Mary Roberts Rinehart's short stories. Mother reads her, and I want to see what sells to book publishers and magazine. I want to write, Alan. I need the *Saturday Evening Post.*"

"Well, don't let me stand in the way of your ambition. I'm sure you can do anything you set your mind to. I don't understand your passion. But if that's what you want to do . . ." He pushed a pile of magazines aside and sat down on the sofa with his engineering journal.

Fiction—stories he called what she read—were mysterious to him. His reading consisted of the *Lincoln Morning Star* with his morning coffee and his monthly issue of *Engineering News Record.*

When *The Great Gatsby* arrived in the mailbox a few days later, Mignon escaped to Long Island from her chair in the living room, absorbed in another world. Like the young girl whose mother had scolded, "You're going to ruin your eyes . . . you can't read all day. It isn't healthy. Get outside and get some fresh air."

Mignon envied Fitzgerald—his success, his exciting life, even his notoriety. Reading him was like a nag. She needed to be writing. Like Fitzgerald. But, realistically, maybe in the vein of Rinehart.

She unearthed the novel she had started writing three years ago—before Alan. If she was ever going to write anything, this was the time and definitely the place. There was *nothing* to do in Valentine.

Alan helped her set up a table in the spare bedroom on the second floor which faced west with a view of the Sand Hills and of the sunset. Admittedly a beautiful view. With a desk of sorts, her notebooks, a supply of sharp pencils, and the stack of paper she had been moving around since they married, she was in a place and in a frame of mind to write.

When Alan left that Monday morning, she sat down at the desk, opened the notebook with the novel she had started now more than three years ago, and read. The voice and words were unfamiliar. Like reading the words of a stranger. Did she like it or not? Was it good or not? *The Dark Corridor.* Maybe it would work as a short story for one of the detective magazines, instead of a novel.

This woman sitting at the desk in the Nebraska hills was not the student immersed in college and literary life who wrote *The Dark Corridor.* She was in this strange, desolate place and her life was defined by Wife—

Engineer's Wife. She wrote a few words about that in her notebook. Then the ideas and words flowed. She didn't have the temerity to put her need for sex on that paper but writing about the rest of this strange life was therapeutic and a much easier task than working at a revision of *The Dark Corridor.*

We live in the outback, she wrote. To the south are buttes rising like buttressed castles and canyons. On the north and west stretch the Sand Hills, dotted with sagebrush and yucca and tumbleweed that rolls unceasingly. The Sand Hills meet the horizon. You feel like you could fall out of the sky.

At dusk, the sun's shadows slant and a pink rim 'round the horizon contrasts with the solid turquoise blue of the sky, giving the first hint of approaching night. The sky becomes deep sapphire and then fills with the glimmer of stars.

There is much here though that is anything but beautiful. Winter is wicked. When winter comes, I am desperate to escape to the city.

My husband is a civil engineer. And we are here because of his work. I am obliged to set up housekeeping in this strange place because of his work.

The engineer is not talkative or effusive. He is also modest. In this age of confessions and self-advertising, he has few words to say about himself. For all his literalness of mind, he does have a flame of imagination—and sometimes genius —that I don't understand. Because of his education, his training, and his thinking habits, he sticks to facts. He does not compromise. Reason, logic, proof are the keynotes of his mental processes. Engineering is an exact science.

However, I leap to conclusions. Before my husband makes a decision about anything, he thoroughly explores all the alternatives. He asks—Is this true? Why? What does it prove? And once he makes a decision, it is as firm as the concrete on his bridges and roads. We are very different. I am spontaneous, and I have to admit that all this gathering of information and deliberateness sometimes causes the fur to fly.

Engineers are unique men. Everything must be in order. He has no truck with our housekeeper who puts his shoes in the wrong place or disturbs the order of his pencils on the oak desk in his study. He only tolerates the hair of the dog because, unfortunately, we have no children.

It takes a strong woman to live with an engineer. Serendipity is not in their nature. Neither is metaphor. I really don't care about the construction of bridges. He is not interested in my poetry.

But we enjoy a game of cribbage every evening when he is at home, and we share great pleasure in reading. He isn't interested in the novels I read, but we have traveled the world and enlarged our knowledge of everything from the planets to earth science with his.

She needed to work on the novel, but kept going back to writing about this life in the outback with Alan —Alan the engineer. She knew the engineer. She *thought* she knew the engineer. What she didn't understand was the man. The affectionate, warm, brotherly loving man. *What kind of marriage was this? What was wrong with them? With her?* She couldn't even write the words to describe what was missing in their marriage, what had been missing now for two years. She blushed even thinking about the words for it, much less putting them in black and white, and she couldn't share her distress with anyone.

She wrote and rewrote. Read and revised. And she liked it. Good writing, she thought, as she finished the final draft about her life in Valentine.

She had never submitted anything for publication, but found the publisher's address on the inside cover of Alan's *Engineering News Record* at McGraw Hill in New York and sent the manuscript with the unwieldy title, "And Far Away: The Candid Observations of a Civil Engineer's Wife."

Three weeks later an acceptance letter and a check for $40.00 arrived from Editor Frank C. Wright of the *Engineering News Record*. He would publish the essay in the spring issue of the journal.

She paced from room to room waiting for Alan to get home. Met him at the door.

"My first publication, Alan, in *your* professional journal. And they paid me." She laughed, waving the check in the air.

"Congratulations. I'm proud. You should have a typewriter. You could use that to buy one." And with his usual segue to earth: "I've been thinking about it. I've done some research."

Of course, he had.

He summed it up at the dinner table: "Four companies make good portable typewriters. But the Underwood and the Royal are best," he said. "From what I've read, the Underwood's touch is more solid and precise. More uniform than the others. But the Royal is lighter, snappier. You might like the finish better too. It has a brown wood-grain hand-painted look. A trip to Lincoln must be in order."

"I thought you were too busy to leave Cherry County and your bridge projects."

"Maybe it's time to take a few days off. I can check in at the State Highway Department Office in Lincoln."

"Just tell me when we can leave," she said. It wasn't Chicago, but it was "city."

When Rita Rose arrived the next morning, soon after Alan left for his bridge, Mignon told Rita that she didn't intend to retreat to her writing room. "And you don't need to dust and vacuum either. You can help me pack for a trip to Lincoln."

They climbed the narrow stairs to the attic under the eaves where the neglected traveling bags were stored—the dust a witness to months' long disuse. Rita helped Mignon drag Alan's large tweed and leather suitcase, the largest of her collection of leather bags, her cosmetic case, and her hat bag down the stairs.

Ordinarily silent and timid, creeping around quietly cleaning and cooking, Rita clapped her hands and laughed as Mignon flitted from one closet to another, trying to decide which dresses and hats and shoes to take. "You are so excited, Missus."

"I know. I am excited. A few days in the city! You must see Lincoln someday, Rita. Restaurants, theatres, dance halls. I wonder where we will go for dinner. What play might we see? Music? Even dancing?" She ran her hands through the filmy skirts of evening dresses in the closet. "We haven't danced for months."

She hadn't thought about the city and the things she loved about city living until a reprieve was imminent.

Writing had so occupied the days, she had quit dwelling on the rural foreignness of Valentine.

Alan came home in the midst of her packing. Stood in the doorway of the bedroom watching her flit from the closet to her open suitcase.

"Aren't you excited about going to Lincoln?" she said. "Aren't you excited about a couple days in the city? Getting away?"

He shrugged, noncommittal. Was he ever excited about anything? Was his self-control so absolute? He punctured her enthusiasm. Made her feel like a child.

Early morning, Rita packed sandwiches and fruit in a basket. Filled a thermos with coffee. Mignon and Alan loaded the suitcases into the back seat of the Pierce Arrow and set off for the day-long trip to Lincoln. Mignon spread a map of Nebraska out on her lap and traced the route: three hundred and six miles from one corner of the state to the other. Three hundred and six miles. A diagonal across the state from the northwest to southeast. Valentine was at the northern edge of the Sand Hills, and the Sand Hills spread before them in the distance like an ocean.

"It will take us seven or eight hours," Alan said.

A world away. From a village of one thousand five hundred people in this back country to her city of fifty four thousand.

Alan tipped back in his seat, put his foot on the gas, and pushed his treasured vehicle to its limits. Mignon leaned over frequently to check the speedometer.

"This is like riding a bucking horse, and you are up to forty-five miles per hour," she complained.

"It's the gravel roads. Always rough driving. We'll get onto the pavement in a couple hours."

They arrived at her mother and father's home in University Place just outside of Lincoln in time for dinner.

The next day she met Carmen for lunch at Nebraska Wesleyan faculty club, where Carmen had entré as Professor Charles Hornsby's spouse. They rushed towards each other in the lobby and wrapped arms in a tight hug.

"Here we are," Carmen said, stepping back and taking in Mignon from head to toe. "I've missed you so much."

"Me, too." Mignon looked at her. Hatted and gloved. Both of them dressed up for lunch in the city. They grinned in one of those "we are turning into our mothers" recognitions.

"Tell me about Charlie and all about your life," Mignon said, after they'd settled at a table in the dining room.

"I didn't know it could be so wonderful to live with someone, be with them day after day."

Mignon looked at her lap and pulled her white gloves off, one finger at a time.

"He is so intelligent. I knew he was smart, of course, but I just realize it more every day. He's a great conversationalist and has such a sense of humor. We like the same books!" Carmen grinned, talking with her hands, leaning across the table. "We read and discuss books. He's so serious and then he's sexy." She blushed.

"I didn't know how wonderful sleeping with someone could be. You didn't tell me about the bedroom part."

No. Mignon hadn't told her anything. "It's different for everyone," Mignon said, rearranging the forks, lining up the knife and spoon. Afraid to look at Carmen. "Marriage is different for everyone. We have wonderful times together." She searched for words, sick to her stomach with envy. "We have some challenges, that's what Alan calls them."

Carmen heard the words, but she didn't hear.

The waiter arrived with their Waldorf salads. He set a plate with the bed of lettuce, green grapes, and red apple slices for each of them on the table. When he stepped away, Mignon moved the conversation on to the evening.

"I assume you're going to Symphony at St. Paul's tonight. Mozart."

"Yes. Premier performance," Carmen said. "We *are* excited."

"Mother and Father are joining us. And I get to dress up," Mignon said. "Long gown and gloves. Do you realize how long it has been since I had a reason to dress up?"

Carmen laughed. Mignon wouldn't get any sympathy about her life in Valentine from Carmen. Too wrapped up in her own new wonderful perfect life.

Alan joined Mignon after lunch to shop for the Royal typewriter and then back to Mother and Father's for dinner and the evening at the symphony. Music the balm and the emotional connection for them.

Most of Mother and Father's set were there, people Mignon had known since she was a girl; sister Helen and her husband, of course; and college friends who lived in the area.

The second day in Lincoln, she had her hair done, they dressed up again, and stepped out on the dance floor at the Cornhusker, Lincoln's newest and latest hotel ballroom. Alan hadn't lost his light touch in their months in the outback, nor the warm smile he always wore when he twirled her 'round to face him in the waltz. She wondered again why he didn't feel more than that warm smile. Why the emotion didn't lead to anything more.

Back home, Alan off to his dam site, Mignon sat at her desk and delved into a copy of Michael Joseph's *The Commercial Side of Literature,* a guide to writing and publishing she'd picked up at the University of Nebraska bookstore. In the first pages Joseph wrote that if he had to nominate one type of novel or series of stories that would provide the most promising opening for a new writer, it would be the detective story.

That was Mary Roberts Rinehart's secret of success —detective stories with a hint or more of romance. Even Carmen was reading her books.

Joseph also said that publishers were so keen to discover new talent they gave as much attention to the promising manuscript submitted directly by an unknown author as to one sent under the imprint of a leading agent.

That information and the acceptance from *Engineering News Record* gave Mignon confidence. She went to work revising *The Dark Corridor* and mailed it to *Flynn's Detective Weekly.*

When she saw the return label on a letter a few weeks later, she ripped the envelope open right there in the Post Office and waved it at Mr. Peterson, the postmaster. "They accepted my story and sent me $300." He grinned.

It would have been "unseemly," one of her mother's common admonitions, to skip the six blocks home, but she felt like skipping. Another publication. A *paid* publication. Affirmation. Her insides bubbled. Now the novel.

The desolate Sand Hills were the perfect setting for a murder, but she couldn't come up with a plot for the place. The old mansion and the gloomy grounds of the hospital in Lincoln kept coming to mind. And the nurses. Rinehart had written a couple popular novels with a nurse detective.

Summer of her sophomore college year, after that hysterectomy, Mignon had spent ten days at St. Elizabeth Hospital, a sprawling, old mansion of red brick and ivy built in the nineties by the wealthy Nebraska Thatcher family. The hospital, which was also a training school for nurses, had retained the solid walls, the gumwood and walnut woodwork, and the large, old-fashioned rooms of a magnificent mansion.

Mignon had a private room after her surgery. The days dragged. The nights were endless. Most of the patients were sleeping, the work on the wards minimal, so Sarah, one of the night nurses in the training program, would check on her and stop to talk. They became friends.

"You're here *every* night?" Mignon asked.

"This is my assignment, and I live here," Sarah said. "Sometimes in the training program, we work eleven hours a day."

"Every day?" Mignon couldn't imagine that kind of work.

"Six days a week for three years. No pay, but I've wanted to be a nurse since I was little. After these three years, I will get a diploma and can take the Nebraska licensure examination."

"Do you live in the hospital?"

"In a dormitory. It isn't too much different than your sorority house—a sisterhood of sorts like yours. Not a sisterhood of nuns! The nuns don't live with us, though some of the rules are convent-like. We are to 'maintain discretion, daintiness, and self-control.'"

"Daintiness . . . sounds like a doily. I can't imagine it!"

"I forgot 'courtesy.' Maybe you noticed. We have to stand when a physician walks into the room. Oh, yes, and leaving the hospital or the dormitory without permission from the house mother is considered immoral and grounds for dismissal. Sister Dominique also warns us repeatedly about getting involved with male patients, as if anyone in a hospital bed would be appealing."

Remembering that and thinking about Sarah, Mignon decided she wanted to create a strong woman protagonist in contrast to the young nurses she met in the hospital. She would tear down the whole submissive, subservient, demeaning role.

She spent every morning working in her room with the view of the Sand Hills. When Alan came home after his day's work, Rita Rose served dinner and then he settled into his easy chair in the living room. Sat across from Mignon, Jericho at his feet. He lit a cigarette, prepared to listen to what she'd written that day. He gave her his full attention. His eyes focused on her, listening, concentrating. Sometimes, when she read descriptions of the hospital, he interrupted with a miniature lesson on the qualities of concrete or the bearing walls of the building. He was too literal for metaphor and psychology, but he was perfect for catching implausible facts or a faulty sequence of events. And he appreciated and complimented what he referred to as her "skill with words."

She finally finished. Wrote the title on the first page —*The Patient in Room 18*. She couldn't resist walking up the stairs to look at that stack of pages on her desk several times a day, reveling in the satisfaction of the accomplishment. But she had no idea where or how to get it published.

Joseph's *Guide to Publishing* listed eight publishers. For no significant reason besides liking the alliterative name, she decided on Doubleday, Doran, and Company in Garden City, New York. Then she spent an entire day writing and rewriting, changing words and sentences in a submission letter. Finally, signed her name, wrapped the manuscript in heavy brown paper, tied it with string, and walked downtown to the little Post Office, smiling all the way.

She was a novelty and curiosity in Valentine—a citified woman who didn't do her own housework and who was purportedly writing a book. The postmaster, Mr. Peterson, presiding as he did over the town news and gossip, had never known a writer.

"We have to put enough postage on this so it will reach New York with the least delay," he said like a co-conspirator. "There's insurance too. It won't cost you much. I think we should do that. We don't want these precious pages to get lost."

She just smiled and fumbled for the wallet in her black leather purse.

She counted the days, waited two weeks after the momentous mailing, and then checked the mailbox anxiously every day. She had no idea how long she would have to wait, what to expect, how timely editors might be in reviewing and responding to manuscripts. She had no idea how the publishing world worked. Four weeks later she got the response:

> October 5, 1927
>
> Dear Mrs. Edwards,
>
> Doubleday is pleased to accept your novel, *The Patient in Room 18*, and I have been assigned your editor. I have been with Doubleday for over a decade and represent many writers including Stephen Benet, Upton Sinclair, and William McFee.

You will be hearing from me regarding the editing process and the publication time lines. You will want to secure an agent's services to help you monitor the publisher's accounts and help you manage things like the earnings due from Doubleday. We advise you to affiliate with the literary agency Brant and Brant of New York City.

Women writers will find your Sarah Keate an interesting protagonist and the plot engaging. I look forward to working with you, and I hope you are writing a sequel.

Sincerely,

Harry Maule, Editor

An editor. Her own editor. A literary agency. She sang inside and talked to the dog. "I can and will produce more than one story, Harry Maule."

With Alan at the dam site most weeks, Jericho was her constant companion. Ironic because it was Alan who had lobbied for a dog. "A dog would be company for you," Alan said. And he was. Company and comfort even in storms.

She woke up one night when a crack of thunder shook the house. Felt her way down the hallway to the living room. Lightning flashed through the closed draperies. She pulled the cord—frightened but too fascinated to move. Thunder rolled and roared like a drum overture above the inky black clouds. Lightning blazed in crooked streaks, flashing nonstop, illuminating the sky over the Sand Hills. The lights flickered. What would she do if the electricity went out? Wind lashed tree branches against the side of the house. Was it the straight-line winds locals talked about? A tornado? Her heart was beating with panic. Her breath nearly a pant. She felt Jericho nuzzle against her leg. She calmed down and realized she had the beginning of her next novel. And a title. Nurse Sarah Keate would wake up and be as frightened as Mignon was. She would put Sarah Keate in a spooky, ancient mansion this time with a comatose patient and the tumult of a summer storm—*While the Patient Slept.*

Life changed. Took on new and surprising dimensions soon after Doubleday published the *Patient in Room 18.* The Nebraska Writer's Guild invited Mignon to conduct a round table discussion on the mystery novel at their spring meeting at the Cornhusker Hotel in Lincoln.

"I've only written one mystery novel, Alan. I can't believe they'd ask me to do this. They assume some expertise I don't have. I don't know if I can do this."

"You should be flattered," Alan said. "I've heard you talk about the people who belong to it. Isn't this a prestigious organization in your literary world? You can't decline."

The Guild *was* a prestigious organization in the literary world. Beth Streeter Aldrich, Dorothy Canfield Fisher, John Neihardt, Louise Pound, and Mari Sandoz had founded it just four years before, and Willa Cather even signed up from New York.

Mignon met Carmen for lunch at the Cornhusker Hotel as usual when Mignon and Alan made one of their infrequent trips to Lincoln. After greetings and hugs and settling at a table, Mignon, near quivering with excitement, pulled a signed copy of the *Patient in Room 18* out of her handbag. She handed it to Carmen across the table. "Here it is," she said. "Thanks for believing I could do it."

"Congratulations. I am really proud of you." Carmen squeezed her hand. "I was afraid you'd given the writing dream up after you met Alan. And then that sybaritic life in Chicago. Nebraska is where you belong. Where you can work."

Mignon beamed. "Chicago was an intermission."

They parted after lunch and Mignon met Alan for a "by invitation" reception at the executive mansion hosted by Governor and Mrs. Weaver. Then, dinner at the University Club, now housed on the top floor of the new prestigious Stuart Building. A whirlwind day ending with a chanted recital of Vachel Lindsay's poems. A perfect ending. Mignon was delighted. Alan endured.

"We don't see enough of you," her mother scolded and hugged, when they finally arrived back at the comfortable old house on University Place. She and Father were anxious to hear all about the day. He passed the tumblers of bourbon, and Mignon and Alan settled on a sofa in the living room to give them every detail of the luncheon with the governor.

Ordinarily, Mignon slept soundly in her virgin girlhood bed, where she wouldn't have indulged in sex if it had been offered. It wasn't. But she tossed and turned, checking the clock every couple of hours, anxious about the morning round table discussion at the Guild.

She had prepared careful notes and lists of questions. It was going well. Then the door opened and Bess Streeter Aldrich, the famous and beloved Nebraska writer of novels and short stories, came in. She sat down in the back row. Mignon stumbled over words and lost her train of thought, recovered, and then, humiliated, lost the place in the agenda when Aldrich slipped out quietly just a few minutes later. But in an afternoon interview with a reporter from the *Nebraska Star*, Aldrich said, "I don't read mystery stories. I don't really like mystery stories. But I did enjoy Mignon Edwards' *Patient in Room 18*. I stopped in at the discussion because I was curious to see what this young writer looked like."

Back in Valentine the reviews of *The Patient in Room 18* came to Mignon in a big brown envelope of press clippings from the man she could now call *her* editor, Harry Maule.

"Hey, Mrs. Edwards," Mr. Peterson called when she heaved open the heavy double door of the Post Office, "there's a big, fat envelope for you from your New York connections." He smiled like a conspirator, glancing at the men who were milling around in the lobby, perusing their mail, and catching up on the local gossip. He passed the package to Mignon across the counter.

When she got home, she opened the brown envelope with trepidation and quickly scanned the note from Harry Maule: "The reviews are very positive," he said. "Readers like the unique setting, and they especially like Nurse Sarah Keate. Doubleday has advance sales of ten thousand copies and has selected it for their featured Crime Club which has four thousand members. That translates to about four thousand copies."

She saved every clipping in a scrapbook. One treasured critic wrote: "with the imaginative storytelling, Mignon Edwards becomes a major figure in shifting focus in crime fiction from strict detection to atmospherics and emotion."

The Saturday Review reported that the suspense was sustained, the action rapid, the atmosphere of the hospital genuine with a lot of thoroughly credible people going through a harrowing experience. "Miss Keate does not withhold any clue she comes across simply to make her denouement more thrilling," the reviewer wrote. "Miss Keate is a model narrator," another said.

Will Cuppy, from *The New York Tribune*, who Harry told her was known for his biting criticism, wrote that the department would disown all mystery fans who didn't buy this one. He said that the book was well-written, amusing in spots, and a grade A.

Critics called narrator Nurse Sarah Keate "peppery" with "tart opinions." They liked the fact that she was loyal to her profession but not a prude. A modern woman who enjoyed a harmless flirtation with detective Lance O'Leary.

That was exactly what Mignon wanted readers to find in Sarah Keate. She was over the top! Alan had built three bridges while she worked on the novel, and her hard work had paid off—in acclaim *and* in sales.

She would buy a car. Edith Wharton said that the only way not to think about money is to have a great deal of it. Then she bought a car with the award money from the Pulitzer—a 1925 gray and *black* Lincoln with red wheels. Mignon's earnings from *The Patient in Room 18* were enough for a car, her own car.

Then a reporter from *The Nebraska Tribune* called. "We'd like to feature you in a Sunday edition. Photographs where you live would interest our readers, Mrs. Edwards. Even locals think of the Sand Hills as the hinterlands. You're a curiosity to city folks."

Yes. Yes. And *Yes* to recognition in the hometown. They made an appointment.

What to wear? Not country clothes. Casually elegant. Thanks to Chicago shopping, definitely not Valentine, she had a full closet. The day of the photographs, she pulled out a dark gray, below-the-knee afternoon dress and took Alan's gray suit and fedora from his closet.

"I know you want to look good. Us to look good." He chuckled as he put pants and shirt and tie on. "A three-piece suit seems a bit much . . . but it's okay. I understand." He grabbed his jacket. "I'll go downstairs and have a cigarette while I wait."

That would be more than one cigarette. She needed at least two hours to do hair, makeup, and dress.

Finally ready, Alan put Jericho in her new blue Packard Phaeton, got in the passenger side, and Mignon drove to the river.

The Niobrara runs along the northern edge of the Sand Hills beyond Valentine, and Alan was working on the Spencer Dam—an appropriate, even significant, setting for these photographs.

They posed and posed. Mignon alone. Alan and Mignon. Alan and Mignon with Jericho.

The story with the photographs traced her life in Lincoln and included childhood photographs of Helen and her which her mother must have given them. What Mignon cared most about was the information about the option of *The Patient in Room 18* as a Broadway play and her life as a writer and wife of a civil engineer.

> September 20, 1929
> Dear Mignon,
> I read the story in the *Sunday Trib*. Quite a spread. Great photographs! The mink coat was an elegant touch. You have made it as a Nebraska writer! I am proud!
> My news is that I'm pregnant! I'm anxious to tell you all about it in person next time you come to Lincoln. We are taking different paths, but it's what we dreamed of and all good!
> Love, Carmen

She'd ripped the letter open as she walked home from the Post Office. Sat down at the kitchen table and read it again when she got home. Carmen pregnant. She hadn't seen that coming. Naïve. Just assumed Carmen wanted to teach for a few years. And they were this twosome. Even husbands outside of the bond. They were career women. Independent. A baby? Mignon didn't want a baby. But didn't know if she wanted Carmen to have one either. It changed everything. They were on different paths. Carmen with a happy marriage. Now a baby. Mignon had her novels. It had to be enough.

Alan and Mignon celebrated the success of the two nurse Sarah Keate novels with a trip to Chicago. She hungered for the city. She needed a city fix, and the timing was perfect to attend Constance's performance in *Romance,* a drama sponsored by The Cameo Salon in Chicago.

They took the train from Lincoln to Chicago and stayed in a suite at the Edgewater Hotel on an enchanted island in the middle of the city. She watched the waves from the dining room. Walked *to* the beach and walked *the* beach to watch the sunrise over the water.

They didn't take advantage of the tennis courts alongside the hotel, but Tommy Dorsey was there with his band, and they danced and danced on the marble floor of the open-air pavilion.

Whatever else was unsettling in their married life, whatever shadow hovered with nothing resolved in their sexless married life, they danced.

They had missed opera in Valentine and were anxious to see the new home of the Civic Opera House which had just opened in July. Constance and Aunt Nelle accompanied them to a matinee performance of *Le Jongleur de Notre Dame.*

The Opera House was spectacular. Shaped like a giant chair. Art Deco exterior. Forty-nine stories high with 3,563 seats. Inside was an explosion of lustrous fabrics in bright orange and red and yellow. Floral designs in the upholstery, the carpets, and even the draperies. It took her breath.

Alan wasn't interested in the colors or the carpets or the draperies. Art Deco were just words to him. He wondered aloud about the design and the "supporting members," which he explained to Mignon again were the columns reinforcing those forty-nine stories.

Mary Garden was still the prime diva and manager of the Civic Opera. Mignon telephoned several times and finally reached her.

"Oh, yes," she said. "Mignon . . . How nice to hear from you. And where did you say you had been?"

How insulting. No point in carrying on that conversation.

"She doesn't even remember that she called you for help," Mignon told Alan. "Her knight. Her rescuer. We're just another paragraph in her book of adorations. She's moved on. One of those celebrated egotists who blithely discard people along the way."

He didn't respond. Did he care? What did he feel deeply about?

Mignon left Alan at the Edgewater for a day of indulgence in book buying. Brentanos Books first, then Kroch's where all the clerks knew books—Virginia Woolf's latest novel and her autobiographical *A Room of One's Own* and Edith Wharton's *The Writing of Fiction* and Faulkner's *The Sound and the Fury* and Hemingway's *A Farewell to Arms* and Sinclair Lewis' *Dodsworth*. A banquet of books. Books to feed her soul. She added

Erich Remarque's *All Quiet on the Western Front.* An afterthought. Maybe Alan would be interested in reading it though it was unlikely. He was too practical and factual for anything but real life. The only place he wasn't basic, predictable, ordinary, and expected was in bed. Her husband the mystery.

The clerks, delighted with her purchases, both extensive and wise, wrapped the novels in their book-title imprinted paper, tied them with string, and arranged for the packages to be delivered to the Edgewater.

Day three she pampered herself with a manicure and a Marcel before lunch with Aunt Nelle who proposed introducing her to Fanny Butcher, the "Literary Spotlight" columnist for *The Chicago Tribune.* They met in the Golden Empire room at the Palmer House.

"I'm delighted to meet Nelle's young writer," Fanny said, in the patronizing tone of the rich and famous, the older accomplished woman to the naïve. Despite the condescension, Mignon smiled spontaneously, still enamored with the recognition as a writer and flattered by the label.

"I have news for you," Fanny said. "Just this morning I learned that *While the Patient Slept* has been awarded the Scotland Prize for mystery. I'd like to announce it in my column tomorrow."

"Yes, of course." Definitely a boon for Fanny, but great publicity for the novel.

With meeting Fanny Butcher and good news of the award singing, she treated herself to an afternoon of shopping with Constance. She found a sleeveless black, silk, beaded, below-the-knee afternoon dress; a floor-length peachy pink lace with a bow at the hips; a Patou on sale—deep blue long-sleeved velvet with a dropped waist, below the knee, embroidery at the neck and along the dropped waist; and a red and tan printed street-length Chanel day dress. A smiling clerk wrapped those in lustrous silver packages and tied them with ribbon bows to be delivered to the Edgewater. She had no idea where she'd wear these luscious gowns in Nebraska. She didn't care. She'd enjoy looking at them in her closet.

Saturday evening, they went to the opera again with Aunt Nelle and Uncle Oscar. Constance was in the cast of *Rigoletto*.

A week of rejuvenation. The Sand Hills gave her the solitude to write; the city energized her. Movies. Dancing. Opera. Book Shops. She was revived. Now she could go home and work.

You must continue with Nurse Keate and the charming Detective Lance O'Leary, Harry wrote. Readers like dependable characters they feel they know. They will look forward to reading your next novel if you stick with Keate and O'Leary.

She needed a different setting though. Some critics said Nurse Keate's last assignment in the old mansion was contrived. Maybe Alan's hunting lodge . . .

Alan's engineering friends from Chicago enjoyed hunting in what they considered the wilds of Nebraska. Several lavish hunting lodges were scattered across the northwest part of the state. Alan especially liked to take them to the Hackberry Club. It had a spring water lake with bass and ducks and rangeland for hunting prairie chickens and grouse, he told Mignon. The clubhouse is big, he said. Two dining rooms, six bedrooms, a parlor, kitchen, sleeping porch, and a view of the lake.

A unique setting for a mystery. She needed to see it for herself. But Alan objected when she proposed the trip.

"The roads are difficult once you leave the highway," he said. "It's gravel. Not a smart thing to do. You aren't used to driving on gravel. Wait until I have time to take you."

That only made her determined. She needed to get away—by herself. She set off in her Phaeton for the three-hour drive. An unbelievable trek across a sea of sand. One of the most desolate places she had ever seen in her life. Barren reaches of sand with pine-dotted buttes. The hills like rolling waves to the horizon. One big emptiness.

She held fast to the steering wheel when she reached the gravel road. Geared down as the car lurched from side to side on the loose gravel of the narrow road leading to the lodge.

There it was. Alan's refuge. His bond with his hunting buddies intrigued her. She grew up in the city. She didn't have brothers, and her father wasn't a hunter, so the relationship was a mystery.

When the hunters came back to Valentine after their days at the lodge, they sat at the dining room table for hours after dinner, enveloped in cigarette and cigar smoke, whiskey glasses and bottles at hand, reliving the hunt. They told the story of this hunt and retold the stories of the hunt before and the hunt before that, laughing, clinking glasses.

"Remember last fall when Jericho got into the porcupine."

"And John never forgets the tomato juice for skunk stink after his dog's encounter."

"Remember Jim and Tony standing over a pheasant, kicking the ground, a hen at their feet. Hoping the rest of us wouldn't discover the illegal shooting."

These men had traditions and stories like a family, like an exclusive club, closed to women. She envied the intimacy. The common interest that created the bond. A part of Alan's world she didn't share. Didn't understand. She had never had a group of women with a bond as intimate, nor any group of women in Valentine. She had Carmen.

However, those hunters and that hunting lodge and desolate, barren place were perfect settings for Nurse Keate's next crime adventure.

When she got home, she pressed Alan for the information she needed for her story. She didn't understand the satisfaction in killing animals nor the hunters' fascination with guns.

"Why do you need a collection of guns?"

"Specific guns are needed for different birds, a different gun for grouse than for prairie chickens and pheasant," he said.

After his hunting trip, she had watched him clean his treasures with painstaking patience and care. He disassembled each gun and laid the pieces on newspaper he'd spread on the walnut dining room table to protect the top. He attached a brush to a metal rod to clean inside the barrel. That done, he put an oiled cloth on the rod and pushed it inside the barrel. Finally, he cleaned the outside of the barrel.

"Oil so it won't rust," he said, as he polished the stock to protect the wood. He handled each gun as gently as a baby and slid each back into a padded case ready for the next hunt. Jericho the hunting dog sat next to the table panting with excitement. All gist for the novel.

Alan drew a schematic of a lodge to suit the plot and the number of characters she envisioned: a log building, the main door opening into a large room with deep fireplaces of native, unfinished rock at both ends.

He designed six bedrooms with shared bathrooms along the west wall of that main floor. A door at the south end led to the kitchen. At the left of the kitchen doorway, an open stairway led upward to a narrow gallery that ran around three sides of the room and protruded out over the room. There were five bedrooms and two bathrooms on this upper level. Perfect for her cast of characters. She'd struggle, she knew, to get into their heads, to write about it. A male point of view. Hobbled by her femaleness.

In February, Doubleday Doran Crime Club invited her to a celebratory tea party in New York City. It had been a bitter winter in Nebraska. Frigid winds and snow swept across the Sand Hills day after day, and even Alan was ready to get out of Valentine. Mignon packed the day dresses and evening gowns she had purchased on her Chicago shopping extravaganza, excited about the opportunity to wear them. They drove to Lincoln and got on the Burlington Railroad to Chicago, spent the night with Aunt Nelle and Uncle Oscar there, and boarded The 20th Century Limited to New York City the next morning.

It was a twenty-hour train trip, and they could have reserved a bed closed off from the aisle by curtains, but the Limited had a Pullman car with compartments, and they were feeling well-heeled and deserving of luxuries. They reserved a compartment and then enjoyed the other amenities aboard. Alan went to the barbershop. Mignon used the secretarial services to answer some correspondence before dinner in the dining car where glass globes on the walls lit each table. Made it elegant. They sat in the soft light. Watched the dark countryside glide by.

"I'm going to have the filet mignon," Mignon announced, glancing at the menu after the Black waiter put the bone china place settings and silver on the pristine white tablecloth. He smiled with perfunctory indulgence and the east coast superiority of knowing this woman came from a place where one simply ordered steak. She tried for nonchalance as he hovered over the serving.

"He's laughing at me," she said when he walked away.

"You're hypersensitive." Alan sliced hunks of his juicy porter house. "You read into everything." He had accused her of that more than once.

After dinner she did relax in the deep cushioned easy chairs of the club car. Enjoyed the luxury and every puff of the last cigarette of the day.

Harry Maule met them at Penn Station. Mignon and Harry had exchanged reams of letters and drafts of her novels, but they hadn't met. Mignon and Alan stepped off the train, surprised by the biting cold. A tall, broad-shouldered man in a gray fedora and a navy cashmere topcoat hurried toward them.

"Mignon," he said, in a deep baritone, enclosing her hand in his, warm from the leather gloves he'd tucked into his pocket. He was one of those people who wore a smile; even his eyes smiled. She liked him immediately.

He was much like Alan: courteous, calm, the soul of decorum, a deep voice that inspired confidence. He and Alan appreciated each other instantly.

Harry dropped them off at the Ritz, and it was ritzy —a brown sandstone facade, thirty-six floors, taller than any building in Lincoln. They walked into a luxurious lobby—one wall Levanto marble. She recognized a Giacometti painting of St. Moritz on another. A thousand rooms, the doorman told her. Four hundred of them directly facing Central Park. And they had one of them.

She'd lived in the boondocks long enough to be very impressed. Carmen would no doubt accuse her of always being impressed by luxury.

Harry had arranged for her to have dinner with Frank Nelson Doubleday, the founder of Doubleday Publishing. Accompanied by Alan, of course. It would have been unseemly for her to dine without an escort. No matter she was the writer under contract with Doubleday.

She fretted about what to wear. Went through her usual trying on and discarding of skirts and blouses and dresses in the three bags she'd brought from Valentine. Ah . . . the forest green with ruffled sleeves to the elbow, tying with a soft bow at the neck. Smart, she hoped, but not flashy. The chunky black strapped shoes. She needed to make a favorable impression.

They met in the Crystal Room, the rooftop Ritz restaurant decorated with oriental hangings and seating under canopies.

Frank stood as they came to the table. He grasped Mignon's hand and shook Alan's. "Good to meet you."

"You have been launched," he said, nodding and smiling at Mignon. "*While the Patient Slept* is even better than your first. Reviewers are using words like 'eerie atmosphere, surprise, exciting clues,' all the ingredients of a first-rate thriller. You have joined the august company of Mary Rinehart, Carolyn Wells, and even Agatha Christie.

"It's the Golden Age of books," he went on. "Novels are popular. People are reading more than ever. Our sales are increasing by ten percent every year. We need you to keep writing."

She did feel, if not "launched," at least "arrived."

The dinner with Frank was the prelude to the Crime Club celebration the next day, a tea in the Rumpelmayer Restaurant of the Ritz.

Alan and Mignon stood inside the double doors with Harry taking it all in. Viennese waltz music from a small orchestra in the far corner wafted throughout the room. She reveled in the setting. Crystal chandeliers, dark paneled walls adorned with gilt framed paintings. Suede upholstered chairs at every table in the vast room. Her feet sank into the Aubusson carpet.

"The caterer is Austrian," Harry said. "He's the former chef of the Austrian Prince."

Nothing was too good for the assembled stars of the Crime Club.

"I'll introduce you to Carolyn Wells," Harry said.

The famous Carolyn Wells was married to Hadwin Houghton, heir to the Houghton Mifflin Publishing House. She had written seventeen children's books, edited several anthologies, and published twenty-nine mysteries. Mignon had read some of her mysteries. The sleuth, Fleming Stone, was dull, dull, dull, and the stories repetitive.

"Carolyn," Harry said as he led Mignon to Carolyn Wells where she stood in the center of the room surrounded by admirers. "This is Mignon Edwards, Doubleday's newest star."

The old and haughty Carolyn acknowledged Mignon with a negligible nod, then turned and moved on, uninterested, anxious to join more impressive company.

"Proves your worth, Mignon," Harry leaned close and whispered in her ear. "You have made it indeed. You are a threat to the queen. You have become the U.S. Agatha Christie."

Mignon didn't appreciate the snub. She didn't care much about Carolyn Wells, but she was beginning to resent the constant reference and comparison to Agatha Christie.

Nothing could dim her delight in New York City though. She basked in it. Even the congestion in the streets was wonderful. People pushed and hurried by. Taxis blared. The Elevated on Sixth Avenue swished above them between skyscrapers. She embraced it all. Her eyes on the street, engrossed in watching the people on the sidewalks.

"The women are wearing felt hats and fur-collared coats. Fur is everywhere," she told Alan. "I must at least get a fur muff."

Alan mostly looked up, his eyes on the skyscrapers, and said things like: "I wonder how that's done . . . that construction of towers rising from the park."

He indulged Mignon in traipsing through the city, hailing cabs when they were tired of walking or the distances were too far.

She hungered for art, in this, her first venture into the mecca of the art world, and she didn't want to waste a day. She had made a list of the galleries. Georgia O'Keeffe was the new darling of the New York art world. Her husband, photographer Alfred Stieglitz, had closed his gallery, but some of her paintings were in the Macbeth. Vanderbilt Whitney was showing American artists in her studio in Greenwich Village. And she had to go to the Museum of Modern Art which had opened just last year, only nine days after the Wall Street crash. Van Gogh, Gauguin, Cezanne, and Seurat were showing there. She needed to see it all.

"You exhaust me," Alan said after a day of walking miles, but he gamely accompanied her to see what night had to offer in the sleepless city, even a sinful, sleepless city. Harry had told them they must experience the Cotton Club in Harlem. Duke Ellington was the headline attraction.

Harry and his wife Edna came by for them in a taxicab.

"Louis Armstrong and Ella Fitzgerald perform here regularly," Harry told them as they approached the Club.

Really? Mignon pointed to the "Whites Only" sign posted on the door. Nebraska and her sheltered life in Lincoln hadn't prepared her for the blatant discrimination, nor the irony of Blacks performing in a club restricted to Whites. She was naïve about so many things. She had so much to learn about the world. So many things to experience.

Edna and Harry also invited them for dinner in their Manhattan town house. Edna was a charming hostess, the perfect ebullient partner for the quiet, serious Harry. The kind of woman you wanted for a friend. They gently supported each other's point of view about the publishing world, about life in New York City, even politics. Harry smiled and touched Edna's hand now and then during the conversation. He gave her a small discreet hug as she led Mignon and Alan to the bar for cocktails and then to the dining room.

Their sex life must be wonderful. Mignon had a stomach twist, a churning of envy and then a shudder at even thinking about another couple in their bedroom. But how she yearned for more than hugs and friendly affection.

The last day in the city Alan indulged her in one more trek to Greenwich Village. They took a taxicab, then strolled along, drinking in the atmosphere—the people sitting with their morning coffee reading newspapers at sidewalk cafés, the delicatessens from every country in the world, it seemed to Mignon. Doors open to entice customers. The aroma of everything from spicy sausage to curry.

She studied the streams of people hurrying by, hoping for a miracle, a chance encounter with Edna St. Vincent Millay. According to *The New Yorker*—which Mignon read religiously to keep up on the writer world —Millay lived here in a nine-foot long, six-foot wide apartment, in the narrowest street in New York City. *My candle burns at both ends/It will not last the night . . .*

Edna Millay. And there she was. It really was her, striding purposefully by, her red hair bouncing. Touched by an idol. Star struck by literary giants. The perfect end to Mignon's first visit to New York City. She dreaded going home.

Once there, Alan worked on his bridges, and Mignon worked on *The Mystery of Hunting's End*.

Carmen's baby arrived March 7. Right on time. The Western Union boy in his smart uniform was smiling when she answered the door, so Mignon knew this was the news she had been expecting and dreading in equal measures. She slipped her pink-polished fingernails under the flap of the yellow envelope slowly, deliberately. Excited. Anxious. Jealous. Reluctant for the confirmation of the change in Carmen's life and their relationship.

A girl. Named her June. Baby and Mother fine. Charlie

They'd named her after Carmen's mother.

A call from Harry gave her hope for a change.

"You've won the Scotland Yard Prize for *While the Patient Slept*. It's also been selected as a Crime Club choice. That insures you of four thousand sales, plus the publicity."

Before it was published, Mignon had argued with Harry about the title. She didn't want to use "Patient" again. Harry had insisted that using a familiar title would attract those readers who liked her first book.

He'd been right. She was learning that she had to trust his judgment.

Alan knew how weary she was of life in the Sand Hills despite the fact that the solitude had inspired and nurtured her writing. After the New York City trip, she whined and complained.

"My job is here, Mimi. I enjoy my work. You're publishing. What more do you need? You don't even try to be content."

"Content? You expect me to be content? You enjoy your *work* . . . It isn't all about work, Alan. Should I be content with this marriage? How long do you expect me to go on like this? We need a change."

"What sort of change do you propose?"

"Go back to Chicago. My book sales and the prize money are enough so we can leave Nebraska, leave these monotonous Sand Hills. You could accept the job the Underground Construction Company in Chicago offered you."

She also hoped they could find a doctor in Chicago to help him with his problem and make that part of their life happier, but she wasn't optimistic.

"Maybe you have Peyronie's disease," she had mentioned after reading an article in the *British Medical Journal* about male sexual dysfunction by that name. He had scoffed at that and turned away. Subject closed.

They got a stormy send off—seven tornadoes in a week. The fierce, whirling winds took out a giant and beautiful ancient oak in their front yard, setting it on its side, the enormous roots reaching as high as the top of the dining room windows. It decimated her flower beds. She'd treasured the red hollyhocks along the side of the house. Had carefully mulched the peonies transplanted from her mother's garden so they would survive the frigid winters. The wind flattened all of it. Made it easy to leave.

1930

Chicago

Mignon and Alan moved into an apartment in Oak Park, where they had lived before Valentine. It was an old, but beautiful, red brick building, U-shaped, built around a landscaped courtyard and right across the street from the park. Their apartment on the fourth floor had been originally two apartments remodeled to one by the previous tenants—four bedrooms, a luxury of space. Mignon had a room of her own for writing and Alan had a study.

She worked amidst her stacks of books and piles of papers, the next page or the previous pages of typing within reach. Alan had his own tidy place, pens and papers aligned on the desk, professional journals arranged by month and year on bookshelves. She shared his bedroom out of habit and the comfort of his bigness next to her. Moving to the other bedroom would have made a statement she was not yet willing to make, nor had the courage to make. He was content. She was often sleepless.

Aunt Nelle helped her find a woman for day work, so she could spend her time writing not cooking, cleaning, or washing clothes. Sophie arrived on the city bus promptly every morning at eight o'clock in her starched white uniform, her oiled, coal-black hair sleeked back into a knot. She was tall and buxom, a big woman—probably ten years older than Mignon, but it was difficult to tell with the dark skin. She could have been fifty, her skin smooth and supple, not one wrinkle, just a crinkling around her eyes when she smiled or laughed in a deep baritone.

The first day, she turned her key in the lock and marched into the apartment with authority. She didn't hesitate to let Mignon know that she was the expert.

"I've been a day maid since I was fourteen," Sophie said. "When it comes to household matters, I know what to do. I've worked myself up, ma'am," she said, looking down at Mignon with her hands on her hips. "I don't do maid work for just anyone," she added, to make certain Mignon understood the privilege granted because of Aunt Nelle's connections.

"Christ Almighty," Alan said when he opened the door to his study after her first full day to find pens and pencils clustered together in big white coffee cups at the back of his desk, scales (rulers to Mignon, scales to the engineer) lined up in order of size on the side. How could she have forgotten about his organization of pens, pencils, and scales placed specifically for efficient and methodical work? She'd gone through this scenario in Valentine after Rita Rose rearranged his desk.

She had to tell Sophie—reluctantly and with trepidation—that she might move papers and pens to dust Mignon's desk, but she must not touch Alan's. To Mignon's surprise, Sophie wasn't insulted. She had noted, apparently with pleasure, the neatly squared, ironed handkerchiefs and precisely folded underwear in Alan's bureau. His orderliness endeared him to her, made him a superior being. She catered to him. Muttered under her breath as she arranged and straightened the piles of Mignon's magazines on every available surface, cleaned papers and teacups and overflowing ashtrays off the coffee and end tables.

With Sophie to manage the household, Mignon took her coffee and cigarettes to her room every morning for writing. She was determined to work at it, and her dear Carmen encouraged and nurtured her:

> May 2, 1930
> Dear Mignon,
>
> I know you love Chicago, but I must remind you where you came from. Today's *Lincoln Journal* links your name with our famous Willa Cather and with Mari Sandoz and Bess Streeter Aldrich. One critic surmised that you Nebraska writers "flourish in the poorest of soils." Literally or figuratively, I wonder? It's insulting either way. You were also mentioned in relation to the indomitable Agatha Christie (I know you love that comparison!) and to Dorothy L. Sayers who has just published a new and purportedly very successful *Lord Peter Wimsey* novel. You are definitely on the cusp.
>
> I have time on my hands. Motherhood hasn't numbed my brain, and I'd enjoy reading your next novel. Send me a draft.
>
> Telephone if you come home for a visit. Hi to Alan.
>
> Love, Carmen

Harry expected another novel and soon. Mignon had sent *The Mystery of Hunting's End* to him just before they left Nebraska, and she vowed it was the last novel she would set in those Sand Hills. The problem was that setting came to her first. Vague characters flitted about in her head and began to evolve, but plot grew from the place, and she had to experience a place to create the story.

She sat at her desk and brushed the hair from her perspiring forehead. Fingers sticky. Pen moving sluggishly. Notebook pages stuck to the desk. The fan simply moved the hot air around and around and around.

She finally decided to get outside, walk to the neighborhood market for cold cuts and whatever fruit might be available for dinner.

"There's a line here, lady," a young man pointed when she stepped up to the counter at the market. She moved back. The woman in front of her frowned and sighed, standing on one foot and then the other, shifting her handbag from one shoulder to the other.

"They are so slow," she muttered.

"Have a little patience. We're moving as fast as we can," the owner said as he bagged the bread and milk and root beer his teenaged son brought from the coolers and shelves.

Walking home, thinking about the weather and the way it affected people, Mignon realized that it would be a useful atmosphere for a murder. A summer-time murder for Sarah Keate in a hot, airless hospital.

She recalled a city hospital in Lincoln with an old walnut carved stairway that turned around the landings midway each flight of four floors. The intersecting corridors offered a glimpse of the entire hospital, although a new and modern elevator had been put in next to the stairway. The operating room was on the top floor. Patient rooms and living quarters for the nurses were on the floors between. An orderly lived in the basement at the foot of the staircase.

From This Dark Stairway — a setting and a title.

The Episcopal church across the street from the hospital operated a shelter for men who were homeless because of the Depression. She could make use of that and of her acquaintance with the young student nurses and their dormitory situation from her own hospital experience in Lincoln.

The ideas swarmed like bees. She hurried back to the apartment and her desk.

When Alan came home, he pulled up the window shades they'd lowered during the day to keep out heat, opened the windows, and put a fan on the living room floor.

In Valentine when the sun set, a cool breeze came from the Niobrara River, and nights were pleasant even in July and August. No night breeze cooled here. The evening air was still and heavy with the humidity from the lake.

Alan settled into his chair with Jericho on the floor beside him, lit his Lucky Strike, and listened patiently to what Mignon had written. Back to their companionable Valentine evenings.

"You're bringing Sarah Keate's secret love into the story at the last minute this time," Alan commented with a tinge of criticism when she read *From This Dark Stairway*. "And Detective Lance O'Leary is getting all the credit for solving the crime."

"They aren't lovers. Sarah is older than Lance O'Leary by nearly ten years. My readers like a hint of their affection for each other. The older woman attracted to a young man. It's taboo. Maybe she is attracted to him because of a sad love affair in her past. Or maybe she is longing for love she has never experienced. Or, love in all of its expressions."

He had no response to that. And she couldn't bring herself to disturb that pleasant evening, that warm blanket of intimacy, with a confrontation. With angry words about her own need for love in all its expressions.

"Contrasting Lance O'Leary and his quiet confidence with a new blustery, disagreeable detective feels like a good change, an interesting change," she said. "I want Sarah proud and in charge, superior to this new detective. She can sum up the evidence logically, but turn it over to Lance O'Leary with her modest, maidenly pose. They both know who really solved the crimes."

"I wasn't criticizing," Alan said. "Just noting."

He wasn't a good critic because he didn't read fiction, but reading aloud was productive and important for her. She needed to hear the words to know what was working, and he was a stickler for detail. Caught her when she glossed over things. She was grateful that he willingly spent his free evenings listening. She couldn't envision life without him, but they were a strange pair in a strange marriage.

She lived in her imaginary world while Alan worked in the real world designing a method for bracing and timbering a tunnel which extended from Kostner Avenue to Cicero. *The Chicago Tribune* photographed two of the inspection trips—a view of the eight and a half foot brick sewer tunnel showing the curve and cutting of the proposed manhole with Alan; William Hale Thompson, mayor of Chicago; M. J. Faherty, the president of the Board of Local Improvements; and A. J. Schafmayer, Engineer of the Board of Local Improvements.

Mignon was proud of him, but couldn't have been more ignorant. "They talk about brick *or* concrete tunnels. What about the designs? Are they different?" she asked Alan after reading the newspaper.

"The design," he explained patiently as to a child, "is adequate for both brick and concrete. The amount of effort is different in terms of getting the concrete into the excavation or using bricks. Bricks are usually more labor intensive but less problematic. I designed the bracing and timbering. The contractor decides what to use."

He slipped into formal, impersonal language, like a textbook when he discussed his work. She wanted to say, *Don't you realize how boring that is?* And she remembered that first essay she wrote before murder and mystery—*Engineers are unique men.*

They resumed the life they had led in Chicago before the move to Valentine. That summer they enjoyed the Ravinia Festival again. They shared a love of opera and classical music. She had Alan to thank for that. They had both missed it in Nebraska.

And thanks to Aunt Nelle's introduction and her collaborations years ago, their friend Charles Wakefield Cadman honored Mignon with a song titled "Mignonette," part of a song cycle he titled "White Enchantment." Alan's cousin, Constance, performed it at Kimball Hall in Oak Park.

"Mignonette" recalled dreams of love in an old-fashioned garden where only the Mignonette, of all other flowers, remained true. Was Charles aware of her fascination for gardens? She had told him once about the peace and tranquility, the serenity that came over her in Aunt Nelle's English garden. Had he read her novels with all the descriptions of gardens in the settings for murder? Not likely. And dreams of love? How could he possibly know about her dreams of love? Must be his creative imagination. He and all of Aunt Nelle's artistic entourage saw her as a romantic.

The poignancy of the story came alive with Constance's light soprano. The singing touched Mignon's heart. Shivered her skin. She willed away tears. Alan sat beside her, crossing and recrossing his legs, uttering an under-the-breath sigh now and then. The message in the art song didn't reach him. He preferred the drama and spectacle of opera. The music of a full orchestra.

Mary Garden still reigned at the Chicago Opera House, and they had enjoyed her. Had both enjoyed her. "Maybe you should call her," Mignon told Alan.

"She's moved on," he said matter-of-factly. "And I don't have time." A fleeting and unemotional attachment. He moved on easily.

And Chicago as always had surprises for Mignon. "Sin City." One Saturday evening a friend and colleague of Alan's invited them to join him for an evening at the Royale Dinner Club. They walked into a Romanesque setting: marble pillars, massive urns of exotic flowers, a mahogany bar at one end of the room, tables set to face a maroon velvet-curtained stage at the other. A string quartet played in the background.

"Ritzy," Alan said.

Mignon glanced around, trying not to gape. "I have never seen so many women and so few men in one place."

Their host smirked, no doubt at her naïveté. What can you expect from a girl raised in the shadow of Wesley Methodist Church in Lincoln, Nebraska?

Dozens of women in party dress and a few men dressed to the nines were crowded at the bar. Others were circulating among the tables, cocktails in hand, stopping to chat, obviously acquainted. A stunning woman, dripping in diamonds from dangling earrings to silver pendant, made a grand entrance.

"My God, she's beautiful," Mignon said noting the white platter hat with white feathers, a white feather boa, a form-fitting sequined gown.

"Not a woman," Alan leaned close and whispered in her ear. "Most of the women you see milling around and dancing together are men in drag."

"Drag?"

"Women's clothes. The dancing couples and the singers on the stage are female impersonators," he said.

Female impersonators. A night club for homosexuals. Saturday night entertainment for other patrons. She had never even thought much about homosexuality. Another of those things only whispered about in the presence of nice girls. She'd never known a homosexual person. Or she'd never recognized anyone she knew as a homosexual. Considering it at all hadn't occurred to her. But she wouldn't let this experience or exposure or whatever it was go beyond the curtain in her head now.

She worked at her writing and shopped. Her therapy and entertainment, as always. Shopping. Clothes shopping. Marshall Field's had a new store in Oak Park where she indulged in filling her closet and lunching often with Fanny Butcher on the elegant fourth floor tearoom.

Fanny liked Mignon's writing and gave Mignon as much publicity as she could. She also enjoyed the one-upmanship in her own world of competitive journalists and gossip columnists. It was Fanny who made the announcement of a London theatre's plans to dramatize *The Patient in Room 18* in her *Chicago Tribune* column, "The Armchair Playgoer." A boon for Fanny and for Mignon.

Mignon sent *From This Dark Stairway* off to Harry.

"I want one more Sarah Keate," Harry wrote. "Sarah is still selling. Random House considers a novel successful if it sells five thousand to ten thousand copies.

The Patient in Room 18 and *While the Patient Slept* have sold well over ten thousand. Your Sarah Keate mysteries are a phenomenal success."

The Depression hadn't had any effect on book sales, Mignon's or others, according to Harry. Women were reading more than ever. They liked Mignon's confident, assertive female protagonist, and the hint of romance, Harry said, and he was waiting anxiously for the next novel.

But she was tired of devising mysteries for Nurse Sarah Keate to solve. Bored with Detective Lance O'Leary and their unrequited love. Not unlike her own. Seven years. A roller coaster relationship. No. Not the exhilaration of a roller coaster. Not blood pumping through your veins excitement on top of the world. Then down to the depths. There were highs. The fun of new experiences. Shared. The lows of her need. The gnawing need for sex. His indifference. Disinterest. But his calm. The peaceable, tranquil life. His support of her writing. Her equalness.

She wished she'd never met Alan Edwards.

Harry prevailed, and she succumbed to Sarah Keate but with a different approach. She decided to begin *Murder by an Aristocrat* with Sarah's own words, her last words—

"My nursing practice is beginning to suffer . . . My patients are beginning to grow nervous when they discover that my name is Sarah Keate . . . They watch me with a faintly wary look. They are restless and ask to have the night light burning. They don't want this red-headed nurse. I've had too much traffic with murder. But I am a nurse. I am not a detective. There's a growing custom of doctors to ask for me when the case is what they blandly call extraordinary. I later learned that's why Dr. Bouligny asked for me when he telephoned the Registry office. He also wanted a nurse with discretion. This is the story of what happened in the Thatcher house one summer week."

She sent that prologue and a draft of the novel to Harry.

October 12, 1930
Dear Mignon,

Your signature old house with the balcony for overhearing conversations, the sumptuous, lush surroundings with glittering bathrooms and extensive gardens works for these aristocrats. I like your description of the family as "thoroughbreds" with their dinner tables of "lovely old china, sparking crystal, and gleaming silverware." Their coverup of a murder to protect one of their own. And their suspecting each other are problems for Sarah Keate.

I suggest that you look at the end lines of each chapter. Leave the reader with a clue or a situation that is climactic. A clue that foreshadows the events of the next chapter. This is effective in any event, but it will also make it easy to publish in a magazine serial without extensive revision.

For example, conclude Chapter 2 with "I bent and picked up an envelope. There was no address, and it was not sealed." Chapter 3—"Murder! Murder! He's shot all to pieces." Chapter 4—"There was blood on the rug. But it was the wrong room." Chapter 5—"Emmaline stood near the bed with the egg basket. In her other hand she held a revolver." You get the idea.

It is actually what you have done with Chapter 10, last line—"You knew about the letter—my letter." Chapter 11, first line—"Yes, I did." Chapter 13, last line—"You can't question Dave ever again." Chapter 14, first line—"Murdered or took the Veronal accidentally."

I like the minor role of romance. This is a clever and complex plot, Mignon. It evolves like an intricate puzzle. The leisurely pace of the investigation echoes the aristocrats' lifestyle.

Your readers will appreciate Sarah Keate's summing up of the evidence as she always does about three-quarters through the story. Some of your readers may be disappointed at the confession which ends the novel and leaves Sarah in limbo, so to speak. But it is a clever departure from the Keate formula and will appeal to readers who admire the detective puzzle.

I look forward to your revisions.

Warm Regards, Harry

Her working path was clear and focused, but the Underground Construction Company's contract was complete along with Alan's resident engineer position. The Depression had even touched professions like engineering. Alan had no job prospects. Mignon was tired of Chicago, tired of Sarah Keate, and restless.

They were unhappy, or at least she was unhappy, though they ignored putting it into words. Mignon, the wordsmith, didn't have the courage to throw the rock into the pond. The ripples might reach further than her want. What did she want? Right now? A change of scene.

"I have award money left. Let's go to Europe, Alan. I've always wanted to go. We can spend the winter. We can afford it," she nagged.

"I don't yearn to see it like you do. But getting out of Chicago is appealing. And there's no job in sight."

Alan was interested in the Cunard Line's *The Mauretania*. Fascinated with what was referred to as an "Ocean Greyhound" and the "Grand Old Lady of the Atlantic," launched in 1907, but refurbished from coal to oil turbines a few years ago. He enjoyed all the details and determinedly, relentlessly, shared his store of information. He related the intricate and endless details to Mignon over and over, referring to the ship as "she."

"She has a steel hull. She has four funnels, two masts, a shelter deck of steel with wood sheathing, and steel in fore and aft holds. She has eleven watertight bulkheads and six decks. The doors between the bulkheads can be closed from the bridge where the captain stands one hundred feet above the sea level. Her four funnels are each 155 feet high, and the two masts are 216 feet high. She has three anchors weighing ten tons each and anchor chains of 1,800 feet."

Boring details. Mignon was not interested. She *was* interested in the fact that "she" had accommodations for 563 first class passengers, 464 second class passengers,

1,400 third class passengers, and a crew of 938 officers and men. A very big ship. An adventure.

Alan booked passage. Mignon sent Harry the final manuscript for *Murder by Aristocrats*. They sublet their apartment in Oak Park to her college friend, Grace, and her husband, Glenn Hefner, and sailed from New York.

1931-32

Europe

The Mauretania met all their expectations. The size and the powerful engines impressed Alan. He spent hours in the bowels of the ship in the steamy, hot boiler rooms, getting acquainted with the men and learning the details of their work.

Despite their reading about *The Mauretania*, the pride of the Cunard line, supposedly bigger and more luxurious than *The Lusitania*, Mignon's eyes opened wide and she couldn't help but grin with the first sight of the accommodations. French Chateau and Italian Renaissance dining rooms. Richly carved African mahogany paneling in what was called the living room. More extravagant than the Ritz Carlton.

She had yearned for Europe and envisioned it since college European history and literature courses, but, when they planned the trip, she had wondered about the four days in the middle of the ocean. What did a person do all day in a floating hotel?

Once settled in their first-class suite, she wandered on the main deck from the spacious and luxurious living room to the dining room. It was equally luxurious, rivalling any first-class hotel. Noting her interest and obvious delight, a white-coated steward interrupted her exploring to tell her that the second-class dining room was also "well-appointed."

"Third class is pleasant too," he said. "Long banquet tables and benches. But you aren't allowed down there, ma'am. Mostly emigrants."

"No. I don't intend to go down there. I was just curious about the different accommodations," she said. She moved on to what they called the reading and writing room.

After that first day, she found quiet and aloneness there in the early mornings. Most passengers slept in, met their friends and companions to indulge leisurely in the multi-course breakfasts. Mignon had the spacious bookcase-lined room to herself. Serious writing required more sustained time, but she sat contentedly at one of the lovely large desks and made notes about the ship and the passengers and the moods of the ocean. All the ingredients for a new novel—*Death in a Fog.*

Afternoons she usually read there ensconced in a comfortable chair. Doubleday had just published Virginia Woolf's *The Waves*, and Harry had gifted it to her as they embarked. Whether he meant it to be or not, it was an appropriate read for an ocean voyage.

"Aren't our rooms and the dining room and the lounges wonderful? Isn't the food just exquisite?" she exclaimed at least once a day.

Alan responded with his information from what he called the bowels of the ship. "Sixty-eight-thousand shaft horsepower. It's steamy hot down there. But not as hot as when she burned tons of coal before the boilers were converted to oil."

Did he really think she cared? His intermittent participation in racing *petits chevaux*, the mechanical little horses gambling game the men played on deck, did amuse her. Interested her more than his encyclopedic knowledge of the ship engine. She yearned for more of that playful Alan.

After four days on the ocean enjoying all the luxuries of *The Mauretania*, they arrived in London on a cold, rainy day. Autumn, they had been told, was much like balmy autumn in Nebraska and Illinois, so they had anticipated sunny sight-seeing weather, not chilling rain.

Mignon first sighted a dull, gray foggy London through steamy taxicab windows—a disappointment.

The driver escorted them from the taxicab to the Mayfair Hotel entrance under a big, black umbrella. Inside, they waited. Waited to check into their suite. Waited for a bus boy to take their luggage to the elevator and to their suite. The crowded lobby buzzed—"Is he here? Have you seen him?" A legion of servants passed them pushing carts with a mountain of bags.

Alan, ordinarily the patient one, couldn't control his irritation. "What is going on?"

"Your countryman," the desk clerk sneered. He pointed at the front page of *The London Times* on the desk. "Charlie Chaplin has just arrived."

They happened to arrive the same day at the same hotel where Charlie Chaplin would begin his legendary European tour. His face covered the front page on *The London Times*.

They didn't get a glimpse of him. But every day they read about him in the newspapers. England worshiped him. According to *The Times*, thousands of people stood outside the theatre just to get a glimpse of him. Who knew he was that famous? He met with Winston Churchill and Mahatma Ghandi and Bernard Shaw and then traveled to Berlin and dined with Marlene Dietrich at the Hotel Adlon. After connecting with Oscar Straus in Vienna, he went to Paris, and, as Alan and Mignon did later, took the train to the French Riviera. The tabloids dripped with names of the famous.

"I am not about to stand in line with throngs of people to see Charlie Chaplin," Mignon said. "I could do that in New York if I was interested. What is the charisma? He is small and unattractive. I have never enjoyed his movies."

"You're just jealous of his fame." Alan laughed at her.

His perception annoyed her. But it was truth. Jealousy—the deadly sin she suffered from most. She didn't want to hear it though.

When the clerk handed Alan the key to their room when they finally got to the room that first day, he said, "Dinner at 8:00 in the dining room."

Alan raised his eyebrows. "8:00? Dinner at 8:00?"

"Yes, sir. Tea is served in the parlor at 5:00."

"We best get back here by 5:00 then," Alan the man of rituals said.

Mignon had read about English tea, of course. All those British novels. But she had no idea that English tea was an important meal with the most delicious and varied finger sandwiches—tinned salmon and cucumber, thinly sliced cucumber with cheese, ham with mustard—then plain or fruit scones with butter and jam, and finally, if you could eat another bite, fruit cake and chocolate cake and tarts.

"I am going to take the teatime practice home," she told Alan.

"Right. That will be quite a hit in suburban Chicago, or are you planning a manor house somewhere in rural Illinois?"

She ignored his disdain. London excited her as she'd dreamed it would. Cars honked. Taxi drivers yelled. People scurried by. It reminded her of New York City. She had an agenda for day and for night. No matter the chilly weather.

She bundled up in her wool coat and pulled the fur collar around her neck, and they boarded the new double-decker trolleys that clinked and clanged up and down the streets to Windsor Castle and Hyde Park and Piccadilly Circus.

They danced at the famous Kit-Cat Club in Haymarket which, lucky for them, had reopened after closing down twice in the past few years. The glass-fronted entrance looked like the entrance to a hotel. They walked into a huge lobby with showcases and into a cloakroom and then into a lounge. Alan finally found the staircase leading to the ballroom, the restaurant, and the grillroom, which were two floors *below* the street level.

She had never seen a ballroom like it—ivory, gold, and turquoise Italian Renaissance. Tall royal blue and gold pillars right up to the roof. The balcony had painted heraldic shields on the balustrade and a floral edging.

"It's eighty by sixty feet," Alan said. "I read about it."

Of course, he had.

A wide balcony circled the dance floor with a recessed space for the orchestra. They sat at a supper table set up in one of two parallel rows at the sides of the room.

The club opened for drinks and dinner at 10:00 p.m. Dining at 10:00 p.m.—Mignon couldn't get over the adventure and fun of it. And then they danced to kaleidoscopic shafts of purple, blue, and orange light projected onto the dance floor from above. At about 11:30, bejeweled women in evening gowns and men in tuxedos crowded in. The theatres must have closed. A medley of languages surrounded them. At midnight singers, dancers, acrobats, and jugglers came on the stage. What an experience!

There was no evidence of the Depression in London. It was light and color and dance, music, and laughter. And dancing always brought Alan and Mignon together, the most intimate thing they shared.

Carmen kept her apprised of life at home and piqued her conscience—fleetingly.

October 30, 1931
Dear Mignon,
The ship you sailed on sounds wonderful. What a luxurious way to travel. You mention that the third-class passengers were emigrants. I wonder what

country they were originally from. Were they going back? Leaving the U.S. because of the Depression? Did you try to get down to just see who those people were?

Nebraska is bleak as is all the Midwest and the South. We have drought and grasshoppers, dust storms and unrelenting heat. People are losing their farms. We hear heart-breaking stories of auction sales —families forced to sell their land and possessions after generations of farming. Many of them leaving for California.

Ironically, the area where you lived in Valentine is the only financially stable region. The ranchers there have water from the Niobrara River and are still able to grow hay to feed their cattle.

There are no jobs in the cities either. Unemployment in Lincoln is higher than any time in my life. You see homeless, jobless men on the streets everywhere. Men from the cities are hopping onto trains, riding until they get to the country, and hopping off in hopes of work or food or both. We hear about hobo camps and the fear these bands of men engender. Last week I saw a man selling pencils outside the Lincoln train depot with a hand-lettered cardboard sign that read, "Veteran." I presume a soldier from the Great War. It's depressing.

Many of our friends are affected. You remember Harold and John Rahn? They left for California in Harold's Ford coupe a couple of weeks ago. Harold lost his job, and Peter finished his law degree at the University of Nebraska, but law firms aren't hiring. They plan to work their way to California, picking fruit, Peter said, if nothing else.

I understand Grace and Glenn Hefner are renting your apartment in Oak Ridge. The future for them was bleak here. They were wise to leave. Even their old friends shunned them after his bank closed.

We're fortunate. So far enrollment at Nebraska Wesleyan is stable, and they're retaining faculty, so Charlie's position is secure, and Jackson High still needs me in the English department.

Enjoy Europe—

Love, Carmen

Mignon didn't want to think about the Depression. They *were* enjoying Europe. Now moving on to Paris— the train from Victoria Station to Dover, a ferry to Calais, and the train to Paris.

They stayed at the Crillon on the advice of New York friends who had told them they were pampered there, treated like royalty. It was a marvelous hotel on Place de la Concorde at the foot of the Champs-Élysées with one hundred twenty-four guest rooms, forty-six suites, three restaurants, a bar, a health club, an outdoor terrace.

"This is too expensive," Alan said. "We're spending too much money on fancy hotels."

"I'm enjoying it," Mignon scoffed. "We can afford it. Harry just wired. *Mystery at Hunting's End* has sold eight thousand copies."

She had hoped for some entré to Gertrude Stein's Saturday evening salon on 27 rue de Fleurus, but that didn't come about. She and Alan had some contacts with moneyed people from Chicago and New York living in

Paris, but no one from the artistic world to drop Mignon's name. In any event, Gertrude would no doubt have said, "Who? A mystery writer? I don't think so." Mignon comforted herself with the fact that the expats she idolized and most wanted to meet had left Paris. Hemingway had moved to Florida. Zelda Fitzgerald had been at a clinic in Switzerland, but she and Scott had gone back to the U.S. by the time Alan and Mignon got there.

People said Europe was on the cusp of change. The roaring twenties were over. But Paris was as beautiful, as romantic, and as exciting as she had hoped.

They strolled down Saint-Germain-des-Prés. They found Les Deux Magots and sat down at a table for two under the wide awning. Laughter and charmed chatter of French surrounded them. A tall, slim waiter in black pants and vest with a white towel over his arm, exuding nonchalance, came to their table.

"Deux pastis." She'd been waiting forever to order that sweet anise drink in Paris. "Here's to you, Ernest." She raised her glass to clink Alan's. "Hemingway hangs out here. Anais Nin met Henry Miller in one of these sidewalk cafés," she said.

She'd been reading about Paris forever. You knew Europe and Paris if you were a college English and arts major. You knew it from "English Lit" and "Literary Masterpieces." She'd enrolled in French every term, three years of French. And Edith Wharton lived in Paris.

The magic of being there gave her a lilt of happiness she wished Alan shared. He seemed oblivious to things that made her giddy with delight.

He did appreciate Parisian architecture and the bridges of the Seine, of course. They walked for hours along the Seine, stopping to watch the sidewalk artists, crossing frequently at a bridge to explore the neighborhoods on the other side.

They took a taxicab to Montmartre and trekked the streets.

"Montmartre isn't what you envisioned, is it?" Alan said, as he traipsed behind her on the cobblestone streets and up the steep steps to the Basilica at its top. "You live in a dream world, Mimi. Picasso and Braque and Modigliani are long gone."

She refused to let him spoil her delight. "Look at the view. Paris is before you. You can see the whole city from up here. You can see all the buildings you admire." She grabbed his hand.

She couldn't get enough of it. Picasso and Braque and Modigliani had been replaced in the streets around the Basilica by dozens of artists, young and old, some quite disreputable-looking, their easels set up to face the busy streets or cafés, their paints on the ground beside them. Everything for sale.

"Only ten francs, Madame. Only ten francs."

"*Ici, ici*, Madame. Take a bit of Paris home with you."

"The perfect souvenir, Madame."

The hawking accompanied the street musicians in a melange of voices and haunting saxophone. Black artists performed jazz in the bistros and bars everywhere in Paris, but they saw them especially in Montmartre. She had read about Montmartre. It was a story book. Euphoria. She floated.

They had always enjoyed music—from dancing music to opera, but they discovered new things about each other's interests on this trip. She searched out every exhibit of Monet and the other Impressionists. Discovered Berthe Morisot.

"Do you think Gertrude Stein would have included Berthe Morisot in her salons?' she mused as they walked along the narrow gallery of Morisot's paintings tucked behind the grand galleries of Monet.

"You told me Gertrude prefers the company of men," Alan said. "She would probably be jealous of a woman like Morisot."

He trudged along to the art museums on her list— The Louvre, Musée d'Orsay, Musée de Montmartre.

"I've had enough of the Impressionists," he said one morning. "We can walk to the Rodin Museum from our hotel." He'd found a place he wanted to see. She was pleased, happy to follow.

She put her old-lady, black tie shoes on and threw a black cape over her black ensemble. (She'd taken note of the French women hurrying along with their grocery carts or strolling the hallways of the museums in elegant black.) And they walked the four miles from the hotel to the cobblestone streets of Hotel Biron, home of the Musée Rodin.

Inside the stone walls—the famous *Thinker*. Mignon and Alan stood side-by-side in the garden staring up at the larger-than-life figure. She was really here! She was seeing this in person—with Alan.

They moved on to *Eternal Springtime* and *The Kiss*. Marble and bronze come to life. Powerful. Sensuous. Raw emotion. She reached for Alan's hand. He grasped hers—firm, warm. He looked down at her with one of his rare smiles.

On the way back to the hotel, after the long blocks of walking, they stopped to rest at a sidewalk café. Sat under an awning in the warm afternoon sun. Ordered *café au lait* and chocolate croissants. A day to remember.

Alan made return trips to the Musée Rodin in the early mornings before Mignon got out of bed. She loved him for it. It healed her heart. Intrigued her too. A side of him she'd never seen. Never anticipated.

At the end of those days of sightseeing, after walking miles and miles, they put their tired feet up, lit their Gauloises, and sipped a cognac. Alan slipped into bed and sighed with contented tiredness, unmindful of the acute physical longing the place engendered in her.

Mignon wanted to stay in Paris, but Alan had his fill. He was ready to settle down somewhere for a few weeks. Paris was for lovers. Not for the Edwards.

"Why don't you see a doctor before we leave?" she said. "You don't really know what the problem is, Alan. There are experts here in Paris. Surgeons in Europe have been treating problems like this for decades. It's nothing new."

She waited for a response. Anything. But he wouldn't indulge her.

"It isn't normal. It's just never talked about. Especially in the U.S. But sex shouldn't be unmentionable."

"Mimi, I'm not ignorant. I know there's a problem. I know you aren't happy. But surgery isn't the answer."

"Maybe it's psychological. I've read some things about psychoanalysis."

"I'm not going to be psychoanalyzed."

"You are stubborn and self-centered."

"And you shouldn't fling the self-centered label at anyone."

She didn't want to ask him just what he meant. Turning the heat of the argument away from sex to a competition about self-centeredness was pointless.

They left Paris for southern France in an unspoken truce.

Ah . . . *Nice la Belle*—Nice the beautiful. The city rose from a flat beach into gentle hills, bounded by the mountains. They had intended to go on and spend the winter in Florence, but the blue sea and blue sky and sunshine were alluring. They settled into a hotel in what was the Russian colony with an Italian manager, where most of the people staying were English, and French was the common language. A mixed flavor. Interesting and stimulating.

The gardens were lovely—roses, violets, all kinds of other flowers, orange and olive trees, winding little paths with steps and benches. Behind the hotel, Mignon walked the terraced path that led to the top of the hill with a view of the maritime Alps, blue sky, and blue sea.

She took deep breaths into the air of the writers and artists. Hemingway wrote here. The Fitzgeralds spent the early winter. Alan and Mignon had just missed them here as well as in Paris. That did not interest nor impress Alan, nor did the fact that Chagall and Picasso and Renoir and Cocteau had lived and painted here. He was no romantic.

She wrote every morning. She had told Harry she needed to travel. She needed to find new settings for her novels, and the Alpes-Maritime was certainly a new setting, a long way from the Midwest and even from New York City.

The Alps plunged straight down into the blue sea from the craggy coastline, a great setting for a murder. She filled her journal with notes. Strolled along the shore of the ocean for hours watching the waves, absorbed in the rhythmic wash of sound, creating stories, and lulled into calm from frustration with Alan who seemed to need people less and less. Or she was more aware of it than she had been before. She could work for four or five hours alone, and she did that, but people stimulated and energized her.

"I'm tired of the glitter and the artificiality," he finally said. "All these rich English and nouveau riche. Crass Americans flaunting their wealth. The men with diamond rings on their fat fingers, their glittering women adorning them."

I'm not an adornment, she thought. *Nor am I adored, though it would be nice to be adored now and then. And I wouldn't mind him finding me physically desirable.*

When Alan did feel like leaving the villa to explore the Riviera, he preferred to drive their rented roadster though there were eighty-nine miles of trams in the area.

"I don't want someone else determining what's important or interesting. I want to be in charge of what I see," he said when she suggested taking advantage of the trams.

He did indulge, with resignation, her interest in the Casino de le Jetée, an opulent Belle Époque casino, perched at the end of a long pier which seemed to float in the bay.

"I don't care about the gambling," she said when he objected to spending more than one evening there. "It's a stimulating atmosphere. Wealthy winter residents from all over Europe are in the crowd."

Alan obviously preferred the quiet evenings in Valentine by the fire, Mignon reading her day's work to him, Jericho by his side. He was bored and restless in Nice. She was neither. There were concerts, the casino, theatre, and she didn't even find enough time for massages and shampoos and waves.

"I thought you wanted to work," he said.

"I am working no matter what I'm doing. I'm working out stories and characters. They occupy my mind no matter what I'm doing. When I'm walking, I'm working on plots and mulling over the action. When I'm in the car, I may be looking at the scenery, but my head is in a story. It doesn't all happen magically sitting in my room at the typewriter. I thought you understood that."

After several weeks, they moved to a little hotel-pension place in the Alps north of Nice. The season was slow, so the proprietors gave her, for no extra cost, a small attic room to write in. But she couldn't work there without a sweater, her fingers were always cold, and the windows faced a brick wall so no view. No distractions from her work. Ultimately little inspiration either. A wordless room.

The domestic problems didn't help. She spent hours hunting for maids, and every cook she found grew restive and temperamental just when she was into the book and temperamental herself.

She worked on a setting in the Alpes-Maritime—*The White Cockatoo*—if Harry approved that title. One of the most arduous tasks in the early stages of writing a new novel was to make a time chart. She needed to know where her characters were and what they were doing at every moment of the time, so the mystery could evolve. This was her first attempt at a story without the red-headed nurse Sarah Keate. She had to let Sarah Keate go. She struggled to write a male protagonist and narrator, trying to get into a man's head. Her working relationships were with men, but the only man she knew well was Alan. Or she thought she knew him. Was he typical? She didn't think so.

She wrote the dedication. The easy page. This novel to Aunt Nelle, her gift in Chicago, their entré to the music world, and to Charles Cadman for the song he had composed for her.

The south of France was a feast, the Depression, a myth here. Life was gay and amusing, and she was finally working. Pleased with her progress, she had just pulled a third page from the typewriter the morning after an entertaining evening at Jetta, when Alan burst into her attic haven.

"Serving as your escort is getting old," he announced. "I need to do meaningful work. Been idle way too long. I've a job offer from the Illinois State Highway Department. We need to get back to Chicago." They left Nice April 30.

1932-36

Chicago

"Junior Engineer. What a title," Alan grumbled.

"You were the one who was sick and tired of traipsing all over the globe," Mignon snapped back. She didn't care about his job. She didn't care about his frustrations. She certainly didn't care about his title.

He left for work. She settled into an easy chair with a cup of coffee at her side. She lit a cigarette to fortify herself. The reviews of *The White Cockatoo* had arrived in the morning mail. First, the *Cleveland Plainsman:* Bruce Catton called it a "bell ringer" in his syndicated column. A bell ringer. That would be read in every newspaper that carried his column. She smiled to herself and opened the *Saturday Review of Fiction.* Their reviewer described it as "an ingenious story with a rapid-fire narrative, a skillfully contrived plot, a mystery well sustained, and a solution that neatly tied all the threads of the book together." She laughed. Then read that lengthy comment over and over. It said everything—everything she hoped to accomplish in her novels. She scissored it out and pasted it in the scrapbook she'd started in Valentine when Harry mailed her the reviews of *The Patient in Room 18*—before she had subscribed to those newspapers herself, before she even understood the significance of reviews.

A letter from Harry polished her ego.

> May 1, 1932
> Dear Mignon,
> With the exception of *The New York Times*, the reviews of *The White Cockatoo* are good, theirs the only reviewer who suggested the story would have benefited from the voice of Sarah Keate.
> Your readers like the Alpes-Maritimes setting. Life is dreary. The adventure in romantic Europe is an escape from their daily life. Women are heartened and entertained by your novels.
> *Mystery Magazine* has contacted us regarding your writing a short story for their monthly issue. You might consider having Sarah Keate solve a mystery in a hotel in Avignon.
> Warm Regards,
> Harry

Nice had been a boon. She could write in spite of Alan's restlessness and discontent. In spite of her unhappiness with him. She could write a good novel.

In that frame of mind, she put the tip of her sharp silver opener into the corner of the envelope of a letter from Carmen and slit it with a smile, anticipating Carmen's usual admiration and approval.

> May 1, 1932
> Dear Mignon,

The mailman delivered my copy of *The White Cockatoo* on Friday. I read it this weekend. You always tell me that you must experience the setting, and your sojourn in France has certainly produced a dark, mysterious, cold, and windy place! I hope your hotel wasn't quite as bleak as the one you described in the novel. I couldn't help but think about your letters from Nice, your "la belle France." Are you craving romance? There's more romance in this than in the Sarah Keate novels.

Marriage must be more challenging than you have admitted, my friend. I know the years in Valentine weren't idyllic, but I had hoped Chicago, and especially Paris and Nice, would make it better.

The adventures in moving from one place to another with Alan are apparently no longer intriguing. Are you longing for stability in the words you attribute to your engineer protagonist, Jim Sundeen: ". . . the same routine, the same home year after year, the same people?"

Are these your own sentiments: "An engineer should not marry." (An engineer should not marry?) "Marriage and engineering don't go well together."

Jim's wife has a bad time of it—no kind of society, living in all kinds of wild places—camp, shacks, hideous little hotels—no family, no friends, no music, no theatre, no "gayety."

What's happening to you? You don't seem to lack any of those things. You escape to the city often enough to nourish your soul more than a little. And you don't exactly live or vacation in shabby places, nor are you deprived of music and theatre!

Where does the fiction begin and end? Exploring your own feelings?

It sounds like marriage to Alan is getting you down. I hear you in Jim's words: "I am not an imaginative man; engineers like exactness and are inclined to discredit impulses, feelings that cannot be definitely labeled."

Is that Alan? You two are very different. But I've assumed you appreciated the differences? He excited and fascinated you in the beginning.

What about those first years in Valentine? I remember Alan's listening to you read in the evenings, and his drawing the schematic for you for the hunting lodge story, so your readers would have a better sense of the place. What has happened? If I read you through your hero in the novel, you're disillusioned with Alan and with marriage!

I'm no doubt the only one who sees those few paragraphs about engineers and marriage as personal and significant. Your readers will be, as always, fascinated by the characters and the suspense with the three murders. The howling mistral wind and dark shadows of the creepy hotel will satisfy them. But I worry about you.

Love, Carmen

Mignon wanted feedback about the novel. She needed Carmen's opinion . . . her approval. Of the novel. She didn't need or want Carmen analyzing her life. *Where does the fiction begin and end! It's a story, Carmen. I'm a writer. It's not my life. And you make me feel like a howling mistral.*

In that murderous mood, she ripped open the second envelope paying scant attention to the name and return address. Then looked more carefully at the unfamiliar handwriting. Faith Baldwin! Faith Baldwin, the most well-known of the romance writers and one of the most highly paid. She remembered her mother reading Faith Baldwin years ago in *Ladies' Home Journal* where her novels were frequently published in six-part serials.

> May 1, 1932
> Dear Mrs. Edwards,
> I have just read *The Patient in Room 18,* and I am enchanted with Sarah Keate. Harry Maule tells me you make frequent trips to New York City. Please contact me when you are next here, so we can arrange to meet for lunch.
> Sincerely, Faith Baldwin

A personal letter from Faith Baldwin! Faith Baldwin made $300,000 on her books last year, according to Harry. Mignon had seen Baldwin's novels described as "ripe, full of sunlight, crowded with romance," and what intrigued her most, the description of her characters as "people making do with each other." What did that mean? Baldwin didn't write about sex. Mignon didn't write about it. Nice women didn't talk about it. Certainly, didn't admit they wanted it.

After they had become close friends, Mignon asked Faith about that reflection on marriage and the significance of the characters in her novels who "made do with each other."

"There are many reasons to stay in a marriage," Faith told Mignon. "Women can 'make do' if they're respected. If a husband doesn't stand in the way of their professional fulfillment, for example. Or if there's real equality, not subservience." Mignon would remember that in the coming years.

And the Junior Engineer's discontent with his job took a new path. Politics crept insidiously into their lives. Alan was obsessed with the Depression and the presidential election.

Franklin Roosevelt, the governor of New York, won the Democratic nomination, and he broke tradition by boarding a plane and flying to Chicago to accept the nomination instead of waiting to announce the formal news at his home. All of that elated his supporters including Alan. Roosevelt promised a "New Deal." The broadcasting world and newspapers went crazy with the excitement.

Over the years, Alan and Mignon had paid scant attention to politics—the political world peripheral, certainly not central.

It had never occurred to her that they could disagree so vehemently. How could their views be so different? How could they have been married this many years and not realized the differences?

Alan sat at the kitchen table and read the *Chicago Trib* from first page to last with his morning coffee before he went to work, and Mignon got a thorough account of the presidential campaign. He read aloud what he thought she should know.

In the evening, he barely shed his coat before turning on the radio. They listened, not only to the news broadcasts, but also to the reporters' accounts of Roosevelt's travels, his stumping for the election from one end of the country to the other.

After one particularly obnoxious and hour-long evening broadcast, she burst.

"How can you believe that the government should step in?"

"Something has to be done, Mimi. Hoover's hands-off policies aren't working."

"A bank moratorium?"

"It couldn't be worse than it is now. People have lost the savings they'd worked for all their lives."

"A pension? He calls it social security. For everyone? No matter what work they do? Or how they manage their own finances? What about personal responsibility?"

"Not everyone comes from your privileged background, Mimi."

"Father worked hard for everything he has."

Nothing she said would change his views. And she wasn't about to agree with his.

"I know we can agree about one thing," he said before he went off to bed. "You can't legislate morality." He picked up her empty bourbon tumbler and waved it at her with a smile.

Roosevelt's promise to end Prohibition had even turned her Woman's Christian Temperance Union mother off. "I can't vote for him," she said. "No matter his 'New Deal.'"

What Mignon remembered about politics growing up was a sedate conversation at the breakfast table the morning of elections with Father reminding Mother of his choices, naming each office and the candidate to vote for. No argument or discussion. She had an image of her mother standing in front of the hallway mirror in a proper navy suit with navy pumps to match, turning to check on the seams on her hose, putting the pins in her hat before she and Father left for the polling place together.

Mignon and Alan had no such amicable understanding. And then there were the radio chats. When Roosevelt was governor of New York, he went directly to the people with monthly radio chats. Now with his magnificent voice, he broadcast regularly on national radio. Alan insisted on listening.

"His language is so informal, I can't take him seriously as a president," Mignon said.

"Hoover sounds like he's giving a sermon," Alan countered. "You're a snob. And in the minority. He appeals to all the frustrated people out there without jobs, standing in food lines. They don't care about his proper English."

She was surprised by her own flash of anger. She didn't utter the "I hate you," but she hated him at the moment. Everything wrong in their marriage condensed and found voice in these political disagreements.

"He's a rich aristocrat with a rich man's schemes to get us out of the Depression," she said, but she was no match for Alan's logical, point-by-point defense. "You act like this is a college class debate. I didn't take a debate course. You back me into a corner."

"You're too emotional. You can't always have the last word, Mimi. And you know I'm right about Hoover's incompetence."

"How could we have been married this long and partisan politics were never important?"

"Things change," he said.

On election night, Alan tuned into CBS then settled into his armchair with Jericho on the floor beside him. Mignon put her ash tray next to her on the sofa across from him and lit up. It took hours for the state-by-state election results to come in. Many cigarettes and a tall bourbon, and then Roosevelt's theme song, "Happy Days Are Here Again," crackled over the air waves. "An astounding landslide for Roosevelt," the announcer said. She wept in disappointment.

"Happy Days Are Here Again" played on and on. After the Illinois election results were officially announced, she couldn't stand anymore and went to bed.

No matter who was president or what the political situation, Mignon could escape in her work. Writing— her obsession. Her passion. Writing, like a nag, demanded her attention.

And women writers were making money for publishers, so Harry, her mentor, also a premier editor for Doubleday, encouraged her, with light-hearted suggestions like, "broaden your scope and sharpen your skills."

His latest recommendation was for her to read Edith Wharton's *The Writing of Fiction*, published, not by Doubleday, but by Scribner's.

Mignon resented the suggestion, and she resented the implication that she needed better skills, but Wharton had always been one of her idols, and she set to reading. What she found was a history of the novel more than a book of advice for writers. And pages and pages about what Wharton called "the present penchant for stream of consciousness writing." Interesting, but not relevant for a mystery writer. She exposed her petulant self in a note to Harry:

> It's a disappointing book. I'd like to review it, and not with Bennet Cerf's accolades. Wharton condescends. She's a literary snob. Arrogant. She wrote those interminable sentences in lofty language to impress literary scholars. And she has no pertinent advice for me, Harry. Nothing to say to me as a mystery writer. Wharton claims that "a writer would never do his best until he ceases to think of his readers and his editor and his publisher and begins to write, not for himself, but for that other self with whom the creative artist is always in mysterious correspondence." On and on and notice the "he."
>
> I don't believe her. I don't believe that Wharton doesn't consider her readers or care about what her editor would think of the work or care if it would be published. She doesn't need to earn her living, but she does care about recognition and fame no matter what she says.

Even Virginia Woolf admits that she cares about reviews. "We all care about reviews," she once said, adding that she wanted to be taken seriously as a writer, but that brisk sales and financial independence were very important. She wanted to afford nice things. I do too—want to afford nice things, that is. But you know that!

She did crave recognition. But she didn't like to admit it. Recognition by other writers and competition fed her hunger to write. And she depended on Harry for editing and advice, but she needed another point of view, a woman's point of view. She trusted Carmen. And trust was essential. Writers bare themselves with their words. Even though Carmen's comments about her marriage irritated her, Carmen was a perceptive reader, and Mignon was learning to value her opinions about the writing. She asked Carmen to read a draft copy of *The Dark Garden*—

Mina Petrie, wealthy recluse dying of undisclosed ailments. Her friend and companion, Charlotte Weinberg, killed in a fog.

August 4, 1933
Dear Mignon,
You always engage me with your descriptions of the place—the mansion, rain and fog this time. And then the first sentences with the provocative point of view of the woman who is murdered.
But I'm not sure about your new detective Crafft. You describe him as a very little brown man,

and as an ugly man with a brown face. A brown face? What sort of prejudice will the reader infer?

Then the lovely young Katie is given an opioid to sleep after the accident. Must you give opiates to your young protagonist who hits and kills another woman in the fog? Is she that helpless? Are young women that helpless?

I am fascinated by the cremation of the rich reclusive aged aunt. How did you come up with that? Cremation isn't all that common.

More questions than answers! But I'm always happy to oblige you with my opinions!

Love, Carmen

Mignon took the comments seriously. She read the manuscript again, considered the case of the new detective, decided she liked him, and sent the manuscript off to Harry.

Alan was complaining about his work with the State Highway Department. He said his experience and expertise weren't recognized. He wasn't interested in traipsing around to every social event in Chicago this winter either, he said. The "traipsing" a common censure flung at Mignon. They plugged along, trapped in unhappiness.

"We have to talk about it, Alan," she said when she'd mustered the courage. "It isn't just your job or social life in Chicago. You are as unhappy in our marriage as I am."

"I'm not unhappy with our marriage."

"Our marriage isn't normal. There must be a physical reason. This is not normal. Or is it just me? Would it be the same with any woman or just me? Why won't you discuss it? We need to talk about it."

"You are arguing with yourself," he said. "You rant and work yourself into a frenzy. There is nothing to talk about. It's just the way it is."

An impenetrable wall of stubbornness. She didn't bring it up again for months and months. She filled her notebooks and wrote and wrote and wrote—four novels in the two years since they'd moved back to Chicago.

Meanwhile, the book world buzzed with Isak Dinesen's arrival in New York. Harry called to tell Mignon. "You must meet her," he said. "You must come to New York and meet her." *Really go to New York just to meet Isak Dinesen?*

People were referring to her as the "Danish Baroness" and were enthralled with her exotic life in Kenya which she had now given up. According to Harry, Random House had published her *Gothic Tales* after a long haggle, and despite her insistence on using a pseudonym. Mignon couldn't believe the pampering. The woman's real name was Karen Blixen, Dinesen her maiden name, and Isak, the Danish version of Isaac. Yet she didn't want to be mistaken for a man. What a hypocrite. Wouldn't you know the book was a best seller, and Book of the Month Club accepted it immediately.

Even Hemingway was besotted with her. He was quoted as saying the Pulitzer should have gone to her rather than him. What nonsense! Mignon did not intend to take the time to read the book though she couldn't avoid the newspaper coverage.

Dineson obviously loved to be photographed too. The newspapers described her as "striking" and "glamorous," as if there were no American women writers in her class. *And Alan teases me about my preoccupation with clothes.*

The New York Times called Dinesen one of the most picturesque and flamboyant literary personalities of the century. "A dramatic persona who relishes the sweetness of fame and the company of the great and the glamorous," the reporter said.

"I'm not interested in her. I really don't need to meet her," Mignon told Harry. "But thanks for the invitation."

"Green-eyed," Alan said.

She wanted to challenge him. *Not true.* She hated that he read her. She could pretend she wasn't jealous of other writers if it wasn't said aloud. The truth was that jealousy even drove her to write.

Alan was now working as a sales engineer for John I. Herman Company, a heating and air conditioning business in Oak Park.

"I hate selling . . . pandering," he complained at the end of every day. And sat, sullen and silent, in front of the radio.

"It's a job. Not the job of your dreams. You're discontent about everything. It doesn't help me. I'm struggling with this novel."

"Is that my fault?"

A stupid remark from him. She'd never blamed him for the struggle in writing. It was an encounter with words and a search for words to tell a story and describe characters. If anything, she retreated from him when she was in the thick of the writing battle.

He was absorbed in the plans and the development of the grounds and buildings for the World's Fair. Read Mignon the stories about it from *The Chicago Tribune* every day.

"The land along the shores of Lake Michigan is owned by the state, not the city. Chicago has strict building codes, but they don't have to be followed . . . The theme of the fair is A Century of Progress, a reference to Chicago's Centennial . . . Architects and engineers are using new techniques and designing buildings that used man-made materials."

Really.

Maybe Carmen would be interested. Mignon invited her to come and visit. As an afterthought, "bring June."

Alan had a plan for their day at the Fair. He never set out on an adventure without a plan. First, they would see the Homes of Tomorrow exhibits and the automobile exhibits with the latest models he had been reading about.

With June between them, holding their hands, Carmen and Mignon trailed behind him as they threaded their way through the throngs of women in the Homes of Tomorrow and then to the automobile exhibits. Alan led them from the Cadillac featuring their V-16 engine, to the new Nash, to the Lincoln limousine with the rear engine, and then his favorite, of course, the silver Pierce Arrow. He waved his hands, beaming with the pleasure of pointing out the significant features of each display.

Then quite unexpectedly he said, "I think Carmen and June would enjoy the Sky Ride," and he took June's hand. They got in the queue for tickets, and he bent down to say, "The transporter bridge will take us along the lake shore from one end of the fair to the other, June."

He sat next to her on the Sky Ride, pointing out the sights as they moved along the lake shore. They got off at the carnival, and he walked ahead with her. She rode the merry-go-round and the miniature cars and the airplanes going around in circles, grinning, and waving at them. Mignon experienced a vicarious, through-a-child's-eyes enjoyment she hadn't anticipated.

"Please, please, please take me on the Ferris wheel," June begged her mother at the end of the airplane ride.

"No," Carmen said. "And not the roller coaster either." Neither Carmen nor Mignon liked those rides. They hadn't even liked those rides when they were teenagers, gathered with giddy high school friends at the state fair in Nebraska.

"I would be happy to go with you," Alan said.

June looked up at him, smiled, and took his hand.

Carmen and Mignon stood beneath the monstrous wheel and waved each time their chair rocked to the bottom.

They ended the day driving through the exhibits and the grounds in a motorized wicker vehicle that Alan rented. But Mignon was dying to go back for an evening at "The Streets of Paris" exhibit where Sally Rand was doing her famous Fan Dance. She had performed some Lady Godiva-inspired appearance at the gates the day the Fair opened and now danced three evenings a week to screaming crowds. Alan wasn't interested, but Carmen and Mignon couldn't go without an escort.

"I can't leave June," Carmen said.

"Well, we can't take her with us. You really can't miss this opportunity to see Sally Rand," Mignon told her. "You can't miss it because of a six-year-old. She won't remember that you left her. She will be asleep most of the time we're gone. Our housekeeper, Mary, will take good care of her."

"She is just a little girl, and she's in a new and strange place, Mignon. Mary is a stranger," Alan said. But he and Carmen both gave in to the cajoling. They said good night to a tearful June and left her sitting on the floor with Jericho's head in her lap.

"Jericho will keep you company." Alan patted her small blonde head. "Mary will tuck you into the big bed in the guest room and let Jericho sleep on the floor beside you."

Sally Rand was a stunning 5'1" blonde with a perfect figure—35-22-35. She danced behind two seven-foot ostrich fans, screening parts of her body provocatively. She looked nude, but they suspected she wore a body stocking of some sort. Delighted men cheered. Mignon was glad that Alan was solemn, unmoved, indifferent, or at least that was his demeanor.

The trio agreed that it was one of those events you were glad to have witnessed both because it was the talk of the town and because you knew it would become part of entertainment history and lore. A couple weeks later, Alan and Mignon received a thank you note from Carmen, and a sweet note from June.

Dear Mr. and Mrs. Edwards,
Thank you for taking me to the World's Fair.
And the Ferris wheel and the roller coaster.
Sincerely, June Hornsby

A charming child. Carmen, like her mother and Mignon's, had taught her the importance of thank you notes. The note reminded Mignon of Alan's obvious enjoyment of their time with June. It had surprised her. Seeing him in a new, unexpected role made her wonder . . . Did he regret their childlessness? She couldn't see herself as a mother. She wasn't as comfortable around June as Alan seemed to be. She couldn't imagine life with a child. Would a child compensate for lack of sex in their marriage? Would they be happier? How could she possibly find enough time to write with all the demands a child imposes? How could they travel with a child?

That fall, after living in Paris for thirty years, Gertrude Stein came home. The literary world tittered with the news: "Gertrude Stein and Alice Toklas are touring. Gertrude is lecturing in Los Angeles . . . in

Kansas . . . in Chicago. Gertrude Stein's opera, *Four Saints in Three Acts,* is premiering on Broadway."

"We have to go. I have to see it. It's her only opera. You love opera. It's supposedly a portrayal of saints as Black," Mignon told Alan. "An all Black cast and singers. It's directed by Eva Jessye. She's a prominent Black choral director."

"According to *The New York Times,* Gertrude's words are verbal nonsense and the score is a collage of non-operatic American-style hymns, marching bands, and parlor music," Alan said. "I have absolutely no interest in it."

"You could go because it's something I want to do," Mignon said.

Guilt didn't move him. Then Fanny's fiancé read the script. "I understood about one line of it," he said. That cinched it for Alan.

Annoyed and as tempted as she was to just get on the train to New York, she couldn't envision herself walking into the Met alone; it just wasn't done. But Fanny had known Gertrude for years.

"She's coming to lecture and teach a two-week seminar at the University of Chicago. I'll arrange for you to meet her and Alice."

Mignon was late for the arranged lunch. Gertrude, Alice, and Fanny were already seated in the Biltmore Dining Room when she arrived. Gertrude stood up as Mignon approached the table.

Mignon had seen many photos of Stein over the years, but she wasn't prepared for Stein's commanding appearance. She was a massive woman with a head like a Roman emperor on a body like a modern stone sculpture.

"This is Mignon Edwards." Fanny introduced them. Mignon felt like curtsying and kissing her hand when Gertrude held it out, but she restrained herself and shook it.

"I like your work," Stein said.

Mignon couldn't think beyond a quiet, "Thank you."

"You know I'm somewhat obsessed with detective stories."

"Yes," Alice added. "We met Dashiell Hammett in Los Angeles, and then we stopped in every drug store in every hamlet from California to Illinois picking up detective novels."

"I read your *White Cockatoo.* It's good writing," Gertrude interrupted.

Good writing. From the doyen. Mignon smiled. Overawed. Stein and Fannie chattered, Alice nodding or assenting in the background. They had finished the entrée before Mignon relaxed enough in the presence of this legend to engage in any conversation.

"I appreciated the comments you made to the *Washington Post* reporter about my novel," she blurted. "Thank you."

"The setting in southern France was charming and quite familiar to me, but what I'm interested in is how you develop your plots? Where do you get the information for your murders? How do you decide who will get murdered and how? I am obsessed with murder," Stein said, leaning toward Mignon, her hands clasped. "I have even arranged to ride in a squad car with a couple Chicago policemen tomorrow evening."

She turned, looked at Alice, and smiled. "Alice thinks it's absurd and could even be dangerous. Ridiculous. It would just be a bonus to run into one of the Capone gangs." She chuckled in that famously deep, hearty way of the legend.

Like the trip to Paris, meeting Gertrude was fantasy realized.

Alan lasted one year as a salesman. He didn't have the "hail fellow, well met" spontaneity necessary. Too serious a demeanor. He gratefully accepted an offer from the Chicago Underground Construction Company where he had worked before their trip to Europe.

"Now we can afford that $50,000 house in River Forest." Mignon had been nagging him for months. River Forest was referred to as "the village" and only ten miles from downtown Chicago. The houses there were grand, and grand people lived in them.

The house she coveted was just down the street from Frank Lloyd Wright's "Winslow House," built just ten years before. Her house was white stucco—Spanish Renaissance with floor-to-ceiling, stained-glass windows, marble floors in the dining room, living room, and library. Terra Cotta in the kitchen and breakfast room. It had two fireplaces and a sunroom, only three bedrooms, but a separate guest house set in wonderful gardens—lush green lawn and hedges surrounding a pool. She couldn't wait to move in.

And she had finally joined the ranks of Faith Baldwin who was in such demand by the women's magazines!

"*Ladies' Home Journal* wants to publish *Fair Warning*, in serial form," Harry wrote.

"You must revise the novel for six installments. Take into consideration that the chapter published each month must end in such a way as to keep the reader in suspense and anxious for the next installment," he reminded her.

She read the endings and beginnings of chapters in the novel with that in mind and began the frustrating and tedious work of revision.

It worked. Carmen approved.

December 10, 1936
Dear Mignon,
I just finished the last installment of your *Fair Warning* in *Ladies' Home Journal*. It's your best yet. I waited impatiently for every issue. Your new detective, Jacob Waite, is a pleasant change from Nurse Sarah Keate. I liked her, but she was becoming predictable and boring. You must have been bored writing about her too. Do your characters begin to bore you? I do hope you are working on another story with the somber and intriguing Jacob.

The constant rain in this novel is like another character. I feel the drizzle and the dampness, its weight on the bushes and the clusters of sedum and wild phlox in the garden. The relentless sounds on the roof and on the French windows inside. It enhances the gloom and the sense of foreboding! I wish, though, that Marcia wasn't quite such a delicate flower! I do like the way you describe "tears raining down her cheeks" instead of sobbing. That is real and not too melodramatic, but I would like her better if she didn't need seclusion and a sedative to calm her after the murders. Nor a nurse to keep her company.

The romance between Rob and Marcia is tender, but I enjoy the mystery, so don't stray too far from mysteries into romance. You've done a superb job of casting suspicion on several characters in the small caste, and in setting the scene—so much darkness, so many black spaces and shadows, pools of shadows as Marcia creeps up and down the staircase and into the library at night. So many lights that must be turned on to get rid of the shadows.

The suspense builds with the interesting accumulation of incidents and clues from each of your characters. And the story zips right along. Seems like more so than with Nurse Sarah Keate. Does that have anything to do with your writing it for serial publication?

As always, I enjoy your descriptions of the clothes! Ah—the cedar closet with the broadtail coat, the sable choker, and the white ermine evening wrap in brown paper envelopes tied with twine. Beatrice's summer things labeled in the wardrobe—green taffeta wrap, white quilted wrap, three knit suits, white linen suit. I suspect that all these things are in your own wardrobe and cedar closet. What a clever idea to give a summer wrap significance and make it a clue to the murderer!

Life goes on boringly in Lincoln. Like many of your readers, I escape in stories of your charmed world.

Love, Carmen

Harry had been concerned that she was emphasizing romance over suspense, and her readers would complain. She didn't want to argue with him, but magazines, including *Redbook*, sent requests for contracts regularly now, and the earnings were significant. Their readers were more interested in romance than in mystery—and heavy on the romance. The romance in *Fair Warning* worked. Women readers wanted handsome, virile heroes and beautiful young women whose love kindled in the midst of murder.

Mignon had quit reading to Alan in the evenings or expecting his approval. She was past it. She would have been embarrassed to read some of the romantic scenes in her latest novels to him anyway. She knew he would suspect she was romanticizing and substituting those stories for the lack of physical intimacy in her own life. Or worse yet, that she had experienced it. Though how or when that would have been possible, she didn't know. Alan wouldn't understand about fiction, that when she wrote about passionate kisses and embraces, she was imagining. She hadn't had the experience. She didn't know a man in that way—it was all imagination. Or did the literal, logical, unimaginative man even care?

1937

St. Petersburg

"My contract will expire this month," Alan announced on the eve of the new year. "The end of working for the Underground Construction Company."

"Now what?"

"I don't know. Something interesting will come along."

"Perfect time for a winter vacation. I just got a check for $10,750 from Warner Brothers. Movie rights to the Nurse Keate novels. We haven't taken a winter vacation since Nice. Six years ago."

They had New Year's Day dinner with Aunt Nelle and Uncle Oscar and Constance. Just the five of them in their alcove dining room. A fire in the fireplace. No servants. One of those wrapped-in-calm times. Quiet conversations, catching up on the news from the Chicago music world.

And Alan told them about his expired contract. "Mimi thinks we should take a winter vacation," he said, as Constance got up to bring the silver coffee pot from the buffet. She filled their cups. He lit a cigarette. "She wants out of this icy cold weather."

"Nice?" Aunt Nelle asked.

"*Not* Europe again."

"I think Florida," Mignon said. "We haven't been there. I just sold the rights to the Nurse Keate novels. We can celebrate." She wanted Aunt Nelle to know they could afford a winter vacation in spite of Alan's unemployment, but it would be crass to talk about the money.

"St. Petersburg," Constance said. "Go to the Renaissance Resort. It's a showplace right on the waterfront. Guests are treated like royalty. You would love it, Mignon. Powder white sand beach, two beachfront pools. An 18-hole golf course, Alan."

Mignon made the reservations.

Constance hadn't exaggerated. Their fourth floor accommodations were palatial, and the view made her heart happy. From a desk set in front of floor-to-ceiling windows, she could look up from her typewriter and see the green-blue of the ocean meeting the blue sky. Fluffy white clouds floated on the horizon. She could hear the murmur of voices from the boardwalk, and the rhythmic slap of the waves washing ashore like background music.

She wrote in the morning. In the afternoon she donned a straw hat and strolled along the ocean shore. Lake Michigan had initiated her to the pleasure and joy of water after the many years growing up in dry Nebraska. She didn't have Alan and his friends' comfort playing in the lake, but she'd walked the sandy shore, feasting on the limitless lake and the sky. Here she was on another adventure, a different but endless sea. She walked and walked. A warm wave washing over her

bare feet now and then gave her a shiver of surprise. Her
mind wandered into the scenes from the novel.

The murder takes place the night before the scheduled
wedding of the protagonist, heiress to a fortune, Dorcas
Whipple. Dorcas has known the prospective groom all her
life. They have a kind of sensible, conventional devotion.
There is nothing at all emotional in her relationship with him
nor does she anticipate anything different after marriage.

Surrounded by sea and sky, soft breeze lifting her
hair, the plot evolved with each measured step of her
bare feet sinking into the sand:

The groomsman arrives. Dorcas dances with him, her
head level with his shoulders, she looks up, and her senses
plunge. The prospective groom is found dead the night before
the wedding.

A title came to her—*Hasty Wedding*. Not unlike her
own. Too young. Why had she been so anxious to get
married? Social pressure? Family? Girls were expected
to marry no matter their other plans. Even college grads.
Friends expected it. If you waited too long, the right
person might not come along. She could blame it on
them. But she fell for Alan. Turned away from the
writing she'd barely begun. He was interesting and
more settled than the fraternity guys. His seriousness
had appealed to her. And the excitement of travel and
living in Chicago . . .

She walked the beach every day working out the kinks in the plot, thinking about the characters, storing the information for writing the next morning.

At the end of the day, they ate five-course dinners— Alan called them three-fork dinners in one of three dining rooms with the din of conversation, clinking glasses, and waiters hovering to place a napkin on your lap. Or they called for room service and enjoyed quiet. A waiter rolled a cart into their suite and, with a flourish, swished a white cloth off platters of marlin or grouper or shrimp, all the fresh seafood they didn't get in Chicago.

Alan golfed every day, desperate for something to do and restless as always on extended vacations. They tired of each other. He was as happy as Mignon when Faith Baldwin and her companion Gonnie, also vacationing in Florida, came by to visit.

"We have only a couple days here," Faith said, as the women settled into easy chairs. Alan, the perfect host, stood by.

"My publishers want me to go to Palm Springs," Faith said. "They tell me it's the new playground of the west and a likely setting for a novel. They urged me to experience it. Brooklyn and Manhattan are my milieu, but I am willing to try a new setting."

"Let me get you a drink before Mignon interrupts with her news," Alan said. "A Gin Rickey? Or any other gin concoction? Cognac? An Old Fashioned—my specialty? Vermouth? Always have triple sec on hand. Mignon will have bourbon, of course."

Mignon couldn't wait for Alan to serve the drinks. "We do have great news! We bought a house in North

Stamford. Long Ridge Village District. Not far from you."

"She had to live in River Forest where important people live. Now she wants to live near you," Alan said.

Mignon and Alan had looked at houses there several times when they visited Faith and Gonnie, but Mignon hadn't told them they'd found a house they liked.

"It's a lovely house. Nearly a hundred years old. Built when the Greek Revival style was in vogue. But it's been completely updated and renovated."

"What do you think, Alan?" Gonnie turned their attention to him as he handed her the Old Fashioned with a smile. He passed highballs on to Faith, then Mignon. She was curious about what he would answer.

"What do I think? When Mimi is restless for a different house, it doesn't matter. It's a colorful place. Ashlar walls trimmed with red sandstone. Framed by columns. Colorful but structurally substantial."

"What about moving from Chicago? That's been your place."

"Mimi claims it isn't convenient for her anymore, and I don't know where I'll be working next."

"We can live in a lovely place with gardens and a country feel, and I can take the train from Stamford to New York City and be at Doubleday and Harry's office in an hour." Mignon glared and waved her cigarette for emphasis.

Later in the evening, they drank champagne and ate shrimp étouffée to celebrate the new house and Faith's contract with Warner Brothers for *Love Before Breakfast*.

She was excited and anxious to announce that Carol Lombard would play the lead.

Faith and Mignon were an unlikely pair of friends with the age difference, but they had much in common, and the four of them were compatible couples. Faith and Gonnie were fond of Alan and he of them. They enjoyed each other's company, but perceptive Faith felt the tension between Alan and Mignon.

She found Mignon in the living room alone before they left, put her arms around Mignon's shoulders, and said quietly, "We writers are a little mad, my young friend. We manipulate situations and characters and cause everything to come out right. Then we think we can do the same thing with our own lives, and we are astonished when we can't control people . . . Alan isn't like other men."

If she only knew how unlike other men.

"After all these years, you must realize that. You must realize what he is. He isn't going to change. He is a precious partner for you, like my Gonnie."

Like Gonnie? What exactly did that mean? About Gonnie and Faith? About Alan and Mignon?

Mignon couldn't bring herself to confide. Tell the truth about her marriage. Even close friends didn't talk about sex. She couldn't even tell her old friend Carmen the whole truth about her married life. But these two women filled her life. Faith sharing a profession they both loved. With age and experience Mignon respected. Carmen with shared history and keen intellect. She needed Carmen in her writing life. She needed to keep in touch with Carmen.

January 10, 1937

Dear Mignon,

Thanks for your note from Florida. Winter in the sun. It's difficult to imagine with the biting cold and the snow-covered streets in Lincoln. How nice it must be to walk outside without hat and gloves, boots, and heavy wool coat. To feel the warmth of summer in the midst of January. You and Alan lead a charmed life. I know you aren't always in accord, but maybe the change in scenery and stimulation of new people will put new vim in your marriage. Maybe you and Alan will both fall under the spell of Florida's charms. Sometimes, if you love a place, you love each other more.

Speaking of cold and snow, my copy of *Danger in the Dark* just arrived in the mail. Talk about a cold world. You captured all the damp, the chill, and darkness of winter both inside and out. I can feel the wet snow on my feet with Daphne when she walks to the springhouse in those first pages. And I am shivering with her when she is trying to get a fire going in the fireplace.

You know I judge a book by the first pages and your opening sentence had me hooked: "The day before the wedding, Dennis Haviland returned." Did you begin with just that sentence in your head or did you know who was murdered and why, and then play with ideas about the opening?

I appreciate your introducing all the characters within the first two pages although some of them are most unlikeable! I can't help but speculate about who they are in your real life.

Gretchen is particularly bizarre, and her brother Johnny is particularly wimpy, or so you lead your readers to believe. He's the perfect fall guy. And the big, broad, obnoxiously dominant Ben Brewer, the perfect person to bump off.

I'm glad you decided to use your detective Jacob Waite again, telling us more about that bored-looking little man with large, morose dark eyes.

Do you think you are revealing prejudices again with the "small, warm strain of Jewish blood" that makes him "deeply imaginative and perceptive?" I am kidding you, of course. I am wondering though when and where you met this Jewish man?

Enjoy the sun and your swanky abode.

Love, Carmen

Despite all those women reading her novels, she was always concerned about Carmen's reaction. Happy to know the plot of *Danger in the Dark* entertained her. She wanted simply to entertain her readers. No sociological comments. No economic theories. No symbolism. She would leave that to Willa Cather, the literary Nebraskan. No theories of government, peace or war, or psychology or philosophy lurked between the lines. She just wanted to excite and baffle the reader with a mystery and keep her reading.

But she needed to tell Carmen that the characters were genuine. Some *were* people Carmen knew. Some composites of people they knew in Lincoln. Jacob Waite though wasn't anyone Carmen or Mignon knew. Just a figment of her imagination and brief encounters with that sort of man in New York City. Not a stereotype. Or she hoped he wasn't a stereotype.

Harry was concerned about the romance. "You are getting too far afield from the mystery," he told Mignon. "More romance than suspense, especially with the serial stories in magazines."

But one of the reviewers from *The Boston Transcript* had complimented her on effectively combining love and mystery in *Danger in the Dark*, so Harry's concern wasn't warranted.

1938-39

Stamford

After winter in Florida, Alan and Mignon moved from Chicago to the Connecticut house near Faith and Gonnie. In the spring Mignon's father died.

When she heard Helen's voice on the telephone, her hand began to shake. Her head and racing heart knew something bad had happened. Helen and she rarely spoke. Their mother conveyed their lives to each other.

She flew to Lincoln for Father's funeral, nursing the usual regrets and guilt of the one who left home and rarely returns. On the long flight from New York City, she thought about her life in Nebraska.

When Easterners introduced her to their friends, they liked to add, "Mignon is from Nebraska." *Nebraska.* They emphasized it. A place more foreign than Europe. When eyebrows raised with wonder at this strange intruder in their midst, Mignon the snob, embarrassed by her Midwestern roots, responded with, "It's a good place *to be from.*"

The truth was that Lincoln and University Place had given her a solid basis, sound values. They'd had a comfortable life, a lovely home, and a prominent place in the community thanks to Father. And the Nebraska Sand Hills, dreadfully desolate as they were, had given her the impetus to write and the solitude that nourished those first novels.

The taxicab ride from the airport to the house on Warren Avenue was too short. She wanted to delay the reality.

She opened the door of the broad entryway to the suffocating sweet of white lilies. Funeral flowers. Dorothy, who'd been Mother's dependable housekeeper since Helen and Mignon were children, came to her, and they wrapped their arms around each other for their one moment of quiet mutual grief.

Vases of flowers covered the buffet and the table in the dining room, the coffee table, and every end table in the living room. The house was full of women. Mother's DAR and Junior League friends bustled about, taking covered dishes to the kitchen for Dorothy and her helpers to deal with.

Mother's southern charm and genteel manners belied her strength. Father's death had been sudden and unexpected, but she and Helen had made the funeral arrangements immediately and efficiently with all the traditional and accepted rituals. Helen had telephoned Mignon with the detailed plan and instructions for what was expected of her. Father would have smiled at that.

Dorothy came to make breakfast for them early the morning of the funeral though grief filled them too much for hunger. Just Helen and her family with Mignon at the table. After the bustle and commotion of the day before, a blanket of quiet had settled over the house and over their conversation.

"Don't forget your black gloves," Mother reminded them when she came into the dining room dressed for the day in mourning black. "Do you need black hose, Mignon?

"Wear comfortable shoes because we'll go to the cemetery after the service. You'll be walking across the lawns of the Memorial Garden to the gravesite. There'll be chairs for the family, but after the burial, we'll be standing in the church vestibule for the reception." She paused with her frowning Mother look. "It's a family obligation to greet everyone who comes." She looked at each of them, and went on, all business. "Your Father's man, Herb, will drive us to the Roper's Funeral Home in the Buick. We'll get into limousines there to follow the hearse to the church."

Mother noticed Mignon tearing up, waved her hand dismissively and shook her head. Weeping was not an option then or later in the long day. Mother's example was firmly ingrained. You endured tragic or unpleasant events by observing the rituals with stoic determination. You grieved privately. You didn't make an unseemly scene or make other people uncomfortable by public weeping. You smiled and said thank you when they expressed condolences. You thanked people for coming, shook hands, and endured hugs.

Their small family, in their black mourning, walked down the center aisle of the church. Mignon looked straight ahead, tried to focus on the cross on the altar. Packed pews. A suffocating nearness. Made the aisle feel small.

So many people. She didn't know why she was surprised. Mother and Father had attended Wesley Methodist from their first days in University Place — when she and Helen were babies. Father's friendships reached from the suit-coated men in the business community to the farmers and ranchers who bought his horses. They were all there.

She couldn't stifle the tears when the soloist began "Nearer My God to Thee." One of Father's favorite hymns. Father. Such a likeable man. He wore his smile. She could hear his booming laugh.

And after the tributes and the hymns, they followed the casket down the aisle, heads bowed to avoid eye contact, and out the door. The traditional ceremonies went on. Limos to the burial site. At the Memorial Garden, Mignon sat on a metal folding chair under a white canopy with Mother and Helen and Helen's family.

It was the best of Nebraska's spring days — meadow larks singing, a hint of warm sun, clear blue skies, a gentle, warm breeze. Father would have liked this day. He wasn't without pride in the city and of his accomplishments. "I provide a fine living for you." He liked to remind them. But he loved the Nebraska countryside. An Oklahoma farm boy at heart, he took them for leisurely Sunday afternoon car rides, meandering through the back roads to look at the crops. Mignon could see him, his elbow resting on the open window, hand on the steering wheel, humming.

After the church reception — coffee, cookies, and condolences — Mother and Helen and Mignon put their smiles on and played hostess at the house. Wearying of that, Mignon abandoned her post beside them to join Carmen and other old college friends.

"The prodigal daughter returns," Helen said, looking over her shoulder as she walked by on her way to the kitchen.

"Thanks," Mignon said. She tried to think of something more sarcastic than the caustic *thanks*. But in the pause, she heard Father. "Hold your tongue, Mimi. Don't respond. Think about what you really gain by responding." A wise man. Gave her counsel beyond his lifetime.

Her ambition and work ethic were her inheritance. She had depended on him for advice and support. "I'm very proud of you, Mimi," he said after every announcement of a new novel. Never could ask his advice about her marriage though. He liked Alan from the beginning. Approved heartily of Mignon's marrying Alan. He wouldn't have understood her standing by his gravesite alone. He wouldn't have understood her unhappiness either. She was never able to talk about the intimacy. The lack of it. Father believed in the sanctity of marriage. It was best he didn't know the charade of hers.

In January Alan proposed a new venture with Aero Motors Corporation.

"I've never done anything like this, but I've always been interested in motors. My role is to help develop plans for airplane motors and to test prototypes," he said. "But I need to invest some money."

"How much?"

"It's a new venture and company, so as much as we can. We'd have to use some of our savings. We should get some royalties eventually."

"I trust your judgment about it."

She had published five novels and had three movie contracts that year. They sank hopes and their savings into the venture. Alan tested motors and lived in Chicago. Mignon stayed in Connecticut.

Her critic friend wrote:

> April 4, 1939
>
> Dear Mignon,
>
> You know how spring comes to Nebraska—flowers bud, then flakes fly. We had a spring snowstorm, and I indulged in a weekend of reading *Hasty Wedding*. I'm curious about the "large, ugly house in North Shore with all the ornamental wood and cavernous rooms with high ceilings." Is this Alan's aunt and uncle's house, or the home of one of the opera fans? I know you like to be completely familiar with the settings of your stories. The "great, gloomy" house, plus the wind and sleet, and the dark days definitely speak of winter in Chicago and in Nebraska too.
>
> And you know I like the sallow-faced detective Jacob Waite with the somber eyes who walks like a cat.
>
> I have to say I don't like Cary, the mother. She is pathetic. You don't help with your description of her as "childish and fragile" with people indulging her and taking care of her. I'm sorry she has an allowance of only $1500 a month for her clothes and theatre tickets. (Do you really spend that much on

clothes?) And always needing a sedative. Good grief. Quite a contrast to the handsome and well-bred murderer, Sophie, with her social charm and worldliness, her well-made-up, dark hazel eyes, and "fine figure." I'm glad you have included one strong woman, albeit the murderer!

The incidental comments of heroine Dorcas like, "Conventions are made for emergencies" and "maintaining domestic routines for a semblance of normality" are meaningful to a reader who has known you forever. We grew up that way. Your mother, and mine too, coped with emergencies or untoward life events by maintaining conventions and routines.

I am interested in your dedicating the novel "To Alan: Who still listens." I'm happy he still listens. I know you have treasured that, but am I to infer that things are better? Or are you resigned to "sensible, conventional devotion," "no strenuous lovemaking," and "unemotional friendliness" as you describe the feelings of your hero in the novel?

Don't be concerned. I notice these things in your novels only because I'm aware of what is happening in your personal life. When you write in the heroine's voice, "it (the marriage) was not the thing she had expected it to be . . . full of hidden, unplumbed depths and sweeping currents . . ." I hear you.

Love from your old friend—
Carmen

She did hear. Mignon had worked on that novel in Florida. Poured herself into it. But she'd moved on now to writing *The Chiffon Scarf:*

Twenty-six-year-old Eden on her way from St. Louis to her wedding in the Bayou meets engineer Jim Cody.

In May she sent a draft to Harry.

May 20, 1939
Dear Mignon,
I'm returning the draft of *The Chiffon Scarf* with my notes. How fortunate that you have an in-house expert, so to speak. Using Alan's experience in airplane design, espionage, and the specter of war, are perfect plots for this precarious time in our country.

You need to cut down on the romance if you can. I know you like your formula of two beautiful young women rivals, but, in this case, you are successfully capturing the reader with the mystery. The pacing creates good tension and suspense. Sending your characters to the dude ranch is a completely unexpected turn of events, and effectively opens up new possibilities for the identity of the real villain.

I am trying to steer you away from the romance somewhat because the mystery in this novel is especially good. Keep the romantic setting of the lover's first encounter—the warm summer night, candlelight, the sweet perfume of red roses, but cut back on the protagonist's romantic thoughts thereafter and take the reader more expeditiously to the test flight.

I am having trouble with the metaphors, e.g., "He drew her nearer . . . that was as irresistible as the course of a river, the strength of a tidal wave, the whirling of the earth and sun." A little far-fetched? Excessive? Do women honestly feel this way? Think about it.

I can't argue with your success though. Your readers are clamoring for more!

The dedication to Alan with your thanks for the information about airplane engines is a nice touch. I know Alan will appreciate it. You are good for each other.

Looking forward to your revisions.

Warm Regards, Harry

1940

Woodsedge

A New Year. She lived on hope.

"I found the house I will be happy to live in for the rest of my life," she told Alan. "It's called Woodsedge. A hundred and fifty years old! Part of it rebuilt and part added onto and updated only thirty years ago."

"You want to move again? One year. We're barely settled."

"The house is in a wooded neighborhood, Alan. We'd have a little over an acre with stone walls and hedges for privacy. There are flower gardens around the entrance. A stone walkway leads to cutting gardens with cosmos and zinnias. Something would bloom every season. The owners converted the stable to a garage. They added a guest house."

"Your life is a sequence of moves. A different city. A different house. The next will be the best and last. Is this one the setting for your stories or the dream of a perfect life? What are you looking for?"

"I promise. I won't want to move again. I love this house, and it *will be* a great setting for my stories.

"It has high ceilings, big bathrooms, a wide entrance hall with wide stairway and lovely old railing. You'll like it. The entrance has pillars and a hundred-foot flagstone terrace in front, wisteria and a privet hedge around the balustrade. You like hedges. It has a lovely hall. A paneled living room. It's very English in feeling with ten-foot ceiling and bookshelves between panels. Seven fireplaces and five bedrooms."

Alan scowled. Shook his head.

"It's too big for us, I know, but we can have many guests."

"How do we afford this monstrosity?"

"Three novels, Alan. Three."

He succumbed. That was how they compromised. His job ventures. Her houses.

The Realtor had told her the neighbors were important people. "Elliot Dutton of the E. P. Dutton Publishing Co and his wife Marjorie." He pointed to the house across the street as they approached the stone walls and green hedges of the place he referred to as Woodsedge. "Marjorie writes children's books," he said. "You know Orville Prescott, of course. Reviews books for *The New York Times*. Lives down the street."

"Interesting," Mignon said. She glanced at the houses as he slowed, not about to admit that she was impressed with the neighbors. He had done his homework about this client.

They had never lived in a place of neighborhood. Someone hosted a cocktail party or garden party every weekend. Family affairs. They'd never experienced that. Children were often included in dinner parties. Alan especially enjoyed Elliot and Marjorie Dutton's daughter, and they saw the Duttons frequently. Four-year-old Emily would run to Alan as soon as they arrived. He would pick her up, she'd giggle and laugh as he swung her around. He'd put her down and she'd run off to be with the other children, but whine and look at Alan with big brown beseeching eyes when her nanny came to take her to bed.

Children. Mignon saw Faith and Gonnie and Faith's four children nearly every day. Faith never spoke of her husband, nor was he ever in the picture.

Mignon was curious. In spite of Faith's prominence, no one commented on Hugh's absence or on her relationship with Gonnie whom Faith referred to publicly as Mademoiselle X.

"I had a capable, kind friend with me at the hospital when the twins were born," Faith once told Mignon. "That is my Gonnie. After Hugh and I separated, she came to live with us. She runs the house and manages the children so I can write." They hadn't discussed it since.

Even the tabloids left it alone. Not a whisper. Ironic because the gossip columnists published salacious stories about prominent people with no regard for the truth.

What was the truth of the relationship? What were they to each other? Mignon didn't want to dwell on that.

On most issues, Faith had a conservative bent, but decidedly not on marriage. At a dinner party, seated down the table and across from her, Mignon looked up, startled to hear Faith openly express her views when an absent neighbor's divorce came up.

"I can't for the life of me see how any thinking person can contend that a marriage from which love and respect have disappeared should continue," she said. "Divorce is not a crime."

What about sex? Does marriage without sex warrant divorce? Respect and love are mutual. Sex and love? Mignon wished she could ask Faith privately what she thought. But . . . discussion of sex . . . taboo.

Mignon admired Faith. Treasured the friendship. Faith had ten years on her and phenomenal success. Dozens of books and movies. *The Times* noted that Faith had earned over $350,000 the year past. Working women and housewives, young and old, identified with her characters. Mignon didn't feel competitive though. Not envious either. No curdle in the stomach envy that punctured her confidence when writers her own age were successful.

All the socializing in the new neighborhood made it difficult to exercise self-discipline and keep to a morning writing routine. Mignon wished inspiration to fall from the heavens in glorious bursts. It didn't. She had to spend long steady hours plugging away at her desk. Fortunately, she had Harry nearby in New York City now, and he harassed. "You have to publish two novels a year, Mignon. Your readers look forward to reading you, but they're fickle and will forget you easily."

"Easy for you to say, Harry. I have pages and pages needing revision. A clutter. Stacks of pages on my desk and on tables that need order. I'm not getting anything done. I can't concentrate. No creativity."

"Get a typist. A secretary like you had in Chicago."

She went to her mentor. Faith always had connections and, of course, a solution.

"Try the Katharine Gibbs Agency," Faith said. "I just met Katharine Gibbs at a dinner party in New York City. She's had Schools for Secretaries in Providence and Boston. Now opened on Park Avenue."

Mignon phoned the agency for information.

"Our young women are taught English, speech, and manners as well as typing, shorthand, and dictation, and they are expected to be well-groomed and well-mannered." The spiel went on. "Most of them work as private secretaries or in large offices as company stenographers." Not even a pause for questions. "Fortunately, some of them prefer a private employer and a more companion-type relationship. We'd be happy to send someone."

They did and after the first day, Paula arrived in her hat and white gloves on the train from Brooklyn every morning. She cleaned up what Mignon had written the day before. Mignon revised and rewrote, preferring to move right along with her story until Harry reminded her that he needed copy. Then she let him take over. He knew what changes had to be made, and Paula could sometimes pick those red-marked pages up at his office before she came to Woodsedge. She took care of all business correspondence too, even dealing with a massive number of fan letters.

All that left time for the children appearing unexpectedly in her life. When Faith and Gonnie went to Europe, they left Faith's sister, Lena, in charge of the four children. The first time Mignon and Alan dropped by to check on her, Lena pulled them in the door. Desperate for help entertaining the children, she suggested a game of croquet.

"Thanks," Mignon said. "You know how I love games. And how good I am! I'll sit here on the patio with my lemonade and a cigarette and watch you."

Alan took over, explaining the rules to the children. In simple language. Amazing. Then he placed his hands over six-year-old Johnny's on the mallet to show him how to strike the ball and get it through the wicket. The four of them celebrated every successful hit, racing each other across the rolling lawn, arms waving, screaming with delight. Infectious joy. Mignon and Alan laughed with them. The children loved Alan. He treated them like small adults, worthy of his serious attention. Mignon loved him for it. The together fun of days like that distracted her from their problem. Was he honestly happy? Was he as oblivious to her unhappiness as he seemed or just ignoring it?

In June they spent a long day at the New York World's Fair with Lena and the four children. A mob. Hundreds of people pushing and shoving to get in lines for exhibitions and carnival rides. The featured World of Tomorrow exhibits were out of the question. The children clamored for attention. Mignon and Alan and Lena divided them. Gripped their hands. Shouted at each other. Tried to stay together and get them on rides. Mignon thought about Carmen and the Chicago Fair years before. Much more enjoyable than this. First experiences can't be recaptured. And four children were a crowd and a challenge.

Life would have been different with children. She watched Alan with them. Did he regret not having children of his own? He would have been a good father. *Was that the crux of his problem? Their problem? Was it her fault? No point in sex?*

He wouldn't have had the flexibility in his professional life. Flitting from one job to another. She wouldn't have had the time to travel and write. Faith managed it, but she had Gonnie and her sister to take care of her children.

Harry kept her on schedule with writing. *The Chiffon Scarf* had been published, and *Brief Return* would be out in a couple months, so that was two in '39, seven novels in three years. A productive three years for writing while her marriage limped along.

She had achieved notoriety and some fame at home in Nebraska too:

> August 15, 1940
> Dear Mignon,
> I just picked up a copy of *Guide to the Cornhusker State*, one of the Works Project Administration art initiatives. You probably read that the House Committee on Un-American Activities declared the Theatre and Writing Projects "hotbeds of Communism" and ended the funding. I read that over a hundred writers were working on guides for every state. Fortunately, Nebraska's Guide was completed before the funding ended. It is an

interesting and thorough picture of the state and impressively well-written. I understand that faculty from the University and professionals from the Historical Society edited the work of the writers in the field.

Lincoln is one of the eight cities featured in Nebraska. Also, sections on every facet of life including a chapter on Literature. Williams Jennings Bryan is mentioned. Willa Cather's novels discussed pretty thoroughly. Bess Streeter Aldrich, of course. You, Mignon Starks Edwards, are there, along with Mari Sandoz, in a list of recent novelists who have "gained national recognition."

"Mrs. Edwards is one of the most tasteful and competent of modern detective story writers."

I thought you would like to know that you are still considered a Nebraska writer! I know you don't like FDR nor all his social programs, but that Writing Project has apparently been a godsend for writers not as fortunate as you.

Thanks for sending *The Chiffon Scarf*. I like the image the title brings to mind. It's also an impressive dedication.

"To Alan with his wife's thanks for supplying the information about airplane engineers for this story, and in hope that she has not taken too many liberties with her rival in his affections otherwise known as The Cruiser."

Telling? Are you concerned about rivals?

You did get me caught up in the mystery of the mysterious plane, the foreign buyer, the crash on the ranch with the rancher a former detective. Great suspense! One of your best. You could take the romance out of it, although the heroine's musing about her marriage speaks to me. I hope you and Alan are working it out.

Love, Carmen

1940

Jamaica

They would remember this as the winter before the war. Life revolved around the war. When Alan came home from work at the end of each day, Mignon joined him in the living room, and they turned on the radio. How far did Hitler's invasion go today? Would France fall? Could Churchill hold out? The news from Europe occupied their conversations at home and at every lunch, dinner, and cocktail party. The distress and heightened feelings threatened even their close friendships.

"Roosevelt is maneuvering," Gonnie said, at the dinner table the night before they left for a Jamaica vacation. "He is determined to get us into this war."

Alan, ordinarily noncommittal and unfailingly polite in social political discussions, attacked. "Do you understand what Germany is doing?"

"I do. And do you remember that we fought them twenty years ago in what was supposed to be the war to end all wars?"

"Hitler is moving across Europe. England is standing alone in this," Alan said. "We have to get into it."

"Well, not everyone idolizes Churchill. You and your president are in the minority, Alan. Americans don't want to get into this war. It isn't our problem."

Faith and Mignon stayed out of it, and Mignon hoped Alan and Gonnie were both sensible enough to put it aside when she and Alan returned from Jamaica. Friendships were too precious to discard over political differences, although the potential for war had everyone on edge. Suddenly they were aware of prejudices and opinions that had insignificant social consequences in the past.

"You can't ignore the war in your novels. You have to recognize your readers' concern with the war," Harry reminded Mignon, and Alan inadvertently gave her an idea with his penchant for reading her bits of the news, a habit that annoyed her because it seemed not a very subtle reminder that there was more to *The New York Times* than the fashion section.

"Did you know that the United States has as many as four hundred of the helium airships providing protection of some sort for the west coast?" he read. "England is using helium balloons, and our Navy is doing extensive testing of helium airships."

Helium? She vaguely recalled helium from high school chemistry, a class she'd struggled through and hated. An item on the Periodic Table?

"What is it?"

"A colorless, odorless, tasteless gas," Alan said.

A provocative subject for espionage and murder. She needed a resort, an ocean, and two unrecognizable cities some distance apart and outside of the U.S. She didn't know of such a place. It would have to be a place she had never been, a new adventure. She knew she could work out the plot and the characters there.

Faith had suggested Jamaica to attract her readers. Women would think it exotic. A perfect escape for the war-weary.

Mignon needed to know the geography and topography—the feel and look of things, the tropical setting and the clothes people wore. Even Alan wanted escape. She convinced him to make the trip with her.

They flew from New York City to Miami Beach and taxied to an airport consisting of one room not much bigger than their living room in Woodsedge. A drafty, tumble-down building with a temporary feeling like a place cobbled together. The few seats were taken, and when one was finally vacated, Alan motioned for her to sit. He paced from one end of the room to the other restlessly, walked outside, came back in.

Mignon took her notebook out of her bag but was too excited and then too tired to take notes. Five hours. They waited five hours for the small prop plane. Then the last leg to Kingston was a hold-your-breath, clutch-your-partner flight. The plane shuddered and plunged up and down, like a bucking horse. Women shrieked. Men swore. The doors on the overhead bins flew open. The stewardesses were ordered to buckle in along with everyone else, but one of them lurched up and down the aisles begging, "Please be calm. Please be quiet. The captain knows what he is doing."

The plane finally landed. People laughed with relief. Strangers threw their arms around each other as they disembarked.

Mignon stepped gingerly down the open metal stairs, clutching the railing with one hand, holding her hat on with the other. The wind whipped her skirt around her legs as she crossed the tarmac to the airport. It turned out they had arrived on the tail of a hurricane. Mignon didn't care. Flying was definitely the only way to travel long distances. She would do it again.

Faith never failed to give them great advice about their travels. The Myrtle Bank Hotel was touted as the lost Garden of Eden, a combination of American comfort, English cleanliness, and Italian climate, a glory of opulence. It was all of that.

It was the only place Mignon had ever been where you sat on the veranda and clapped your hand for service. Black boys waited in groups within earshot waiting to do their bidding.

"This is disgusting," Alan said as she clapped her hands for her afternoon bourbon.

"Well, I feel royal."

"You would."

She picked up the highball glass of bourbon from the tray the boy held out. "I'm getting all the information I need for my novel. And it's my writing that makes these experiences possible . . . especially when you're between jobs."

1940-41

Woodsedge & Florida

Within days of their return from Jamaica, Alan announced, "I've decided to invest in the Aero Motor Corporation. Join their design team. And I can't be commuting to Woodsedge. The hours are too long. I need to be closer to the company headquarters. I'm going to rent an apartment in Manhattan."

"Manhattan? What do you expect me to do? Move to Manhattan?"

"You can join me on weekends."

"I do like you better when I don't see you every day, but I am not inclined to spend every weekend in Manhattan."

"Suit yourself. If I want to do this job, I need to be in Manhattan."

"And I need to be at home."

But home—Woodsedge—wasn't as comforting as she expected it to be.

She had always been well. Hadn't experienced physical pain of any kind since nineteen-year-old menstrual cramps, but now she had stomach cramps and diarrhea no matter what she ate. Didn't dare leave the house. Didn't dare travel. No social life. Worst of all no energy to work at writing. She finally dragged herself to a clinic.

"You have colitis," the physician said. "An acute inflammation. There's no cure for colitis. And I'm not aware of any medication that effectively alleviates the pain when you have a flareup. I suggest a soft diet and bed rest for relief."

"Bed rest? That's unrealistic. Lying around, doing nothing is not a solution for me. I have too much to do."

"There is some evidence that colitis isn't all physical." He paused and squinted at her, deciding whether to go on. "Psychoanalysis is becoming a popular treatment for women with disorders of this kind."

The weak mind of a woman thing again. The fragile female psyche. Thanks. She'd put that woman in a novel.

Maybe he was right. She had also read that psychoanalysis could cure a man's sexual dysfunction. Maybe she and Alan should both see a psychoanalyst. Alan would certainly appreciate that suggestion. She had suggested it when they were in Europe. Ten years ago. What was the matter with her? Ten years of this strange marriage.

In the midst of this, Helen telephoned.

"I'm thinking of coming East to visit you. I'll bring Mother with me." She didn't wait for Mignon to respond.

"I'll stay a week, but Mother can spend a couple months with you. Then I'll come back and get her," Helen said.

"Months? I want Mother to be happy, but I can't write with her here."

"You do have some responsibility, Mignon. I have her full time," Helen said.

"But I have to work. You and Mother don't stop to think about that. You're living on Father's inheritance. I'm not. My income depends on my writing."

No Alan. Insomnia. Constant stomach cramps and diarrhea. Mother here. It was unthinkable.

"You have to wait until spring," Mignon said.

Helen hung up. Daughter. Sister. Wife. Only one problem deferred. She had to do something about the Wife. Make some kind of decision.

The antidote to Connecticut winter, quarrels with her sister, and life without Alan was to write about their trip to balmy, warm Jamaica and the ocean, helium ships, and murder. Write away the unhappiness and frustration. Bury it. She was filling her days with the work when Harry telephoned.

"Mignon, I wanted to tell you in person, but this will have to do. I have decided to leave Doubleday and edit for Random House."

Change. A big change. Her hands shook. She reached for a cigarette and a lighter, always handy near the telephone.

"Bennett has been after me since he started Random House fifteen years ago," Harry went on. "The company wasn't exactly limping along but having James Joyce in house and the success of *Ulysses* has lured prominent writers.

"It's an exciting time for Bennett, and I'm ready for a change."

A dramatic change for her. She hated change in her working life. Hated the disruption. Didn't want to leave all the people she knew. Doubleday had launched her. She was comfortable there. She didn't want a different publishing company. Protests winged through her head while Harry worked at persuading.

"Sinclair and Pen Warren and some of my other writers will come to Random House with me. I hope you'll join them, Mignon."

She knew she couldn't do without Harry. "What about advertising and promotion? How does Random House handle that?"

"It won't be any different for you."

"You have to make it clear that my novels can't be promoted in a cluster with other mystery writers. I don't want blurbs about Agatha Christie on the fly leaves. And I don't want to be referred to as the 'American Agatha Christie' in any promotions."

"I know. I know. I'll take care of all that," he said. "I'll make sure you're referred to as the 'First Lady of Mystery.' And I will make sure your copy editors aren't frivolous young women." He chuckled. "I know you prefer working with men."

Harry understood her. He comforted, cajoled, counseled. She couldn't imagine her writing life without him. There was no question about going with him to Random House. All she needed to confirm her dependance on him were his suggestions and edit of *The Murder of Robert Dakin* that arrived in the mail.

September 3, 1940

Dear Mignon,

I received your draft of the Jamaica novel. The opening sentences catch your reader's attention immediately: "The brutal and cold-blooded murder of Robert Dakin was actually a thing of slow growth, with roots that, like a noxious plant, spread slowly over a period of years. But to Elizabeth Dakin, his young wife, it was sudden and unforeseen. She had often been afraid of him, never for him." Readers will feel compelled to read on.

I suggest *Speak No Evil* for the title. You don't want to remind readers of the popular Christie's *Murder of Roger Ackroyd*. You know how you feel about Christie. *Speak No Evil* gives the reader a hint of the motive for the poisoning and the stabbing of several characters, and it casts aspersions on your powerful main male character.

As for Eliza. Let's give her more backbone. She is an especially weak woman, too much of a victim. I don't believe her coddled background of wealth can quite account for her spinelessness. She needs hot soup and tea for comfort too often! It's not Woodsedge. And it's not you. Take yourself out of your novel!

Your "scientist with a microscope," the no-nonsense Paul from London Criminal Investigation Department, is an effective contrast to the dipsomaniacal Robert, and a relief from the number of other shallow men you have in this one!

I look forward to your revisions.

Warm Regards,

Harry

Now the female characters were weak? Spineless? Victims? What was she thinking? What was she writing? Eliza a victim? Weak? Why describe her that way? What had happened to her focus on strong and strident Sarah Keate? Maybe she was succumbing to her own weakness.

Carmen's critique of *Hangman's Whip,* which had been published while she worked on *Speak No Evil,* arrived in the same mail and improved her frame of mind substantially.

> September 3, 1940
> Dear Mignon,
> I just finished *Hangman's Whip.* Amazing how you devise a different method of murder with each novel. This one really took me by surprise. Poisoned, shot, stabbed, bludgeoned, but a hanging! And the golden-haired Eve with soft blue eyes and gentle beauty, a most unlikely victim.
> As usual I looked for your descriptions of the clothes the women are wearing. Now I know what is appropriate for the well-heeled at their summer mansions on the lake.
> I was amused by your giving your hero, Richard, Alan's venture into designing and promoting the manufacture of an airplane. I assume this new venture is turning out well for you or you wouldn't write about it. Or do your write about it because it's a struggle?
> Keep in touch.
> Love, Carmen

Why did she write about it? That venture of Alan's hadn't turned out well. After less than a year, he sold the manufacturing rights to the aircraft motor he helped design and ended his association with Aero Motors Corporation. He didn't have the courtesy to tell her until he came to Woodsedge for the weekend.

"I'm going to work for Starrett Brothers and Eken Company. Assistant division engineer. They're building roads and drainage at Camp Blanding."

"Where? Where are you going?"

"Florida. Camp Blanding. The camp will eventually house seventy thousand troops. We're preparing for war."

"You are moving from Manhattan to Florida? It would have been nice for us to discuss it."

"You can join me whenever you like if you can bring yourself to leave Woodsedge."

"I can join you *if I like*? I don't want to leave Woodsedge. I'm getting a lot of work done. My life is here."

"Suit yourself. You always do."

And they left it at that.

She had work to do. Revisions. Revising took the most self-discipline of all the work in writing. She tried to work. In her perfect room—book-lined, cushiony chair, oak table spacious enough for typewriter and notebooks and papers. The noisy, nest-making robins in the treetops outside the window distracted her. The sounds of the gardener wheel-barrowing mulch in flower beds below the window distracted her. She wanted to get up from the desk and call Faith. Ask her to go out for lunch.

Speak No Evil. Give the main character more backbone, Harry said. Too many shallow men, he said. Maybe she just didn't like men much right now.

"The place is a mad house," Alan said when he telephoned from Camp Blanding. "Thousands of men. I'm working with groups of two hundred and five hundred Blacks. We're building a hundred and sixty miles of road and a hospital with two thousand beds."

"Black workers? Why the predominance of Black workers?"

"They aren't part of the military draft, so they're available and they're anxious for the work."

"It's a challenge. I have to coordinate with a white southern foreman with all his prejudices and the Blacks who are clearing the land."

"But you like it?"

"Designing roads is what I do best. There are unique problems in this part of the country with drainage. It's interesting. Challenging. Yes. I'm keeping very busy."

Drainage. If she were with him, she'd get a college-worthy lecture on drainage systems. She missed him. She even missed listening to the boring details of his work. She looked at a map. The camp was west of Jacksonville and twenty-five miles from Green Cove Springs where Alan was staying. Maybe she should rent a house for the season somewhere in the area.

She worked every day. Filled the daylight hours with an obsessive fury of writing. But the evenings without Alan were interminable. She chain-smoked. Listened to inane radio broadcasts of Gene Autry's *Melody Ranch* and the idiocy of Abbott and Costello. Tried to immerse herself in the recordings of operas they'd seen, which only made her think of Alan.

Edward R. Murrow's live broadcasts from London with bombs falling in the background added fear to the muddle of her emotions. She went to bed early, then churned with the frustration of her dependence. Hated herself and hated Alan for making her dependent.

Lonely evenings. Sleepless nights. She needed a dog. In Valentine and in Chicago, Jericho had comforted her and kept her company when Alan traveled. She was never lonely after they got Jericho. When they lost him, they agreed that no dog could take his place, and then moving from city to country and back, and their extensive traveling made owning a pet inconvenient. She'd cope with the inconvenience. But she couldn't bear to have another English setter, so she chose a completely different breed—a French poodle. Named him Beau.

"A French poodle?" Alan said when she telephoned him. "A foofoo dog! One of those obnoxious yippies? Beau? What kind of a name is that for a dog?"

"A Standard Poodle. He isn't tiny. He's tall as Jericho."

"Won't be much good for hunting pheasants in the Sand Hills! Good company for you though. Walking him will give you something to do. A French poodle by your side. That'll enhance the persona."

She ignored the comment about persona. He'd tossed that at her before.

"It isn't about something to do or something to keep me busy, Alan. I have plenty to do."

But the sneer didn't puncture his ignorance of her loneliness. He was oblivious. Absorbed in his work.

She saw Faith and Gonnie and Lena regularly. Dinner. Movies. They enjoyed going to the pictures. Faith was especially interested because several of her books were on the screen, and she was more than a little proud that Carole Lombard and Cesar Romero were starring in her *Love Before Breakfast.*

Mignon didn't know Faith when she created Nurse Sarah Keate, but Faith was a Sarah Keate, a model of the stable auntie or older sister Mignon liked to use in her novels—a calm, in-charge sort of woman. A good influence too. As dedicated, as disciplined as Mignon. They understood each other. Escaped for lunch or a long drive in the country, sharing their frustrations about the tediousness of the work. The discipline writing required. Faith comforted Mignon with her understanding of the process.

Some days Mignon got up from the typewriter after four or five hours, simply stuck with no idea of how to move on in a story. But she learned that she couldn't wait for inspiration, she had to sit down at the typewriter and start again the next day.

Writing wasn't a hobby for either Faith or her. Mignon had to earn a living, although Faith didn't entirely depend on her earnings. Her absent husband came from a wealthy family. Mignon assumed he supported her and their four children although they never discussed it.

Admitting the significance of money and the need for recognition would have been unseemly. But she could crow to Alan when he telephoned. "*The New York Times* says I earned just slightly less than Agatha Christie last year."

"Your nemesis. I'm proud," he said.

She needed him. Needed to be near him. She decided to rent a place in Orange Park, Florida.

The area had changed dramatically with the construction going on and the workers and the troops coming in. The lazy little southern town she remembered from their Florida winter was overwhelmed by the tide of men that rolled in on the wake of the camp. They crowded the streets and stores and hotels, packed the motion-picture theatres, and snatched up every house and every livable room. A town of fifteen hundred persons had become suddenly fifteen thousand.

After days of searching, she found Azalea Manor in a sprinkling of houses along the lovely banks of the St. Johns River. It had a beautiful flower garden with a winding path and bubbling fountain with golden Japanese koi swimming in a shallow pool. Azalea and clipped privet hedges. Live oaks. Spanish moss. Palms. A big house with pleasant rooms. They had a large bedroom opening onto a sun porch with an awning for sunbathing, canvas curtains to shut off the wind.

The view of the river had enticed her. She was always enticed by a view. Especially water. She hadn't counted on the noise of building. Hammers and drills and machines going on everywhere. She sat down at the typewriter every morning with good intentions, but the voices and pounding of the nearby construction disrupted any meaningful work. She had to find a better place to write. Alan was not sympathetic.

"I do not have time to house hunt," he said, when she proposed a move. "You wanted to come here. You're the one who is discontent, Mimi. *You* find a different house if you can't work here."

A Realtor found them a place called Sun Patch Cottage on the river north of Ormond, only ten miles from Camp Blanding, an easier commute for Alan than Azalea Manor, or at least she could rationalize with that as part of the reason for moving.

The Cottage was furnished in white wicker with bright floral upholstery, and they were the first renters. It had three big bedrooms and one small one, fireplaces in every bedroom, two fireplaces in the living room, a little boathouse, and a charming azalea garden. She couldn't imagine needing a fireplace, but Alan's friends assured her that cool, damp nights did occur.

It took weeks to find a cook and a girl to clean and care for the house, but she finally found two Mexican women. Neither of them could speak English, but they were smiling and pleasant, and she managed to communicate with them.

Mornings she worked on *With This Ring*. Lived in New Orleans and the bayou in her writing world. In the afternoons, she sat in the garden, which had a little promontory above the river with chairs and a sundial.

Arches created by great live oaks festooned with ghostly wisps of Spanish moss framed her view of the river. She described it in her notebook. The setting for a story. A mysterious drowning.

She had pages of scribblings in her notebooks and a mess of typewritten pages that needed retyping and organizing.

"I need help," she told Alan.

"You aren't likely to find a secretary here," he said. "Men who are rejected or don't want to join the service find good-paying jobs in construction. Better pay than office work. So, the opportunities for women in offices on the base are endless. Some officers even hire secretaries to act as what they call Listening Posts."

"A listening post? What's a listening post?"

"When orders are called from Washington to the officer, they listen in on another phone and make complete transcripts."

She gave up trying to find a secretary, but she had fodder for a future story.

Harry wrote to tell her that progress on releasing *Speak No Evil* was slow because of the war, and advertising had been delayed. She invited him and Edna to visit at the end of March before they left the area. Harry declined.

In April the construction work at Camp Blanding was finished; Alan was again without a job. He did have an offer from a company in British Guinea where the engineers lived on a boat. It sounded like an interesting place. Mignon telephoned a travel agent and asked about accommodations for families.

"There are no houses to rent there," he said.

"There have to be hotels."

"In Georgetown? No, ma'am. Georgetown is twenty-five jungle miles from the work site. It is no place for women. There is no place for you to live."

"What in the world kind of wanderlust makes you want to go there?" Alan asked. "I don't even want to go there and work on some unknown project."

The Quartermaster Department of the War Department rescued him. Offered him a job as assistant deputy chief civil engineer for highway and drainage work at army camps in the New York and New Jersey Districts. The kind of work he felt most competent and content with. Mignon went back to Woodsedge.

With This Ring was published and she heard from Carmen:

> June 15, 1941
>
> Dear Mignon,
>
> *With This Ring* arrived this week. I lived in the wind and storms of the hurricane in that New Orleans plantation house. The lights going out! Electricity lost! Great atmosphere for a murder.
>
> The women in these last two novels seem particularly hapless and helpless—I presume unlike anyone you know personally. And the men— dipsomaniacs and hypochondriacs! Muddled marriages . . . Muddled marriages!
>
> I hear your voice in the heroine's opinions that marriage has to be built like a small house, one brick

at a time. I worry about you. You need to get out of that marriage.

Love, Carmen

Although Alan's work was war-related, Mignon didn't want to believe the U.S. would get into the war. She listened compulsively to the radio night after night, shivering over Hitler's voice and theatrics, dreading but riveted by the news reports. Alan was too old for the draft, but his work put him in close contact with the military. They kept in touch via telephone and letters.

"I need a lot of men, and, luckily, there's no shortage of young men applying for jobs," he said.

"I thought the country was empty of young men. They'd either been drafted or enlisted."

"I have young men who have been denied military service. Some—Blue Discharge."

He had told her about the Blue Discharge years before, but she had frankly forgotten. In the last war, men suspected of homosexuality had been prosecuted for sodomy.

"Psychiatrists have decided homosexuality isn't necessarily criminal. It's now an affliction," Alan scoffed. "The armed services are using some bizarre tests to determine if a draftee is homosexual. The guys who don't pass the test apply for war-related jobs. They're joining my crews."

Why did she need to know about that? Why did Alan even tell her? Why explain it? She refused to think about it. Better to focus on work.

All this talk of war and preparation for war was obviously the time to set a novel in wartime Washington. She called Harry.

"I need some contacts just to get a feel for the atmosphere, not any specific intrigue."

"You should get in touch with Drew Pearson or Bob Alan who writes the 'Washington Merry-Go-Round' column," Harry said. "I'll join you. I haven't spent time in Washington recently. I'll introduce you to Frank Kluckhohn who covers the White House for *The New York Times.*"

What she didn't expect in Washington was to meet Elsa Maxwell. Harry escorted her to a by-invitation-only dinner party honoring the one hundredth anniversary of the publication of Edgar Allan Poe's *Murders in Rue Morgue,* the first modern detective story.

Elsa Maxwell was seated next to Harry with Mignon on his other side. Harry and Mignon were engaged in conversation about the place and the event. Elsa had a martini in hand. She bumped Harry's arm. Dumped the martini in his lap. He jumped up, startled. Others at the table laughed, tittered. But Harry was never discombobulated and never pandered no matter the celebrity. He was also never unmindful of the potential for publicity for one of his writers.

He stood, swiping at his trousers with his napkin, and said, glancing from Mignon to Elsa, "Elsa, this is the mystery writer, Mignon Edwards."

She nodded, dipping her broad-brimmed black hat, acknowledging Mignon with a dismissive smile.

"Elsa enjoys making a scene," Harry said later. "That little stunt with the martini was no doubt purposeful."

To Mignon's surprise, she made it into Maxwell's next syndicated newspaper column, "Elsa Maxwell's Party Line": *Sitting next to editor Harry Maule was a chic, alert young woman who looked as though she ran a fashionable dress shop. It turned out to be Mignon Edwards, a writer I always assumed was a sinister old woman. Her eyes are wide and wistful, and her fluttering hands might well be an inheritance from a Southern Belle ancestress.*

Fluttering hands? Wistful eyes? Southern Belle? Mignon would have the last word though. Elsa Maxwell had the potential for an excellent protagonist. Mignon put her in the orange notebook.

In October, Bennett and Phyllis Cerf invited her to join them and Harry and Edna on a trip to the Boston Book Fair. Alan was working and unavailable, of course. Mignon was alone so much she might just as well be a widow or divorcee. Alan didn't care about books like these friends did anyway. She accepted the invitation. They took the train from New York City.

The first person she encountered at the Book Fair was Alice Dixon, a reviewer from the *Boston Herald*, and the first thing Alice said was: "I'm sorry I can't review your books, Mrs. E., but there are so many books, and I have space for only the best of the Fair's books."

Both Agatha Christie and Dorothy Sayers had books at the Fair, so that put Mignon in the worst kind of mood—humiliated, insulted. And jealous. She hated that jealous feeling.

"Ignore her," Harry said. "Her opinion doesn't matter."

"You don't even want her reviews," Bennett said. "She's nasty."

"I can't believe you can let one opinionated woman affect you so much," Phyllis added.

Mignon wished she could feign indifference. But she did care what the critics said. She lost sleep and confidence over negative reviews. Especially abhorred the reviewer who made up her mind before she had read any of Mignon's books.

Bennett suggested they fly home instead of taking the train. The bumpy flight reminded her of the flight from Miami to Kingston, Jamaica. The plane struck one snatch-your-breath, long down-draft. Like stomach dropping to the floor on a roller coaster. The stewardess walked up and down the aisle.

Her voice shook. "Keep your seat belts buckled. I have to buckle in myself," she said, waving her arms and pointing. "Drinks and dinner will not be served."

Their heads nearly hit the ceiling as the plane began the descent and spiraled down to LaGuardia. It landed with a jarring thud. The seat belt kept Mignon from launching into the back of the seat in front of her. She caught her breath and wondered why she was entranced with flying, but the experience would be a good scene in a novel.

The attack on Pearl Harbor stunned everyone. Roosevelt wouldn't keep the U.S. out of this war. Now he had a powerful excuse. People were excited and enthusiastic. Hysterical. Rumors flew that the United States might be air raided. The noise of constant air patrols and unusual number of planes overhead added to the hysteria and the anxiety.

It was all anyone could talk about, and Alan and Mignon didn't agree about any of it. He believed Roosevelt could do no wrong. "You are just emotional, not logical," he told her.

"My emotionalism is always your fallback position," she retaliated. "You never admit to being wrong about anything. And you are prejudiced and obstinate."

She cringed at Roosevelt's "Thank you for inviting me into your living room" fireside chats. All of it, the world, her world with Alan, and their disagreements stifled any creativity. She needed to quit listening to the radio and reading the newspapers. Ignore all the political turmoil that she couldn't do anything about anyway. Concentrate on writing. It took more discipline than usual.

Harry said her readers were yearning for Nurse Sarah Keate, so she began work on another mystery/romance with Nurse Sarah as the narrator and protagonist. There was certainly no romance in her own marriage, so she wrote about it. Affection, warmth, kindness, yes. That was it. Alan was not romantic.

1941

Maine

War changed their plans. Alan was preparing to move to Bolivia where he had contracted with Pan Am to work on the construction of a new airport when the military called him to duty. He had served in the Great War when he was only seventeen years old, so it never occurred to Mignon that he could be drafted. But no matter his age. The armed services apparently needed his professional engineering skills. He was commissioned and assigned before she could catch a breath. Or utter her dismay. It wasn't the way she had envisioned them living. She shuttled back and forth from the house in Woodsedge to the apartment in Manhattan and kept writing.

Who knew that writers could be influential in a war effort? Or that writers' voices would be heard? Rex Stout, Pearl Buck, Clifton Fadiman, Oscar Hammerstein II, and John Marquand formed a Writers War Board to write stories, radio scripts, poems, and dramatic skits—a kind of propaganda machine to promote the sale of United States war bonds. The Treasury Department supported them. The Board was large. Mignon joined. Over two thousand writers joined. She didn't even recognize some of the names although all of the

Pulitzers were on the list—Steinbeck, Pearl Buck, Margaret Mitchell, Rawlings.

Faith was asked to sit on the Advisory Council. That group included Edna Ferber, Stephen Vincent Benet, and Fannie Hurst. Even Edna Millay. Why Millay? Millay just hid in her cabin in the Berkshires and was rarely seen in New York. It would have been nice to be included. Recognized for twenty novels. Who chose those people? Literary snobs. Mystery and romance didn't meet their literary criteria.

Alan was stationed in St. Louis as an inspector in charge of the Navy Ordnance plant. Mignon stayed at the Plaza Hotel for a month to be with him. Then he got orders to proceed to Washington "for such duties as assigned." She had followed him from place to place (*wither thou goest*). Tethered. Trying not to complain about living in hotels. Trying to hold onto their marriage.

"I do not want to go to Washington. I do not want to spend the summer in that beastly heat and humidity," Mignon told Faith.

"Don't then. You don't have to follow Alan around. Some of the artsy New Yorkers are going to Ogunquit, Maine, for the summer," Faith said. "It's supposedly a charming, coastal town. No further than the Hamptons which you talked about. Take some time away from him."

According to the advertising, Ogunquit offered a "vibrant arts scene and night life," and the Sparhawk Hotel, a "country hotel," located some distance from the town center, purported "solitude and gentle ocean breezes." The art scene would be welcome, and she needed the ocean. It always soothed her into productive writing. But she didn't want to go to Maine alone.

Faith came to her rescue again with her contacts. This time from Wellesley College. The Wellesley Students' Aid Society, a women's organization, gave scholarships to girls who otherwise couldn't afford Wellesley: "poor and deserving" women, they said in their mission statement.

The scholarship girls required summer employment, but after interviewing several of them, Mignon had given up hope of finding the kind of young woman she needed when Ruth Herborn poked her head in the door with a smile. She didn't wait for Mignon's rehearsed speech about the position but launched into one of her own with barely a breath between words.

"I understand you're looking for a secretary. I'm an English major. Third year. I'm not trained in shorthand, but I am a very good typist. I'm a good writer too. I can compose letters to answer your fan mail, and I'm willing to do whatever other tasks you have."

"You realize that you would be living with me in an apartment for the summer?"

"That would be a luxurious break from the college dormitory."

"You will be on your own at odd times of the day. I work in the morning. Sometimes, not often, late in the evening. I may need you on Saturdays and Sundays. It's not an eight-hour-a-day, nine-to-five type job."

"I'm fine with that. It isn't easy to find a job in my hometown. I have to work this summer. The scholarship is generous, but no pin money. I will lie contentedly in the sun or read a book when you don't have work for me.

"I'm used to organizing my time. I have three younger brothers and a sister, so I can take charge of whatever you need. I can even do a little cooking if you'd like that."

She was confident without the brashness of some young women from those prestigious Eastern schools. Her dark-eyed seriousness appealed to Mignon, a spontaneous smile, but no giddiness. Her midwestern plain-speaking manner and confidence exuded dependability. Instinct told Mignon she would be a pleasant summer companion.

They took the train to Portland and arranged for a car to Ogunquit. Cold and rain greeted them, but Mignon wasn't deterred. Summer would arrive, she knew, if slowly, like it did in Nebraska.

They unpacked. Mignon put on slacks and a wool sweater, tied a scarf around her head, and walked to the beach. The ocean touched the horizon as far as the eye could see. She loved the ocean. Not unlike the infinity of space of the Nebraska Sand Hills. The kind of place she needed to rejuvenate. A transfusion for her writing.

"How do you find time to write?" friends often asked, as if she dabbled in it in spare time, like a hobby interrupting real life. In spite of her published books and the short stories and the magazine serials, even her sister and mother didn't take her work seriously. They were amused by her lugging her typewriter everywhere and hiring secretaries whenever she could. It was useless to try and explain the compulsion to write. She had never wanted to do anything else, and the fact that it earned her a good living was the bonus.

As for the typewriter—that gift from Alan more than fifteen years before. Her orange notebook was always at hand, but she could also set up the typewriter wherever she was living or vacationing. Sometimes words flew onto the page, and sometimes they didn't, but she was more likely to fill a page if she stuck to a routine. And she was more likely to do that if she had a secretary like Ruth to clean up what she'd typed or to type what she'd written.

She did love to dance and go to casinos and night clubs. "You enjoy hobnobbing with the upper crust," Alan had accused her now and then. But her work was serious. She maintained a morning writing schedule wherever she lived, and she was writing all the time in one way or another.

The ocean especially calmed her. At night she lay awake. Tossing. Turning the pillow. Fluffing the pillow. The brown and brass Waterbury alarm clock tick-tocking. Alan. Marriage. Alan. Marriage. But walking alone on the sand beach, she concentrated on *The Man Next Door*, the working title for a spy novel set in Washington.

A spy. A murder. A beautiful young Washington confidential secretary, maybe a listening post, caught in a net of intrigue and sabotage between her and her boss.

She worked out the details as she walked, defining the characters and cooking the plot around them.

"Try to give your hero a more rugged appearance," Harry had advised recently. "Perhaps he should be less kind, not quite as thoughtful. Some critics comment that your heroes are all effeminate."

Walking along the ocean those cold, windy days, watching the white froth of angry waves crash onto shore with a steady rhythm, she thought about Harry's comment. Were her heroes effeminate? She thought of them as handsome, gentle, affectionate. She enjoyed writing tender love scenes—hugs, passionate kisses, clandestine meetings. No sexual scenes. Lord knows she had no experience to draw on. Was Alan effeminate?

When she got back to their rooms after those long walks, she sat at her desk in the bedroom with the ocean view, made notes, and gave them to Ruth to type up. She realized quickly that Ruth was a competent copy editor.

"Mystery romances aren't my usual reading, Mrs. Edwards," Ruth said the first day, "but I hope you won't mind if I change some punctuation and a few other grammatical things if I notice them."

"Please call me Mignon." She warmed. Ruth Herborn was a smart girl. She didn't refer to errors or mistakes. She was sensitive enough to say "change" instead of "correct."

"Is the Shoreham a hotel?" Ruth read and paused, waiting for Mignon's response. "The secretary, Maida, in your novel, and her escort go to the Shoreham regularly to dance."

A critical reader. Perceptive. The Washington, D.C., setting and the Shoreham, so familiar to Mignon, could well be unfamiliar to readers who had never been there.

They settled into a routine. Before dinner Ruth brought Mignon her bourbon and made herself a Tom Collins of gin and soda, the college coed's drink of choice, she told Mignon. "My mom is appalled by my smoking. I assume you don't mind," she said that first evening as she took a pack from the pocket of her slacks, tapped a cigarette out, and lit up. She amused Mignon with stories about her family life and college life at Wellesley.

After an amiable evening of making a dinner together, they quit going to the hotel dining room every evening. Ruth shopped at the village grocery store while Mignon worked, and they cooked together in their little galley kitchen. After dinner they sat with their books in pillow-cushioned easy chairs in the living room facing the ocean. The intimacy, a kind of intimacy Mignon hadn't known, made her wonder what it would be like to have a daughter.

"What are you reading?' Ruth asked abruptly one evening. She looked up from the big high-backed chair where she sat with her legs curled under her, a book in her lap. "Would you make me a list of books I should read?"

No one had ever cared about what she read. No one had ever asked her what she read. She hadn't thought about all the books on her shelves at Woodsedge for years. She made a list. Recalled the novels and the writers with an unanticipated pleasure, like discovering old friends. Old friends to share with this bright young woman.

Over their weeks at Sparhawk, Ruth questioned: "How did you start writing? Tell me about your first publication. How do you get your ideas? Tell me about your life growing up in Nebraska. And in New York City. Tell me about your college friend, Carmen. You still write to each other?"

Mignon's affection for her grew each day, like falling slowly in love. How could you not love a young woman so curious about your life? Who wanted to know about your writing life? Who let you tell your story? A daughter might be interested. A daughter might care about such things.

At the end of the summer, Mignon left Ruth reluctantly at the Portland airport. They would exchange letters and visits for years to come.

1941-42

*Washington &
Woodsedge & War*

The world was as upside down as Mignon's life. After the Japanese planes streaked out of the sky on that sunny Sunday morning over Pearl Harbor, the newspapers and radio were filled with stories of spies and sabotage.

Alan was stationed in Washington, D.C., but making inspections of munitions plants around the country. This time, instead of moving to D.C., Mignon shuttled back and forth from Woodsedge. Washington was a different city than the one she'd known in peace time. The quiet Southern city seethed with people. A boom town.

They ignored the personal problems they'd been ignoring for years now. Mignon had always been an ostrich. Alan didn't procrastinate or avoid a dilemma or problem of any kind, their marriage the one exception. He didn't mind their life, or he didn't want to confront her about divorce. And she didn't want to face what might be the loneliness of single life.

They distracted themselves with dancing. Still found pleasure in dancing. Office workers and civil service employees crowded the Shoreham the Saturday night before Alan left for an inspection tour somewhere in the hinterland. There were also some prominent people in the crowd. The flamboyant Republican Senator, William Langer from North Dakota, sat at a table next to them with his matronly looking, mute wife, a smile fixed on her face. Harry Byrd from Virginia and Alben Barkley sat at a table nearby. Their wives dressed to the nines. Uniforms everywhere. Alan joked about the officers on the dance floor.

"How many ranks can we see?" he said, as the dancers floated by. "I've got three generals and an admiral."

The soft blue- and rose-colored lights were dim. The band played a Strauss waltz—lovely, nostalgic. Reminded Mignon of Vienna and of love and happiness. Perhaps all of Washington and New York and the civilized world were clinging, like Alan and her, to some normalcy. Trying to hold on to something of ordinary life. Dress up. Go out for dinner and dancing. Be in control. They all craved some enjoyment and pleasure. Nerves were battered with the horror of war. People were saying, "Live now. Live now." Try to forget the war with gayety and laughter and waltzing.

Alan was assigned to D.C. for the duration of the war. She had to decide if she should live with him there. He had irritated her even more than usual his last weekend visit to Woodsedge.

"Your rituals and routines for everything from bathing to this," she said, pointing a finger at the coat hanger in his hand, "are obsessive."

He laughed. "Routine is good. Anchors me. Helps me feel in control of some things at least. Gives me power." He proceeded to hang his suit coat on the oak valet. Smug.

"You have a split personality, Mimi. You want to be a strong, in-charge woman like your Sarah Keate. The old auntie types in your novels. But then you're the pampered, fragile young blonde beauty who needs laudanum to calm her nerves. My routine and rituals haven't changed. What's really bugging the fragile blonde now beyond the usual?"

"That's insulting. I don't even like you sometimes. I don't want to live this way anymore."

"Without sex, you mean. Just say it. Nothing has changed in these seventeen years, Mimi. You've known for seventeen years now."

"I don't know what's changed. Nothing has changed. I *have* known it for all these years. I have tried to accept it. That doesn't make it easier or better. For some reason, it's worse. You tell me there are other ways to show love besides sex. I know that too. But I need more than hugs and friendly kisses on the cheek. I could get that from a brother."

"I wish I could make you happy in that regard, Mimi, but it isn't going to happen. You want me to be a virile version of Hemingway and, aside from sharing his interest in hunting, you know I am not. You've known now for seventeen years that I'm not."

"I read about a study in Europe where scientists are isolating hormones. Maybe . . ."

"I'm not going to see any doctors. I am not going to agonize about it. There are no pills or procedures that will change this. I'm content with the way it is."

"*You* are content. I am miserable."

After a tossing, turning night, Mignon found him at the breakfast table, smoking a cigarette with his coffee and newspaper. Infuriatingly calm. "Maybe it's time for a real separation. I'll stay here in Woodsedge."

She slammed cupboard doors and banged drawers shut after he left and finally put a leash on Beau and took him for a long walk to wear out her fury.

Later in the week, she tried to call him in Washington, but he wasn't in. When he finally returned her call, he said, "I took a friend out for dinner."

He was solemn about it. Serious. Just relaying information. She didn't expect him to sit in a hotel and read the *Engineering News Record* every evening, but she was surprised at how quickly he had accepted their separation. Apparently, he simply adjusted his life accordingly.

"I don't want to be married to anyone else," he said. "You know as well as I do that marriage is complicated for me. But I enjoy having dinner with someone."

She certainly didn't understand his seeing another woman so soon. Or was it another woman? The possibility that his affection might be drawn to a man hovered, but she refused to give it any space in her thoughts. She missed him. He was good company. An interesting man. Missed sitting across from him at dinner. They had affection and understanding. Not what she saw in other couples. But a kind of affection she missed.

Marriage. *'Til death do us part.* That was ingrained in her. She had been determined to make a success of it. Hadn't realized the importance of sex. Marriage without a sexual relationship was strange and stressful, and you couldn't share the truth of your need with anyone. Women didn't discuss sex even with close personal friends. She didn't even know how to talk about it. It was embarrassing.

She had tried to ignore it for years. Just worked and worked at her writing. Fortunate to have her work since she didn't have what should be a normal part of a woman's married life.

Faith came by, concerned that they hadn't seen her for many days. "Gonnie and the children miss you," she said.

Mignon did miss those little people and her lunches and long talks with Faith. She enjoyed them all but hadn't felt like leaving the house or seeing anyone, and she wasn't ready to share the real problem.

"Alan's lengthy absences obviously aren't good for you," Faith said. "But isolating yourself isn't healthy for the writer you either. Are you working on anything?"

"Struggling with another spy novel. Spending hours at the typewriter but making very little progress."

"Maybe you should see someone for depression. I'll give you the name of a psychiatrist in the city. Maybe that's the cause of this colitis thing that plagues you too. Depression can have physical effects."

A receptionist led her into a spacious, light-filled room with a view of the Manhattan skyline to wait for Dr. Michaels. A large mahogany desk dominated the room with floor-to-ceiling bookcases on the wall behind it, a cream-colored sofa, mahogany coffee table, and two beige club chairs placed in a grouping in front of it. No couch to lie on like movie settings.

She read the framed diplomas on the wall. Graduate of Yale Medical School. New York State-Licensed in Psychiatry.

Her eyes opened wide with surprise when he walked into the room and introduced himself. His horn-rimmed spectacles didn't detract from his youthful, high-school-boy looks, nor did his neatly trimmed beard which he, no doubt, sported to look professional and older. All she could think was *I cannot tell this boy-man about my marriage. There is no way I can talk about sex.*

He moved to the desk, sat down, and motioned her to a chair opposite the desk. "Tell me about yourself," he said. "I understand you are a writer. What do you write?"

What do I write? That disarmed her . . . gullible as always to interest and to flattery.

"Mysteries," she said, aware that mysteries were held in higher regard than romance novels. And neither was considered serious writing.

"Have you published anything?" Almost a smirk. He raised his eyebrows with barely disguised cynicism.

"Over twenty novels." She hoped her tone of voice would dispel any notion that she was some society dilettante with a writing hobby.

"Prolific," he said. She interpreted surprise. Realized the truth of it. She had been prolific. Worked steadily and successfully over the years throughout a difficult marriage and illness and moving with Alan from one place to another.

Dr. Michaels brought her back to the room. "Tell me about your life outside of the writing. What brought you here?"

The first and easy response. "I'm not sleeping."

"How does that affect your daily life?" he said.

"No energy. I'm too tired to work."

What she wanted to say was *I don't find any joy in my life*, but she felt guilty admitting that. She lived in a beautiful place. In the house she'd always wanted. With enough money to do as she liked. And . . . she had been married nearly twenty years and had never had sex.

"I need to work out my life with my husband," she finally blurted. Wished she could take her cigarettes out of her handbag and light up.

She sat there thinking about her life with Alan. They had a lot of happiness. They saw each other frequently even when they were separated. Wrote letters and telephoned, although Alan didn't want to discuss their problem. He had never understood her need to discuss it as he said, *ad infinitum*. He claimed she was emotional, but that was a judgment he made frequently about many of her opinions.

"It is what it is," Alan said the last time she had broached the subject. "I'm not going to take advice from doctors. I am not going to a doctor. Shock treatments or needles in the groin aren't options. Neither is surgery. Talking about it won't change anything."

"Your marriage?" Dr. Michaels said.

"We aren't intimate." Intimate. The word she'd finally come up with.

"A passionless marriage." He picked up his pen and made a note on the paper in front of him. Her file. If by passionless, he meant loveless, that wasn't true.

He went back to her writing. "Some of your readers may be in similar relationships. I assume your readers are women?" He looked at her and smiled. "They probably identify with you. You, no doubt, work out your own life when you're writing." He picked up his pen again. "Your readers probably find escape from their own negative domestic situations in your little stories."

Her little stories. "That may be, but right now I'm not able to write. I don't get enough sleep."

"I'll give you a prescription for Veronal to help you sleep." He handed her a slip of paper with an illegible scroll. "Make an appointment with the secretary. I'll see you next week."

She didn't feel any better about herself when she walked out the door. He was patronizing. And she didn't appreciate his trivializing her work.

Alan's only response, when she told him about Dr. Michaels was, "You know how I feel about medications, but I hope it helps you sleep." He didn't ask if she had talked about their sexless marriage, and she didn't volunteer.

Mignon went back to work. A war-related mystery/romance using her notes from Florida. The setting, always important for her, was a big old mansion with grounds and gardens leading to a river. Like the house she and Alan lived in the winter they spent there. All fictitious names but she used the Air Force Base and what she'd learned about sabotage. The title, subject to suggestion and revision by Harry — *Unidentified Woman.*

Alan had given her the idea for the plot when they lived in Florida, and he talked about his frustration with the contracting process for the work going on at the Air Force Base. The government awarded a prime contract to a company and issued a check for a percent of the amount bid for the job. The prime contractor subcontracted to smaller companies for materials or work they didn't have the capability or manpower to do in-house.

"In one case," Alan told her, "the prime contractor subcontracted for lumber. They needed prompt delivery. Everything needed to be done at top speed. All they needed to apply for the subcontract was their corporation charter. They might not even be asked to show the charter. Oversight and responsibility were sloppy."

She listened, impatient with the interminable details of his work.

"It's ripe for fraud," Alan said.

Or for espionage, she thought, and for foreign agents. She'd put it all in her orange Rhodia notebook.

She didn't make another appointment with Dr. Michaels. Gave up on therapy. But she felt better and decided to move to Washington, D.C. to live with Alan.

"That would make me very happy," he said when she told him. "I'll take a leave and come to Connecticut and help you move." He made arrangements for Tom Leland, their gardener, to get gas coupons and drive the Cadillac full of possessions to D.C.

There was nothing to rent in D.C., not even permanent hotel rooms which would have been preferable to the house they finally rented—three tiny bedrooms, a tiny but light study, and a small, enclosed garden. Beau could at least have a place to run.

It was a strained and strange reconciliation. She knew she was lucky to have Alan stationed in D.C. instead of Europe, but he was totally absorbed in his new projects for the Pentagon. She saw so little of him, she might as well have stayed at Woodsedge, and D.C. was a miserable place in the winter.

She needed a change of scene. A different setting for a new novel. Faith rescued her again.

"Gonnie and I plan to spend January and February at the Del Monte Lodge at Pebble Beach on the Monterey Peninsula in California. Join us. We can't escape the war anywhere! The old Del Monte Hotel, where we usually stay, has apparently been appropriated by the Navy. Two hundred Navy men are stationed there in preflight school. But we can stay at Del Monte Lodge."

Mignon wrote the ending to *Unidentified Woman* and sent it to Harry. She arranged for Tom Leland to take care of Beau and then went shopping for beach clothes and dresses for evenings in Carmel.

1943

Carmel

The Southern Pacific Railroad took them from D.C. right to Carmel. From her seat on the train Mignon could see the city on the blue sea with the green hills beyond. They took a taxicab to the Del Monte from the station.

Faith had not misled her about the hotel. She stepped out of the taxicab into the spacious courtyard of the two-story Spanish-style building with a red clay roof. The music of splashing and spraying water from fountains set amidst the palms greeted her.

Her suite didn't disappoint—a large living room with a fireplace and a view of the ocean-side fairways of the golf course, a bedroom with a big desk and lamp and a comfortable chair, always her necessities.

That first evening was windless and warm, a balm from the cold north she'd left. She stood on the balcony inhaling it. The stars seemed more brilliant because of the blackout. She felt the havoc slip away.

"I'm looking forward to the Golden Bough playhouse one of these evenings," she told Faith and Gonnie at breakfast.

"Closed," Gonnie said. "Because of the blackout. The entire west coast closed really. No theatre, no concerts, no museums. A moratorium on the arts. Victims of the war."

They took a drive along the beaches of Monterey. Seventeen miles along the rocky shoreline of the blue Pacific. The surf seethed. The crashing waves were like a threat to all that tranquility. She could feel the perfect setting for mystery and romance. There was an "other worldliness" about the place—the startling beauty, the hot sun, the black rocks, the sea.

She settled into working in the morning. Often rode horseback in the afternoons, then cocktails and dinner with Faith and Gonnie, who knew the local celebrities living in Monterey and dining at the Del Monte. Salvador Dali arrived nightly with an entourage. Bob Hope and Gloria Vanderbilt regularly sat at an out-of-the way table.

Mignon reveled in it. She was busy and entertained. Working and playing, she pushed Alan out of her mind.

She sent Harry a draft of *Escape the Night,* and he responded quickly as he always did.

> January 16, 1943
> Dear Mignon,
> The setting in Carmel is charming and described in interesting detail as your settings always are. I believe you must recognize the war in this novel though, not necessarily as part of the romance and mystery, but certainly more than simply in the army enlistments of your male characters.
> Women in small towns and cities all over the U.S. who read your books to escape from their mundane lives and poor circumstances, are now

coping with rationing of essential food items and gas for their cars and shoes for their children. They are going bare-legged because they can't get silk stockings. In some small Midwestern towns, probably in your own Nebraska, every family has a son serving in the war.

Your characters are leading a charmed life with no deprivation, traveling from one end of the country to the other in luxury. Your readers want this escape and the romance of it, but you should acknowledge the impact of the war in some way.

One of our young editors noted that you treat the war in a cavalier sort of way, essentially brushing it off as incidental to your story. She also commented that the love triangle is becoming a formula. You might want to think about that in the future. She is concerned that you are obsessed with clothes, which may be unseemly at this time, for example, in the scene wherein the main character, Serena, "dresses for dinner" after her sister is murdered. The coldness between the sisters may be unrealistic.

I'm sending you some revisions to take into consideration. I will see you in New York. Edna sends her love.

Warm Regards,

Harry

A harsh critique. Mignon pushed herself away from the desk and left her room to walk on the beach. She watched her feet, concentrated on her stomping feet in the sand, oblivious to the slapping ocean waves, lost in her own head. The anger and railing at Harry played itself out. She went back to her room and sat down at the desk with the manuscript and Harry's suggestions.

She pounded out revisions. Added a dirigible searching for Japanese submarines and described the blackouts, including the blackouts on the train she recalled from D.C. to Carmel. She made note of Red Cross work and air raids and rationing. But she brooded about it. Harry had shepherded all her work, and she needed to trust him, but her women readers had always enjoyed descriptions of the stylish clothes, and she wrote about affluent people who generally lived well and who observed certain formalities even in the midst of war and murder. They dressed for dinner. Even the Churchills dressed for dinner during the Blitz.

As for the comment about the coldness between the sisters, Serena and Amanda, and the unrealistic response of Jam, the male character, to Amanda—it was all realistic. She used her own experience. She and her sister Helen weren't friends. There was too much difference in their ages for friendship. Helen had always acted like another mother. Amanda in the novel had some of Helen's characteristics—vain and dramatic, selfish and manipulative. And men responded to Helen's childish drama, so Jam's response to Amanda may have seemed illogical, but it wasn't unrealistic.

She compromised with Harry and sent the revisions. Reluctant revisions. He responded with interesting news of the publishing world.

February 23, 1943
Dear Mignon,

I received your revisions for *Escape the Night*. We planned to have it out by the end of the year, but it may be later. Things are moving more slowly because of the war, but at the same time, you might be interested in some radical developments in the publishing world.

German refugees, Helen and Kurt Wolff, prominent publishers who epitomized and defined European intellectual life, have launched Pantheon Books, with the intention of publishing banned and burned books from Europe, especially those by Jewish writers.

The burning and banning of books in Nazi-occupied countries has fostered unprecedented attention to the importance of books as weapons in the war of ideas. I don't know if you have seen the recent poster (a gigantic book cover) with President Roosevelt's words: "Books cannot be killed by fire. People die, but books never die . . . In this war, we know books are weapons."

This may well be the golden age of literature. I am told that reading Hemingway in Nazi-occupied countries is indicative of resistance!

I look forward to seeing you in New York soon.

Warm Regards,

Harry

The California sunshine had proved productive. It was time to go home—home to Woodsedge for a few weeks before returning to Washington and Alan.

1943

Washington & War

D.C. was teeming with people—service men and government workers and congressmen and congressmen's wives and their families—everyone needing household help. Mignon finally found a cook, but the woman wouldn't cook if she had to help with the cleaning. No luck finding anybody to do cleaning. Though she detested making beds and dusting and vacuuming, after her morning writing, she got out the Hoover.

But life in D.C. during war wasn't dull. It wasn't *just* hoovering. She and Alan dined and danced at the Shoreham even more often than they had in the past. Wartime Washington was full of interesting people, thick with intrigue and gossip. When she wrote to Carmen about it, Carmen responded with more than a hint of disapproval and a lengthy description of the war in her world.

> May 15, 1943
> Dear Mignon,
> You mentioned the exciting life in Washington. There is little gayety here! Every town and village in

Nebraska has been touched by this dreadful war. In some small towns, every family has given a son or a brother.

And everyone has to cope with the rationing, which is especially difficult if you have no connections. New shoes for growing kids in big families is a problem. The farm women are canning vegetables and fruits, but they have had to fill out special applications for more sugar.

The new *Good Housekeeping* cookbook just came out with a special section for rationed foods. That and the government's meal planning guides are helpful for those of us in the kitchen. Charlie and I let our hired girl go. You at least still have a cook!

The only hardship some women seem to have is no silk stockings, nor as many new shoes as they'd like. We aren't suffering beyond having to curtail our pleasure trips to save on the tires and make the best use of our gas ration. Some people don't seem to have a problem getting gas. Charlie says there is a thriving black market for it and, ironically, for sugar.

Winter is grim. We're looking forward to spring and summer when we can drive out to the country and get fresh vegetables from the farmers' roadside stands.

I've been volunteering at the Red Cross as a Gray Lady. I took a training course they provided and work with dozens of other women helping the medical personnel at the hospital here and at the Military Base. There are twelve new bases training pilots in Nebraska.

And everyone I know is knitting. The Red Cross provides patterns and wool for sweaters, socks, mufflers, fingerless mitts so soldiers can keep their hands warm when they are shooting, and even toe covers for use with a cast. Can you imagine? It's a horrific mental image.

The knitting is boring because the clothes have to be knit in olive drab or navy blue. But you feel like you're helping in this helpless situation. I recently saw a photo of Eleanor Roosevelt knitting the stretch bandages they sterilize and ship to the medical units all over the world.

I don't know if you heard, but our sorority sister Fran's son Victor was killed in Africa. After he was shipped overseas, his wife went to Seattle with a friend to work in the shipyards and wait for Victor there. She'll stay in Seattle now. No reason to come back to Nebraska. There's work for her in Seattle, and she needs to work. Victor was the oldest boy and would have taken over the family farm, but his brother Jim will have the farm now. You know these old patriarchal families—the widow is out of luck.

Keep in touch.

Love, Carmen

The comment about silk stockings and new shoes was a direct hit. Carmen had always chided Mignon about her shoe fetish and her obsession with clothes. *It isn't my fault I don't live in Lincoln where the Red Cross and the worship of the knitting Eleanor Roosevelt is important,* she thought. *It isn't as though I just party and dance. I do work. I am working.*

In fact, Harry had just asked her to write a story for the CBS *Cavalcade of America.* Dupont was sponsoring a radio series of war-related programs, and the Writers

War Board was trying to include as many writers as possible.

Alan Lomax, the *Cavalcade* producer, instructed her to use the essence of the government war slogans in her radio script.

The government had printed and posted hundreds of war posters everywhere with slogans like *The Enemy is Listening—He wants to know what you know—Keep it to yourself* and *Loose Lips Might Sink Ships—Don't Talk About Ship Movement or Cargo.* Some posters had garish photographs: a woman with *Wanted for Murder—Her Careless Talk Costs Lives;* a soldier with *If You Talk Too Much—This Man May Die; I'm Counting on You* with Uncle Sam pointing a finger; a woman on the phone and a globe with ears—*The World Has Ears.*

Lomax sent her a working title: "The Enemy is Listening."

"Write a story," he said, "within the parameters of your mystery/romance storytelling. Show the consequences of idle conversation. Or what people consider idle, innocent conversation."

A radio script was a different kind of writing, and the strict limits for time would be a challenge, but she decided to write it like her magazine short stories. Her main concern was the number of characters she needed for all the roles—mystery, romance, *and* message. How could she keep from confusing listeners?

"Don't be concerned about that," Lomax told her. "The actors are experienced. The voices of individual characters will be clear to the radio audience.

"You will have to describe the setting briefly," he said. "No lengthy narrative. No intricate, extensive description of mansions or gardens allowed on radio." He knew her work or Harry had primed him.

Strip the story of setting—a challenge. Setting was basic for her. She worked it out—setting, characters, plot. Sent the script to Lomax and was summoned to New York for rehearsals.

She took the train from D.C. to New York City, then a taxicab to the CBS radio studios. A doorman escorted her to Studio 41 in the Madison Avenue headquarters. She wondered if this was the same studio Edward R. Murrow and Charles Collingwood used to broadcast the war news she and Alan listened to every evening.

Lomax, the producer she'd been corresponding with, introduced himself and directed her to a seat in the first row of a small auditorium. Two dozen seats she guessed, looking around her. All empty. She was the only audience. But on stage—a hum of activity. Actors and actresses sat on folding chairs with scripts in hand. A large white clock above them with "Eastern War Time" in bold letters on its face.

Mignon watched with surprise as an attractive, dark-haired woman, long hair pulled back from her face for headphones, rolled a table-type cabinet onto the stage and arranged various small bells, gongs, a small drum, a xylophone, a strange contraption of wooden pegs, a fan, and a length of chain.

When Mignon asked about the woman later, she learned that three women were now sound engineers for major news corporations. War created opportunities for women.

Lomax stood in front of a microphone, announced the program, and set the stage for the drama—two soldiers on a train in New York City. Two young men got up from their chairs and came to the microphone, scripts in hand.

A technician for the equipment and a music director, along with Lomax, hovered nearby, the woman with the sound effects stationed to the side of the microphone with script in hand. The soldiers read their lines. Then two actresses joined them at the microphone. The voice of Vera Lynn with "The White Cliffs of Dover" and "We'll Meet Again" played softly in the background.

Lomax interrupted. He wanted changes in the script. The music director stopped the recording abruptly. Every fifteen minutes, Lomax called "Cut" for the Dupont commercial. The music stopped. "We need a dramatic moment before the commercial," he announced.

Lomax and his two associates, the sleeves of their white shirts rolled up, ties loosened, leaned over the script with their pencils. Then the actors resumed with an edited version of her story. Her story. Her script. Mignon clenched her teeth.

The bones of the drama were: Two women sit behind soldiers Pinky and Bill on the train to New York City and eavesdrop on their conversation. The soldiers discuss their own surprise of an unanticipated twelve-hour leave. They are on their way home before shipping out to France. As the eavesdropping women exit the train talking about the soldiers and their unanticipated leave, their conversation is overheard by two men following the soldiers. One of the men, Mr. Smith, has a decided German accent.

Background music emphasizes the drama of Smith and his fellow spy whose mission is to discover where the soldiers are going after their leave and how many troops are embarking. Smith follows Pinky home. Pinky and Bill decide to take their girls, Sally and Jami, dancing for the last time. The band plays "I didn't want to do it" and "I'll be seeing you" while they cuddle and dance. Jami and Bill kiss on the balcony with dance music in the background. Time flies, the boys are late, and must hurry. Smith pretends to be a taxi driver and picks them up. Pinky and Bill kiss their girls good-bye and have the taxi drop them off at the wharf. Smith and his spy-buddy have gleaned the information they need about the troop's embarkation and destination.

Last scene—the sound of marching from the wooden peg contraption on the sound engineer's table. A soldier comes to the door of Pinky's parent's home to tell them that Bill and Pinky were killed in a battle in France.

Lomax stood at the microphone and read the final words which he wrote: "The enemy is listening, eavesdropping on a nation. He is listening to the man on the bus, the woman going shopping and you and you and you." *When the Lights go on again all over the world, and the boys are home again all over the world* played softly in the background.

Pinky and Bill's deaths were supposedly the result of the conversation overheard by enemies on the train. Contrived, Mignon knew, and even far-fetched, but it was, she supposed, a patriotic contribution in a way. Not her best writing. Not even *her* writing. A collaboration. But the radio audience was enormous. It never hurt to have her name out there. Her readers would realize that she wasn't ignorant of the war.

And radio had become indispensable. Countries on both sides of the insanity used radio in what some people called psychological warfare. American boys heard Tokyo Rose with her Japanese propaganda. The U.S. had its own anti-Nazi weapon. Marlene Dietrich recorded and broadcast popular American tunes in German. The German boys adored her. And the Germans had the despicable Mildred Gillars collaborating with them in Berlin.

How could Gillars have become a Nazi sympathizer? She was born and raised in Maine, even lived in Greenwich Village. Now she called herself Axis Sally. On her evening program, *Home Sweet Home*, she purred things like: "Hello boys, American boys. I've got your favorite jazz recordings tonight. Remember Glenn Miller's 'You'd be so nice to come home to?' Who are you thinking of tonight, boys? I hope she's being faithful."

Nazi sympathizers. A female Nazi spy. The perfect protagonist for a war novel. Mignon needed to write about a Nazi spy. She didn't care to get into the morass of politics in Washington. And setting a novel in Europe, though she knew it well, created all sorts of dilemmas with accuracy in time and location. Too many details to cope with.

She tried to write it in a New York setting. Couldn't make it work. The problems with Alan weighed on her, and Harry was pressuring her about writing a new novel. She'd been putting out at least two a year the past years.

She finally decided to put the spy and her friends in Mexico which was out of the war and safe. But she always wrote best when she experienced a place herself. She had to go to Mexico. Alan was too busy to care where she went.

1943

Mexico

The challenge for Mignon was getting to Mexico with the war restrictions on travel. Always eager to participate in her adventures for the sake of a good novel, Harry appealed to his friend, Carlene Roberts. She had just been promoted to Assistant Vice President of American Airlines and was being transferred from New York to D.C.

"I'll be leaving New York in a couple of weeks," she said when she telephoned Mignon at Woodsedge. "Meet me for lunch. You can tell me what you have in mind in regard to a trip to Mexico."

Mignon had never met a woman business executive. The only powerful woman she knew was in the literary world—the lioness Diana Trilling, who Harry referred to alternately as a Rebbetzin and a fish wife. Mignon evaded the acerbic tongue, gratefully, because Trilling found Mignon's novels too lacking in literary merit to review. The only other powerful woman she could think of was in government—Frances Perkins, Roosevelt's Secretary of Labor.

What kind of woman reaches that accomplishment in the business world? She tried to picture her. Large.

Manly. Severe. A buxom type with tightly permed gray hair and thick, wire-rimmed glasses in navy blue suit and brown, laced oxfords.

Mignon arrived at the Waldorf and was seated. The maître d' nodded in her direction when Carlene Roberts appeared at his station. People looked up from their plates and paused in their conversations to note the tall woman, head held high, striding across the room to the table. She was not movie-star beautiful but striking. Classic good looks. Taller than Mignon by six inches at least, dark brown hair parted on the side and cut stylishly chin length, saved from severity by a slight curl and flip. Mignon especially noted the pearls in her ears and a single strand of pearls around the neck of a lovely soft gray silk shirt under a dark gray suit jacket, pencil skirt, and matching gray suede pumps.

"I must apologize," Carlene said as she sat down and introduced herself. "I haven't read your books. I do know some of your friends, and I've read about you in Fanny Butcher's column, but I don't have much time for pleasure reading."

I could use a friend unconnected to my writing life, Mignon thought. Especially a friend who isn't a writer and competitor.

Mignon wasn't sure how to respond. How did one make small talk with a woman executive? She read Fanny Butcher though so no doubt knew of Mignon's purported obsession with clothes. That was a place to begin the conversation.

"That is a beautiful suit," Mignon said.

Carlene smiled and laughed. "I was just promoted from what was essentially a secretarial position. I'm being transferred to our Washington, D.C. headquarters, so I thought I would assume a persona appropriate to the new title. I have no imagination. I just bought three identical suits. Navy blue. Brown. And this gray. I'm flattered that you approve."

That confession and confidence, a kind of humility, endeared her to Mignon immediately.

Mignon ordered her bourbon. Carlene started with a martini, and their luncheon lengthened into mid-afternoon.

"Why do you want to go to Mexico?" Carlene asked.

"I want to write about a Nazi spy, but I don't want to set the story in the U.S. or in Europe. I've never been to Mexico. And I need to experience a place to write about it."

"I've been there. You'll enjoy it. Do you always travel to the places where you set your novels?"

"As often as I can. I grew up in Nebraska and have had a hunger to see the world."

"Kentucky for me," Carlene said. "My dream was escape to New York. Make a name for myself on the stage."

"And did you escape to New York?"

"No. The Depression intervened. Reality shattered the dream. I went to the U of Oklahoma. Got a business degree. But then had to learn shorthand and typing to get a job! Got a secretarial job with Braniff Airlines, and fate smiled on me. After just two years, my boss took me with him to Chicago. Then New York when he transferred to American Airlines. I have loved living in New York City. I hate to leave."

They launched then into the art and the music and the stimulation of multi-cultural New York City, and their mutual—from the center of the country—hunger to catch up with those worlds and know them. They interrupted each other, leaning across the table with smiles of recognition at each discovery of common enthusiasms. Their basic rural upbringing. The yearning. The ambition born in them.

Sometimes, when you are in need, affection comes along serendipitously. Maybe fate, Mignon thought. When Carlene and Mignon parted that afternoon, Mignon knew they would be friends. She didn't have a collection of women friends like beads on a necklace. Had always preferred working with men. She was used to men in the publishing world. Some of them were friends. There were only a few special women she cared deeply about. Except for Faith, they weren't writers. They were women who gave her some intangible thing she didn't have, a piece of a puzzle to make her whole. Like Carmen who had a keen mind and ambition and drive but didn't take herself seriously. She had a lightheartedness Mignon definitely lacked.

"Call me when you get back from Mexico," Carlene said. "I'll arrange some trips for us."

The trip to Mexico was horrendous and long—three days, three different flights. After the first leg, New York to Chicago, Mignon spent the night at the Blackstone where she had stayed for years. In the morning, she flew to St. Louis and another overnight. From St. Louis to Fort Worth and, finally, on to Monterey, Mexico.

They landed briefly. Once in the air again, they climbed high into the blazing sun. The cloud-bed beneath them cleared, and they were above the mountain peaks. It was spectacularly beautiful—strange and lovely—and her enchantment with this adventure into an unfamiliar world grew. Anything could happen. They swept so low between the mountains she could see the ruins of the pyramids, the mystery and beauty below and ahead of her.

A few minutes later, they swept down into the valley and Mexico City with mountains rising all around it. The plane flew lower and lower. Its enormous wings brushed the earth, its shadow moving over the concrete concourse. It kissed the concourse with a light tremor. Her breath stopped. Her heart pounded so loud she felt it in her ears. And she had the title for a new novel: *Wings of Fear*.

Mexico City was a hubbub. The taxi from the airport crawled, and Mignon drank it in. The streets were crowded and noisy under a blazing hot sun—cars, buses, smartly uniformed policemen on the corners. The air was filled with the fragrance of tortillas and ears of corn Indian women in bright shawls were cooking on braziers in the street.

The flower markets were a mass of glowing yellows and reds, the paths between the banks of flowers teeming with tourists in sport suits and print dresses, businessmen in dark clothing, Indians with bright serapes and sombreros, Spanish or Mexican women in black, children with round brown faces and twinkling black eyes. Mignon's driver had to brake to miss an Indian man strolling along with a small donkey beside him.

The houses were set flush with the street and secreted behind great closed doors and shuttered windows, or almost concealed behind high walls and shrubbery and trees.

They came to a high, mellowed pink, plastered wall. The driver sounded the horn. Great wooden doors opened magically. An Indian servant stood aside to let the car pass and then closed the gate. The taxi took them up a short, pebbled driveway with thick glossy green shrubbery and suddenly, the house—a vine-covered, mellowed pink stucco house, built within a courtyard.

Harry had arranged for her to stay with friends, and she settled into the routine of her hosts. The patio was the hub, the center of communication, the life and heart of this lovely old Spanish house. They ate on the patio. They lounged there, met for drinks there, had after-dinner coffee there in candlelight.

The bedrooms were on the second floor with balconies overlooking the courtyard. If she leaned over the railing, the patio looked like a stage. When she walked across the sun-flooded patio during the day, and when it was lit by the moon and stars at night, she knew it was a good setting for a mystery. Patches of clouds passed over, dimming the light now and then, making it perfect for murder.

The dining room was low-ceilinged with a long, narrow Spanish table and high-backed chairs carved like miniature thrones—a different sort of house than she had ever experienced—a unique setting for a novel. Coming here was a good decision.

She resumed her morning writing routine. Thinking about Alan and their marriage falling apart persisted like a shadow over her shoulder. It invaded her writing. She found herself creating a man more tender and caring than some of the men in past novels. Her hero puts a warm quilt over the woman he loves and gently wipes her face with a warm cloth when she's ill. Alan had never seen her as a woman to be coddled. Apparently, she wasn't the kind of woman to inspire devotion either. He did express admiration and support . . . and always affection.

Before she left New York, they had danced at the Stork Club. Alan had always been a wonderful dancer. A perfectionist. A perfectionist about every little thing. It irritated her more and more as the years went on. How much would she miss him? His blonde hair, his clean, well-scrubbed handsomeness. His steadiness and support of her writing. Thinking about it invaded her work.

She thought Mexico would be the best place to write a Nazi spy story. The setting was lush and unique. Maybe too exotic for the subject. She couldn't get the story. And she couldn't focus on writing.

After two weeks of that ruminating and languor in the heat and the exotic surroundings, she called him. They hashed out their problems, as much as Alan would hash anything out.

"My parents *never* argued," he had told her once when she launched into one of her tirades about their unnatural married life. Their lack of a sex life. "I never heard them argue."

"Well, that's unrealistic. They must have suppressed their feelings, or they had their disagreements behind their bedroom door."

She was tired of this strange life and this strange marriage. Tired of her own frustration and guilt over the cravings. Her yearning. Her envying married friends.

"I don't understand how you can go on this way without any angst, Alan. Without any concern about it. It isn't normal. You aren't normal."

"You are obsessed with sex," he said. "We need to quit arguing about this. You need to decide just what it is you want."

The maddening calm in his voice fed her fury. "I'm finished. What I want is a divorce."

"I won't stand in your way," he said.

Divorce. It made no sense to stay in Mexico. She wasn't getting any work done. It didn't make sense to go back to New York either. Divorce. She considered Reno but found out that Arkansas allowed simple incompatibility as grounds for divorce and divorce granted in a closed hearing. No publicity. Not even a newspaper notice.

She wouldn't tell her mother or Helen until it was over. She couldn't cope with the "sanctity of marriage" lecture from her mother, nor hearing about Helen's dismay and embarrassment.

She booked a flight to St. Louis and packed her bags. She would take the train from St. Louis to Fayetteville.

1943-44

Arkansas

A sleazy, patronizing attorney met her at the train station.

"Welcome to Fayetteville, Mrs. Edwards. Gertrude insisted on meeting you." He pumped her hand and turned to introduce his dumpy wife.

Gertrude gushed. "I've never met a famous author. I'm so looking forward to reading your books."

Mignon wasn't in the mood to make small talk with provincials who hadn't even read her books. What was she thinking? What an impulsive thing to do. Six months in this godforsaken place to establish residency.

"Since you'll be here several months, we thought you'd be more comfortable in a rooming house," Gertrude said. "A bedroom, sitting room, and private bath. Quite nice. The family lives in the house. Meals are provided."

Not even a decent hotel.

In their town car on the way to the rooming house, Gertrude nattered on about Fayetteville. "We're at the foot of the Ozarks. One of the most beautiful cities in the state. We have the university here," she drawled.

Mignon unpacked her inappropriate Mexico wardrobe. No need for sun dresses and dinner dresses.

Clothes shopping would kill some time. She set her typewriter on the kitchen table. No room with a view here. Paper and pens and frustrated fragments of a novel forced her to focus on the necessity of writing.

Her forays from the rooming house in the following days convinced her that she had no interest in the place nor in the southern culture. Even the accents annoyed her. She'd always used her travels purposely for settings in novels. Every new place an adventure. Not this. This place was alien in every respect.

She filled the days meandering through the nearby campus. Enjoyed the arboretum. Thought of her flower gardens at Woodsedge. Reminisced about her first flower garden in Valentine. Thought about Alan as she wandered by a building with a College of Engineering sign over the entrance.

No Macy's here, but a department store called Dillard's. Carmen would surely appreciate her being able to buy shoes and appropriate clothes. The downtown Dickson Street bookstore on the corner of the city square became a second home. Some days she just sank into a corner nook sofa, surrounded by high shelves of books, and read to get away from the sterile rooming house. Faulkner and Hemingway both had just published new novels. Steinbeck's *Moon is Down* and Pearl Buck's *Dragon Seeker* were Book of the Month Club selections.

"Agatha Christie has two books on the best seller lists," a clerk said as he stacked her purchases on the counter one afternoon.

"I don't read Agatha Christie."

He raised his eyebrows disapprovingly and stared.
She wrote for hours every day. Mornings.
Afternoons. Evenings. There was nothing to distract her.
And having made the decision to divorce Alan freed her
pen. *Unidentified Woman:*

A lovely young heiress introduced to the reader in her
shantung dress, blue linen sandals and wide-brimmed straw
hat. A big old mansion with grounds and gardens leading to a
river near a Florida army base. The chief financial officer of a
big company with government contracts is murdered. The
devoted confidant, housekeeper, is murdered. The
mysterious young secretary may be involved in the espionage
or sabotage.

Mignon talked to Alan several times those months.
She couldn't bear the thought of not seeing him. They
had always been friends. They liked each other. They fell
into easy affection and conversation. He had been
content with their marriage as it was, but that was
beside the point now. She didn't want to live with just
contentment and affection anymore. Kindness and
goodness weren't enough.

It wasn't only that. They didn't want to live the
same way anymore. Their differences had increased as
the years went by. Alan had his life in the field with his
engineering buddies. He ate and drank with them after
work, so when he came home, *when* he lived in their
home, he was happy to settle into his chair and listen to
the radio or read. She worked alone. She wanted to get
dressed up and go out and be with people. Have a social

life. They had lived that way in their early years in Chicago, but he wasn't interested in that kind of life anymore. They were at odds about it most of the time.

All of it, including the sexual frustration, had apparently benefited her writing—twenty-three novels in twenty years of marriage.

This is the best thing. Divorce was the thing to do. She convinced herself during those long days and the toss-and-turn nights in Arkansas.

> October 25, 1943
> Dear Mignon,
>
> I was relieved to hear from you though saddened by the reason for your not returning to New York. Edna and I have always liked Alan, and we're sorry your marriage hasn't worked out.
>
> I am, of course, pleased that you are able to write in spite of the barrenness of Arkansas. I am enclosing notes on *Unidentified Woman* for your revision.
>
> I suggest that you introduce fewer characters in the beginning pages so as not to confuse your readers. If you prefer the large cast, you can introduce them gradually as the action unfolds.
>
> You've done your usually splendid job of describing the big old mansion with stairways and balconies, grounds and gardens leading to the river. Ghostly wisps of Spanish moss and the shadows and moonlight create suspense. I like the hint of espionage right from the beginning, and your details about government contracts are no doubt thanks to Alan's experience on the Base.
>
> Keep working!
> Warm Regards, Harry

In December Harry sent her the final copy of *Escape the Night*. She liked what he had done with it—a list of characters opposite the title page and on the inside cover, a sketch of the courtyard with palm trees and umbrella-like balconies of the villa where the murder took place. The synopsis of the novel on the facing page —*A young girl in love battles against hate and suspicion in this story of murder on the enchanted California coast*— reminded her of those wonderful days in Carmel. The Condit Ranch, the setting of the novel, was the oldest ranch on the Monterey Peninsula, mountains on one side, sea on the other. An enchanted place.

But then Harry mailed the reviews. Publications as sophisticated as *The New Yorker* weren't available in this godforsaken town. One reviewer noted that her readers would find the plot reminiscent of her last four or five books. Another noted with disdain "a familiar theme of unrequited love and the love triangle."

Harry included notes from one of her readers who said she was obsessed with clothes: "Edwards' Serena travels from New York to California in tweeds and alligator pumps."

Her readers had always enjoyed the descriptions of stylish clothes and the women who wore them. Her characters always dressed for dinner. She wrote about people who observed formality—even in the midst of murder. In fact, they coped with life's adversities by observing traditions and rituals.

Devastated by the criticism, she couldn't write, but then the compulsion—half her brain had to be engaged in a story—drew her back to the typewriter. She pounded out her frustrations. She wanted to pound on Alan.

> January 15, 1944
> Dear Mignon,
> I am sending an update of your book sales to cheer you:
>
> | | |
> |---|---|
> | *Speak No Evil* | 10,981 |
> | *With This Ring* | 11,845 |
> | *Wolf in Man's Clothing* | 14,789 |
> | *The Man Next Door* | 12,737 |
> | *Unidentified Woman* | 14,542 |
>
> Note the sales of *Wolf in Man's Clothing.* I know you are tired of her, but Sarah Keate is obviously a popular sleuth, a lucrative sleuth, and you might consider writing another mystery for her.
> Warm Regards,
> Harry

She telephoned Alan.

"It's final," she said. "The divorce is final."

"Are you going to Woodsedge?"

"I don't think I can bear it right now. I'm going to New York."

"How about we meet for Christmas dinner. I have Leave."

She had no idea what etiquette was for divorced couples, but she knew she wanted to see him. "I'll see you there."

She left Fayetteville and flew back to New York and the Hotel Chatham.

1944

Hotel Chatham - New York

Mignon and Alan had often lived apart. His job. Her travels. But he was in her life. Had always encouraged her, bolstered her up. She missed him. No matter how she struggled with a story, he was confident she could fix it. Reading aloud to him when they were together often made things clear, but most of all, he believed in her writing and told her so. His praise was her stimulant.

This was different. Divorced. Living apart in a final way. She had to learn to live alone. Lots of women lived alone. Lots of women were single. Carlene had never been married. Carlene had never depended on a man for company or affirmation. *What is the matter with me?* she thought.

Evenings were hellish. She tried to change her habits and work from three or four o'clock in the afternoon until nine in the evening instead of mornings, but that didn't suit her creative energy. She had to figure it out.

Alan had given her Woodsedge—her anchor and her refuge—in the divorce settlement. She had always retreated to Woodsedge after her forays to find the perfect settings for her novels, but now she had to sell novels for Woodsedge's upkeep. She decided to live at the Chatham while she sorted that out.

The few people who knew her well were aware of her loneliness and constantly finding her companions for the theatre and the symphony. Dating at this age seemed ridiculous and strange, but she did go to the theatre with a casual friend, and then he kept calling and calling. She finally told him she wasn't interested in any kind of permanent relationship. He had, no doubt, found her quite a cold fish anyway.

Harry and Edna accompanied her to D.C. to attend a book fair and to promote *Escape the Night* which had been published when she was in Arkansas. She was still smarting from a reader's comment that the book "suffered" from "Mignon Edwards' standard formula of two beautiful young women competing for a man."

"You have twenty-four novels," Harry said. "Forget it. Your reputation is solid. Publishers put those comments into perspective."

She had never been able to ignore negative reviews. No matter how many novels she'd published. She cared about readers and about reviews. Were her stories a simple formula of two rich, beautiful women competing for a man? Was the protagonist now only a pale imitation of the strident, competent Nurse Sarah Keate she started with?

She also cared about selling her novels. If the novels didn't sell, she couldn't live the way she did. And the novels were selling.

She was trying to work on *Wings of Fear* set in Mexico. When she was there—in that lush place of greens and reds and perfumed moist air, in that perfect setting—the story wouldn't come together. She was too absorbed in her problems with Alan. She did a writer's easy work in Mexico, making copious notes with excessive descriptions of the place. Now she struggled with the characters and with the plot. In this murderous mood, she didn't feel like working out a plot. Writing was very hard work. Life a muddle.

She was even ambivalent about where she wanted to be. So distressed she even asked Myrna, her maid, if she'd like to spend a couple of weeks at Woodsedge. Myrna was not interested in leaving the city. And being alone there didn't appeal to Mignon.

She wrote and revised *Wings of Fear* several times with advice from Harry. Finally finished it and sent it off to him.

Carmen, as usual, forced her out of herself:

> June 30, 1944
> Dear Mignon,
> I'm sorry about the divorce. I've always liked Alan. I know you've had difficult times, but I've always hoped your differences weren't so great you couldn't work it out. After all these years of marriage, I can't help but be sad about it.
> I assumed you'd go back to Woodsedge, but I know you enjoy living at the Chatham with all its amenities. I especially remember the mirrors lining your dressing room!
> I am distraught with the war news. Can hardly think of anything else. Our neighbor's son Tony was killed in Normandy. I happened to look out the

kitchen window one afternoon and saw the Western Union messenger boy in his cap and gray uniform get off his bike, and walk up to the door. I just knew it was that "The Secretary of the Army regrets to inform you" dreaded telegram. Sue was home alone so I went over right away. Her son Tony was with the Third Army in what they are calling "the first wave" of our troops that landed on Omaha Beach. He was only twenty-one years old, just beginning his junior year at U of Nebraska when he decided to enlist. The troops in that first wave were pinned down by the Germans in bunkers on the hills overlooking the beach. According to the newspapers, it was a slaughter. Tragic for his parents to hear. They had begged him not to enlist, to wait and see if he'd be drafted, but he wouldn't listen, of course.

I'm glad I don't have sons! June is enjoying high school. A self-centered teenager and mostly unmindful of the world events. As it should be, I think. There is time enough for worry. This war seems hopeless despite the liberation of France.

It is frivolous to get dressed up and drink tea at the Junior League luncheons, but I am losing my enthusiasm for knitting and war-related volunteer activities that just seem designed to keep us busy.

If the invitation is open, I may bring June to New York for a high school graduation treat. A week of theatre and music would fill my soul.

Thanks for the advanced copy of *Wings of Fear*. I always enjoy your settings—you take me to places I'll probably never see. Mexico is fascinating. When the war is over . . .

Your female Nazi spy is an important addition to the story. I do want to escape ordinary life when

I'm "living" in a novel, but Harry gave you good advice. Ignoring the war is too unrealistic for your readers right now.

Looking forward to seeing you soon.

Love, Carmen

In July, Alan came to New York. Mignon had been anxious to see him. He stayed at the St. Regis, but they had dinner together and talked and talked. And she imagined that people talked about them and their strange divorce, but she didn't care about the gossip.

Alan described his work at the naval base and the poker games and the cocktail and dinner parties. The military had their own social world.

"Seeing anyone special?" she asked.

"You know I don't care about other women."

Jealousy made that comforting.

"I enjoy your weekly telephoning," he said.

He hugged her. They said another good-bye, and she went back to the Chatham.

Homeless and without Alan, she was at loose ends when Faith came to New York to see her publisher and proposed a solution.

"Gonnie and I are going to Miami for a couple weeks. Join us."

Frigid January, rather than summer, would have been a better time to escape New York City, but Mignon had never been to Miami Beach, and this was another opportunity to travel with Faith and Gonnie.

1944

Miami

The sweet, moist tropical air embraced them as they emerged from the plane to step gingerly down the metal stairs to the runway. No matter how often Mignon flew, the change from one environment to another always gifted her with surprise. She never got over the amazement of the transitions that could be made within hours. Just that morning she had been in the skyscraper world of New York City. From bustling, busy streets with people pushing and rushing to a playground where languor lingered in the air. Her breathing even slowed down. She couldn't help smiling. This Miami holiday would be good for her.

They stayed at the Macfadden-Deauville hotel right on the beach. A couple of years before, Harry had reluctantly introduced Mignon to Bernarr Macfadden of Macfadden publishing. Harry wasn't interested in her getting too well acquainted, nor allowing Bernarr to seduce her into writing for one of his publications. He published about a dozen romance magazines—*True Story, Photoplay, True Confessions, True Romance, True Love Stories*, etc. It was enticing to think about writing for him, because his magazine empire thrived, and she could always use money. But she was a literary snob— admittedly not an Edith Wharton writer—but her novels were deeper than what she had read in *True Romance*. Anyway, she didn't have the sexual experience or the imagination for *True Romance* or *True Confessions*, and she was too much a prude to write more than the hints of romance and sex she put in her mystery novels.

The connection with Bernarr was very nice though. Mignon and Gonnie and Faith benefited from the casual acquaintance. Bernarr liked to impress his Connecticut and New York City friends. He gave them a cabana on the beach with a private shower and a cabana boy to serve their afternoon bourbon. It was more than a simple, pleasant retreat from Mignon's cold life at the Chatham.

The Macfadden had three luxurious dining rooms where they foundered themselves on smoked mullet with their cocktails and with grouper and dolphin and sea bass for dinner, none of which they could dine on in New York.

The Macfadden also had the only Olympic-sized swimming pool in any hotel in Florida—maybe in the United States. Guests, all three hundred of them it seemed, lounged in beach chairs in multiple rows surrounding the pool. Waiters weaved in and out, trays of drinks and food held high, people came and went, calling to each other—commotion and joyous noise.

Mignon passed through the din every morning on her way to the quiet and privacy of the cabana right on the ocean's shore. A walkway along the ocean stretched from one end of East Shore to the other, sometimes next to the ocean, sometimes in a path shaded by plain trees and palms. She walked and walked, listening to the symphony of the waves, thinking *story*. Place. Setting. A beautiful, lithe young woman, probably in her early twenties, in a frothy white dress that skimmed the ground, passed by her every day. *The Woman in White.* The protagonist.

Bernarr invited Mignon, Faith, and Gonnie to his exclusive home for dinner on Shadow Island, a short car ride on the causeway that connected Miami to Miami Beach. Islands like emeralds dotted the bay, and a bridge from the causeway was the only approach to Shadow Island by land. For access by sea, the Macfadden had a fleet of boats—sail boats, fishing boats, utilitarian motorboats.

A winding avenue thick with scarlet bougainvillea and poinciana lined the driveway. It was dusk when they arrived, so the shadows created a mysterious atmosphere. A beautiful white house—long, Spanish with lacy grilled iron along the balconies, and lights glowing from inside—appeared, like a setting for a movie, amidst the lush green of palms and bamboos.

The blue waters of the bay were on the south below the house; on the north, an inviting swimming pool, tiled in blue. A house on a secluded island, another setting for a murder.

Bernarr and his Miami dinner guests regaled the New York women with tales of the hurricanes that plagued Florida usually in late summer and fall.

"We're always alert to radio forecasts and the progress of the winds," they said. "All the windows on the house have shutters. We nail them shut . . .

Sometimes all of Miami loses electricity . . . The islands in the bay are often the first to lose power."

More and more information for a murder!

"You're safe in June," they said, "although last year we had an early season. A June hurricane. Thousands of people along the coast had to be evacuated."

Whatever their desire to shock and frighten, or simply impress the naïve easterners, Mignon was gathering ideas for a story. It took discipline not to reach for the pen and notebook in her handbag. She wrote the notes as soon as they got back to the hotel.

Faith and Gonnie knew and respected her morning work routine. She ordered room service for breakfast and worked diligently for the first time in weeks. The heat and the humidity and the ocean, especially the ocean, were seductive in a way crisp New York City was not. She immersed herself in the novel. Put Alan in another part of her mind and wrote.

Shadow Island in the midst of a hurricane. The terrible quiet and then the hurling wind, the slanting brutal rain. The intense dark with shutters nailed shut but clattering and clashing. The woman in white and her lover danced. He danced well. Light on his feet. The music, the rhythm, his arm around her made a tight, invulnerable world.

1944-45

Manhattan

Christmas in Manhattan. Mignon thought about taking the train to Lincoln to spend the holidays with her mother and Helen and her family. But she didn't have the emotional energy to cope with her mother's admonitions, and she didn't particularly want them to see her distress about the divorce. She didn't understand her ambivalence herself.

Christmas Eve, Bennett and Phyllis invited her to their annual dinner, an elegant affair, the guests all "names" in New York City publishing and writing worlds. It was at least an excuse to get out of the apartment and a reason to get dressed up.

Carmen would have been amused to see Mignon finger through the rack of gowns in her closet to find something elegant to go with her new Ferragamo shoes. Carmen chided her often about the walk-in closet and the mirrored doors in the dressing room of the Manhattan apartment. "You're a vain clotheshorse," she would say with affection and only a hint of criticism.

Alan, on the other hand, had often sat in the satin boudoir chair, his legs crossed, cigarette in hand, and watched her choose the dress and then slip it over her head. "Let me," he would say when she was dressed, and then fasten the clasp of her wedding pearls, the perfect accessory for any occasion.

The Cerf's butler met her at the vestibule door of the penthouse. "Merry Christmas, Mrs. Edwards," he said, taking her scarf and mink coat and nodding his head toward the living room. "Go right in."

Phyllis had pushed furniture to the sides of the spacious room so people could mingle and enjoy the view of Central Park's holiday lights from the floor to ceiling windows. Guests were gathered around banquet tables at each end of the room, enticed by sardine pasties, cheese puffs, crab meat, and lobster in crystal bowls of ice, deviled eggs, and cheese balls with crackers.

Mignon recognized Truman Capote moving from one group to another, shaking hands, the darling of the evening. Truman's first short story had just been published by *Mademoiselle*, and prescient Bennett already had him under contract.

"Truman, I'd like you to meet Random House's queen of mystery," Bennett said as he introduced Mignon.

"I am honored," the charmingly confident, very young man said. He took her hand and then bowed as if she were an ancient monarch. He was short, slight, had lovely dark eyes, was just shy of pretty. Unlike the other men in tuxedos, his all-black pants, shirt, and jacket with white tie set him apart as she was sure it was meant to do.

The guests milled around with their cocktails greeting old friends, catching up on the latest news of the writing world, but when they sat down for dinner, the talk turned to the seriousness of the war.

"Tell us about your new poetry book, Muriel," someone said to Muriel Rukeyser.

"Yes, Muriel. We got her *Beast in View* out just in time for Christmas. Rukeyser's gift to her Christian friends." Bennett attempted to lighten the mood.

"It's not a light read." Muriel frowned. "You know me and my causes." She paused. "Books are symbols, you know. Symbols of liberty and freedom. I'm urging my readers to share in the fight by buying war bonds." She looked around the table, piquing every conscience including Mignon's though Mignon decided not to voice her thoughts—*I don't want to proselytize in my books. I just want to tell a story. I don't want to feel obligated to send a message.*

Even Harry, who usually tried to keep conversation light and stimulating on social occasions, was gripped by the war.

"Writers have never been more important. The Writers War Board has produced eight thousand stories, radio scripts, poems, dramatic skits, and slogans. Eight thousand. Just think of it . . . It's the greatest propaganda machine in history." He shook his head.

"Incredible," he said. "The Council on Books and various publishers have sent over a hundred and twenty-three million to the American troops. That includes the titles burned or banned by the Nazis."

"Think about it. Our soldiers all over the world are hunkered down in tents and bunkers reading. Sailors on ships are taking a break and refuge in their bunks reading. Reading our books," someone added.

Clink of forks on plates filled the silence. No one spoke.

Bennett tried to change the subject. "The war's had an interesting and vibrant impact on the publishing world. Salman Schocken . . . he's a refugee . . . has founded Schocken Books. He plans to publish Jewish titles. Hannah Arendt is on board as an editor. And Pantheon Publishing is thriving. Helen and Kurt Wolff . . . they're refugees too." Bennett was always aware of the competition in the publishing world.

Later, Harry cautioned Mignon. "You don't have to wave your patriotism or proselytize, but you can't ignore the war. It's too important and significant in the lives of your readers, Mignon. People are much more aware of the countries in Europe than they were in the past," he said. "Their world is bigger than it was. The Blitz got their attention. Now your readers know where Normandy is, and they're knowledgeable about the German occupation, especially of France. They know about the Vichy government and the French resistance. You have to recognize that in your work."

It hadn't been a productive year. She did have an idea for a novel that would meet Harry's criteria, his expectations about recognizing the war, but her immediate and practical problem was adjusting to a new secretary/typist. When in New York, she'd always had her longtime assistant and friend, Marilyn, who knew just how to create order out of messy drafts. Marilyn was used to Mignon's idiosyncrasies. Knew just when to hand over the typed manuscript, so Mignon could get her scissors out and do the cut and paste for the next version. Training someone new took so much time and so much patience—more patience than Mignon had even when she wasn't distraught and unhappy.

She wanted to get back to a novel about Axis Sally. The novel she'd abandoned in Mexico. Use the information she'd read about the American woman broadcasting propaganda for the Germans. An Axis Sally character along with Nazi sympathizers and expats on a ship escaping Europe. She pounded away on the typewriter, trying to put all that together. *Five Passengers from Lisbon.*

A strong, substantial Colonel named Josh Morgan. Practical and inventive. Reserved with matter-of-fact good sense, not the flamboyant type women are often attracted to . . . Alan.

She worked on the story all winter and was at the typewriter the April day Faith telephoned and told her to turn on the radio. President Roosevelt had died while on vacation in Hot Springs, Georgia.

Alan must be devastated. Mignon listened to the radio obsessively into the evening, wishing Alan was sitting in his chair next to the Philco.

She'd been distressed and disappointed when FDR was first elected, but in this terrible war, he had become a symbol of stability even for her mother and some of their friends who were staunch Republicans. Roosevelt's radio chats with his common vocabulary and trite analogies that annoyed her at first had become comforting. His voice calmed people, and he appealed to everyone, in every walk of life.

On CBS Studs Terkel's voice broke and broke again as he tried to describe the scene. "I'm sorry. I can't stop crying," he said. "Everybody is crying."

A reason and an excuse to cry. When world life is breaking down and your personal life is breaking down, crying was relief.

She turned to NBC, hovered over the Philco, too riveted to switch it off. Alone. Thinking about Alan. Wishing he could be with her to share this. Their evening news habit. He had always indulged her in listening to Earl Godwin, the conservative in the press corps.

"President Franklin Roosevelt died on the eve of what he had hoped would be the inauguration of an era of peace in a world free from want and fear," Godwin said. His voice broke and a colleague took over for him.

Mignon telephoned Alan for comfort and his reasonable view of events no matter how unsettling.

"Have you been listening?"

"Tragic," he said. "I know you don't like him, but it's not a great time. The war. Change in the midst of war."

"I know. I needed to hear your voice. I miss you. It's lonely here."

"You can change that, Mimi. I miss you too. Say the word. It's up to you."

1945

Military Wife

They reconciled without telling anyone. Flew to Reno and took their place in line at the Courthouse the next day. Repeated the familiar vows. When the Justice of the Peace pronounced them Man and Wife, Alan's broad smile made his eyes crinkle. He put his arms around her in a fierce hug and bent for a deep kiss.

They hired a car for the drive from Reno to the Cal Neva Lodge, advertised as having gourmet food and entertainment in a rustic log lodge environment. The kind of place Alan liked. Mignon preferred hotels like the Ritz Carlton, but always delighted in adventures.

They checked in at the Lodge and followed the porter to their suite. He opened the door, deposited the luggage, Alan handed him the tip, and he left. They were alone. Married. Again. Another wedding night.

Mignon watched Alan put his suitcoat on a hanger, smoothing the lapels into place. Watched him put the worn brown leather valise he'd carried for years on the bed and unpack. Put ties and underwear in drawers, arranging them in neat little stacks. Hang his trousers and shirts in the closet, making sure the shirts faced the same direction on the hangers.

He was the same man she'd been married to before. Had she expected him to change? Was she living in some romance novel again? Had she dreamed up a different Alan? Faith had reminded her years ago that writers have no control of the characters in their own lives. She couldn't decide if she was comforted or disconcerted.

Mignon had no such compulsion for immediate unpacking and organization. She picked her cigarette case off the dresser, poured a tumbler of bourbon from the silver flask they traveled with and went out on the balcony to watch the sunset—a heart-lilting view of the sun going down over the clear blue water of Lake Tahoe with the mountains in the distance. No twilight here, just sinking and gone, a flash of pleasure. But then the sobering thought. *What am I doing? What have I done?*

She went back into the room. Alan was sitting, his back against the pillows, enjoying his last cigarette of the day. She smiled at the familiar blue silk pajamas. She unzipped her dress, stepped out of it, and put on a chiffon floor-length nightgown, the kind she'd always worn.

She lifted the covers and climbed in next to him. He put his cigarette out in the ash tray beside the bed and turned to her. She had been so lonesome. She tucked herself next to him, feeling the warmth of his body, and then the physical desire. He put his arm around her. Kissed her forehead. Kissed her nose. A gentle lip kiss. He moved her into the spoon hold where they'd spent the nights all the years of their marriage. What had made her think anything would be different?

She had missed him so much she had let herself forget the reason she'd divorced him. She needed to be content with who he was. A like soul. This was a partnership with a like soul. He didn't care about other women. He didn't prefer men. He didn't want or need sex. And he loved her.

Only the Place for this marriage would be different. In her loneliness, she'd agreed to live with Alan on the naval munitions base in his apartment at Hawthorne while they waited for a house to become available. She had also decided to keep Woodsedge after having it on the market all spring. Woodsedge was the place she always called home.

Life on the Hawthorne Base was not what Mignon had envisioned. Alan had told her that the other officers' wives would call on her. All part of the Base protocol. She didn't expect it to happen two days after they arrived. The tiny apartment in his officer's quarters was military clean, but Alan had had no need for a cook. And she had only his word for what was expected. "Tea and maybe some kind of little sandwiches," he told her. The English version of high tea? Or her mother's Junior League type "Tea." She settled on the latter.

They had arrived on the base on Friday. At 2:30 Sunday afternoon, Major Shaw's wife rang the doorbell and introduced herself and the friend standing next to her, Lieutenant Renner's wife. Alan excused himself. This was a Wives' thing.

Within an hour Lieutenant Wolff's wife arrived. Then Captain Bender's wife with Lieutenant Albright's wife. And Major Meyer's wife. They came steadily, all afternoon—gloved and hatted, calling cards in hand. Mignon greeted and gushed, moving from the door to the tea table she'd set up in the living room. Dazed. She tried to keep track of the ranks and the names attached. Her feet ached and she didn't know how long she could keep smiling.

A tall woman, her white hair pulled back in a sleek chignon beneath her navy-blue cloche, put her gloved hand on Mignon's arm as she prepared to leave. "You're new to this, my dear," she said with a warm smile. "The protocol is that you return these calls within the week. And some wives even serve cocktails."

She had half a dozen calls to make within the week. All part of the expectation for a military wife.

The women were very pleasant, but not very interesting, and there was simply nothing to do on the base but play bridge—which she would not—and drink, which she did. Those formal calls began with coffee and proceeded to cocktails. The women relaxed, and Mignon enjoyed the cocktail hours but found out she couldn't consume nearly as much liquor as some of those women who had obviously been on the base a long time.

In her writing life, she lived on a Red Cross ship, revising *Five Passengers from Lisbon*.

Marcia, the beautiful, young American protagonist, discovered that the man she had sacrificed the war years for, hiding in Europe, was a fraud, but she found steadiness and comforting affection from an officer onboard the ship.

The ship was Mignon's personal escape. As always, she was happiest when part of her brain was engaged in writing. The hospital ship was a completely different environment than any she'd known, although before the war, she and Alan had made that passage from the United States to Europe and back in a luxurious passenger vessel.

The endless cocktail gatherings weren't without benefit. At one of those obligatory events, Alan introduced her to Captain Hagel who had served on a Red Cross hospital ship that transported wounded men home from Europe and Africa.

Captain Hagel was generous with information, happy to condescend and humor this little woman with all his knowledge.

"I was on *The USS Comfort*," he said.

"Tell me about that." The coy, old ploy to encourage conversation and confidences.

"Yes. Dozens of passenger and cargo ships have been converted to hospital ships, you know. *The Refuge. The USS Mercy. The Comfort. The USS Hope.* Those are just a few."

"How are they distinguished from the troop ships? What protects them?" Mignon asked.

"They're painted with a large Red Cross and broad green stripes on the hull. That identifies them. Both on the ocean and on shore. They're protected by the Geneva Convention."

"How many people are on board?"

"*The USS Comfort* has four hundred beds, about forty-eight officers, and thirty-five nurses." Hagel smiled, pleased with his superior knowledge.

And she had all the details she needed for her story.

"Sounds like you are concocting an interesting tale," one of Alan's other officer friends commented, like patting a puppy.

"Probably not something you'd want to read," Alan said. "Her readers are lonely housewives in the hinterland."

Mignon was taken aback. He had always said her stories were interesting. Supported her writing. She turned and left.

"I was kidding," he said when she confronted him about it later. He wasn't a kidder. It nagged at her.

The base was really the damnedest place. The Post Office refused to take her manuscript although she wrapped it exactly the way she had always wrapped and addressed manuscript packages to Harry. She couldn't even send a wire, and it was one-hundred-thirty miles across the desert to Reno where she could. The laundry facilities were inconveniently located in a wash house, and there was very little domestic help available, although she finally found Clementine through an advertisement in the Base newspaper.

"I clean, Missus. I do laundry. And I like to iron clothes," Clementine said when she arrived the first Monday morning. "I do not shop. You will have to make arrangements for grocery shopping."

The food market didn't deliver. Mignon had to do the grocery shopping, and she dared not be picky about Clementine's demands because every officer's wife was looking for domestic help. It was a small and intensely circumscribed world where everybody knew everybody's business. It was a small town worse than small town Valentine, unlike anywhere she had ever lived, the military culture unlike any culture she'd ever known.

She was expected to pay homage to wives appropriate to their husbands' rank even to the point of seating arrangements at dinner parties. She spent hours arranging appropriate places at the dinner table and figuring out who must be invited with whom for afternoon tea when what she wanted to do was spend her time writing.

The only thing she appreciated about the place was the setting. The mountains changed colors with the sunlight. They were different at daybreak than in the middle of the day, and then changed again at sunset, magic shades of pink and red and gold and purple. And Lake Tahoe was as blue as the Mediterranean.

She didn't enjoy anything about the obligations of an officer's wife. Wife was not the be-all and the end-all of her existence as it seemed for the other women on the base. She had never appreciated the simple Wife role. She thought about that first publication in Valentine for the *Engineering News Record* when she wrote about the engineer's wife. A full circle.

She couldn't arrange uninterrupted, unobligated time to get her work done, and Alan wasn't sympathetic with her dilemma. He had also become disinterested in her writing.

"I don't have time to listen to you read," he said one evening as he took his top coat out of the entryway closet to go to his weekly bridge game.

"You haven't changed your lifestyle with my being here. But *my* life is completely disrupted."

"You wanted to come. You're the one who wanted to try again and try again *here*. This is where I have to be right now. This is where I want to be." He put his captain cap on. "You're self-centered," he said. "You've created a persona and now you believe in her. You need constant attention, Mignon."

"Thanks," she said.

She tried that life for three months. Hated the place more every day. Living on the base and serving as Mrs. Alan Edwards to Captain Edwards required too much time away from her writing. And too much emotional energy. Writing was demanding. She couldn't write and run around to parties and entertain constantly. She needed more alone time than that, and she needed sustained hours to work.

All she could think of was their house in Connecticut with the lovely old maples arching over the driveway. She decided to go home to Woodsedge.

There she went back to her morning writing routine and was as content as she could be living without Alan. What she missed was their life together in Woodsedge, but that life was obviously over. Alan moved along in his own world, with or without her.

What was she doing? Alan had changed. Why couldn't she just let him go without the angst? Why couldn't she live contentedly without him? She was like one of those helpless, hapless women in her novels standing on the iconic balcony looking down onto the courtyard at her life.

She telephoned him. "I need to see you. We need to talk in person."

"I have a Leave from the base in November," he said.

"I'll meet you in New York City. This is an insane way to live. We need to talk about an official separation."

1946-47

Mrs. Duncan Perry

Bernarr Macfadden was determined for Mignon to have a social life in Connecticut. He invited her to dinner along with Gonnie and Faith to meet his friend, Duncan Perry. Duncan lived on an estate not far from Woodsedge. His wife had died the year before.

"I'm honored to meet you," Duncan said when Bernarr introduced her. "I've never known a writer."

He brushed a dark lock from his forehead, leaned close, and grasped her small hand in both of his. She had to look up to meet his broad smile. A disarming smile that inspired trust. Made him instantly likeable. And, she realized later, he wore it like a costume.

Mignon was flattered and charmed. She was also lonely. A fateful moment. She abandoned reserve and common sense. Succumbed to his flattery with impetuous affection. Like a teenager with a crush, so enamored she fantasized about him in the novel she was working on:

She stepped back and was in Andre's arms. Close and hard and warm. He held her for a moment and then moved her face with his own so his mouth came down upon hers and held her like that.

Andre kissed her and held her and kissed her again.

She tried to move away . . . "Andre . . ."

"Don't pull away like that . . ."

"But I . . ."

"Be quiet." He kissed her again, long and hard.

She pulled away from him then, and he laughed a little, his handsome face . . .

"I'm not in love with you . . ." She tried to escape his arm, shaken and breathless.

"You don't know a thing about it."

He kissed her again. "You've been in love with me since the moment we met."

"I've been in love with you. We've been pretending it isn't so."

"It's silly. Life is short. You have to take love if it happens. Don't try to run away from it."

Duncan's persistent attention thrilled her. Flattered her. Filled her lonely life. He escorted her to an endless round of dinner and cocktail parties where his friends, though not effusive, greeted her politely, and with undisguised curiosity.

At the first of such parties, martini glass in hand, Mignon moved with Duncan's gentle nudge from one group of his Wallstreet friends to another. She gathered from the conversation that they put on their three-piece suits and crisp, white shirts with monogrammed, gold cufflinks every day and took the train to Manhattan where they managed other people's money. Their wives did charity work, lunched at The Club, played tennis, and managed the servants.

Mignon was the first woman Duncan had brought to their esteemed gatherings and tight social circle since his wife Ann died. They sized her up, suspecting a successor to the perfect Ann, who hadn't been absent from their circle very long, and whose virtues they extolled without restraint. One woman said, "You would have loved Ann."

Really? That must be the difference between losing a spouse to death and losing one to divorce. It wouldn't have occurred to her to mention Alan. Nor would her friends have mentioned him to Duncan.

None of these women had read her novels—if they read.

"Duncan tells us you are a writer," his business partner's wife said. "What do you write?

"Murder mysteries! Oh! Not really my cup of tea, but it sounds like a fascinating thing to do. A lovely way to spend your time."

"Where would I find your books?" This by another woman, standing in the cozy circle, her slender fingers with pretty pink polish clutching a champagne glass. And in an obvious effort to make amends for her friend's faux pas, she added, "And where did you get that lovely frock? Dior? Your shoes? Ferragamo's?" She blubbered on, "I love the high heel. Do you shop in the City?"

The attire passed muster. It was Mignon's strange occupation, and the fact that she admitted to having an occupation, that stunted their small talk. They obviously didn't know how to relate to a woman who had a significant life of her own.

Mignon saw very little of Faith and Gonnie those days. Faith did invite Duncan and her to a garden party in the late summer, but Faith had no patience with most of Duncan's milieu and didn't hide her disdain, especially for the women.

"How can you stand them?" she asked. "They're unreal."

Faith's fiction often focused on the dilemmas and conflicts women had in balancing work and home. The women in this new social sphere of Mignon's were oblivious to that life and ignorant of its challenges.

A month after they met, Duncan proposed marriage. "I need to make you my wife," he said, after a leisurely dinner and a lingering "good night" at her door. He put his muscular arms around her, leaned down, and brought his lips to hers in a bruising kiss. Not gentle. But she had no misgivings. She decided to fly to Reno to divorce Alan.

Louella Parsons and her ilk had a field day: "Mystery writer, Mignon Edwards, divorces again." "Mignon Edwards takes advantage of Nevada's six-week divorce residency." "America's first lady of mystery and romance is living in a motel in the Divorce Capital." "A whirlwind romance."

It was a whirlwind. It was exciting. She was in love. Anxious for the dream to come true. Living in a romance novel.

Like one of her broad-shouldered handsome heroes, Duncan took charge. He planned for her to arrive in Chicago from Reno on October 24. They would have a small wedding on October 26, just a dozen or so of their close friends and Duncan's two grown sons. She hoped Carmen could come from Nebraska although it was a long trip. Her mother and Helen both declined the invitation.

Duncan made all the arrangements. Reservations for dinner at the Arts Club and then dancing at the Drake. A Presbyterian minister he knew from Evanston to officiate. The Episcopal priest he originally contacted wouldn't perform the ceremony because of the brief interval between Mignon's divorce and the marriage. Her Methodist self had a fleeting qualm of conscience about that.

They planned to leave for Connecticut the day after the wedding and move into his house. After Duncan took her there the first time, she had oozed her impressions to Faith. Couldn't wait to tell her all about it.

"Mystic Brook Farm. Isn't that a charming name? But it's a gloomy house with sundry spots and stains on the Aubusson rugs. It smells of cats. You know how I hate cats. And there are no books. Can you imagine? The former Mrs. P. apparently didn't read. And no hint of what hobbies or interests she had besides her cats."

Faith just looked at her and shook her head. "The drapes and upholstery are worn and the walls ugly colors? The furniture is lumpy and uncomfortable. The art ugly. Why would you move in there?" The judgmental tone took Mignon by surprise. "You have exactly what you like at Woodsedge. You love Woodsedge. Why doesn't Duncan move in with you?"

"He wants us to live in his house."

"What is your hurry? Why immediately after the wedding?"

"He wants us to make it my place, *our* place."

"Sounds selfish. Domineering." Faith looked at Mignon. Shrugged and shook her head. Mignon read the disdain. And they changed the subject.

Faith's skepticism was prophetic. Mystic Brook Farm. Not the magic place Mignon naively envisioned, more like black magic. Not the romance she envisioned either.

Her illusions were all short-lived. She should write a novel about wedding nights.

"What's wrong with you?" Duncan said that first night. She had longed for this physical connection for too many years. She had imagined it in a romantic way. There was nothing romantic or gentle about it. He didn't take her gently in his arms, look into her eyes, and kiss her forehead and her nose softly as she had described too often in her novels.

She came out of the bathroom in the thin-strapped, flowing, white negligee she'd bought with such anticipation of this night. He grabbed her arms. She stepped back from him—shocked. He pushed her onto the bed and fell heavily on her, jerking on her negligee to pull it up out of his way. It happened fast. She gasped. And then pain. He grunted, breathing heavily as he pounded into her. She cried out. It was a physical act, simply physical. Nothing like what she had imagined.

"What is wrong with you? You were married for twenty years? What is wrong with Alan?" He sniggered.

It was the champagne and the cognac. Too much cognac. It would be different tomorrow night. It would be different next time. He was just anxious and impatient because of the waiting, her insistence on marriage first.

Her inexperience and the obvious physical pain of those first nights disgusted him. Humiliated her. Erased respect or admiration on both their parts.

The courtly, sophisticated companion. The man who liked telling people his wife was a prominent writer disappeared in the bedroom. And the bedroom man was her daily companion. Domineering. Authoritative. In charge of everything and everyone in his house.

It was a strange autumn. She watched the leaves on the ancient oaks in the yard turn yellow and golden, maples adding splashes of red to her favorite season, but it didn't give her the usual joy. She kept busy with the moving process. Tried to cope with the difficult domestic help. Duncan had insisted on retaining all his servants. He expected her to achieve perfection though plunked down in a strange house. He didn't understand the time or the sheer labor of moving things from Woodsedge. They were both short-tempered and tired. Or that's how she rationalized the rancor.

For twenty years, Harry had guided her through the financial complexities of publishing. Since *The Patient in Room 18*. She'd always left the details in his hands. Duncan asked about royalties and advances. It didn't seem unreasonable at first. She wrote to Harry for the current details.

October 29, 1946

My Dear Mignon,

Congratulations! Edna and I were surprised to receive the announcement of your marriage. We haven't kept up with you as we should. While I wait impatiently for you to send me your next book, I forget you have a personal life. We are, of course, full of curiosity and anxious to meet this man who has apparently swept you right off your feet. We would like the two of you to join us for dinner when you come to New York City next month.

You asked about your royalties. We should discuss this in person. The statement I'm sending is approximate although it is your largest royalty payment ever. You asked about advances. Random House is cautious about paying out advances, but Bennett is happy to do so for you. You have $14,000 upon which to draw. I advise you though to wait to draw on your account until the new year. The Republicans might give additional tax reductions!

I look forward to seeing you in New York.

Warm regards,

Harry

She felt frantic to get the house livable. But the servants, especially housekeeper Hilma, didn't like or trust her. They resented any instructions she gave, still loyal to the first wife. Ann, the perfect wife, according to Duncan. Ann had impeccable taste. Ann had created beautiful gardens. Just look at them. Ann had golden hair and a sweet voice. Mignon's harsh tones annoyed him. Ann was small and frail, but efficient. Mignon was small, dark-haired, and inept at managing his house.

"Nothing like Ann," he said. The contempt rang in her ears.

He expected the house and home he'd had. To resume the life he'd had with Ann. Not a role she could play. And she needed routine and comfortable calm to write. She needed to write. She was becoming desperate. Writers get desperate when days go by without writing.

And then the holidays. "We need to do some entertaining," Duncan said. "Christmas. New Year's. We've always had a dinner for my partners and their wives and a cocktail party for the neighbors. Hilma knows the routine."

"I'm not ready," Mignon said. "My things aren't organized." What she needed to do was get rid of Ann's things. "I want to wait until we are more organized to entertain."

"The house is fine," he said. "You are too house-proud."

"I like an attractive, comfortable home, and this isn't. And yes, I've always been house-proud."

"Your idea of attractive and comfortable is to paint and redo. None of it necessary."

She did work at making it her home, but it was still Ann's house. The servants were still Ann's.

When Mignon walked into a room, they often quit talking. Were they talking about her? Whether they were or not, she slinked away guiltily.

On her way upstairs one afternoon, she met Hilma in her starched gray uniform with the white collar and cuffs coming out of her bedroom. "Did you need something? Were you looking for me?" Mignon asked.

"No, ma'am." She stopped. Looked down at Mignon. The authority of height. Looked directly into Mignon's eyes with piercing defiance. Then sauntered down the hallway.

Hilma had no reason to be in Mignon's room but to look through her personal things. One of the day girls did the laundry, pressed Mignon's clothes, and put them away in bureau drawers and closets.

She checked her desk. Wondered if Hilma had rummaged through the papers. Read the pages of the novel laying there? Opened the drawers? Learned anything important about her?

Hilma had been with Duncan and Ann since their boys were children and in complete charge since Ann died. Mignon obviously posed a threat. She should put Hilma in a novel. Hilma, a spy for a suspicious husband.

Duncan was used to having his way about the house. Alan had left even house-buying up to her, and she had always made decisions about furniture and decorating. Duncan had apparently had the final say at Mystic Brook Farm. She would have to suggest changes thoughtfully. Plan. Plot like a novel, not just go ahead.

She decided to propose her projects on a Friday, always a shorter day of the week in Duncan's office and an earlier commute.

He came in, shed his suit coat, and tossed it on a chair by the door. She was waiting in the living room armed with a sheaf of information. Alan had always been interested in detailed information.

"You're wearing that peach loungie thing with the weird fasteners I like," he said. He smiled. The little wife dressing to please him.

"Yes . . . I am. Pink though. Frog fasteners."

He loosened his tie and sat down in what she'd realized in their first days at Mystic Brook Farm was *his* chair. A great big ugly brown thing where he waited for faithful old Raymond to serve his before-dinner scotch. Over ice. In a crystal tumbler.

When he was settled with his drink, she handed him a folder of paint swatches.

"These are paint samples from a painter I've contracted with before." She sat on the sofa next to him, took a cigarette out of the package, and flicked it with the lighter waiting for his response.

"*You* contracted?" He handed the paint swatches back to her without a glance. "I don't see any need to paint."

"It's dark in here. Gloomy. Lighter colored walls would make a big difference." She leaned forward with the swatches.

"If you think it's too dark, turn more lights on."

Right. She'd have to come back to that later. Would she have the energy to come back to that later?

"What about bookcases? This room would be cozier with bookcases. And I'd like to bring some of my books from Woodsedge," she cajoled. What kind of woman was she becoming?

"Ann always tried to keep the clutter down. Shelves just encourage clutter."

"Books. I'm talking about books." She stubbed her cigarette into the ash tray on the end table between them. "I didn't know you cared so much about the decorating." She stood up, the wad of papers and paint swatches in her hand.

She was afraid to risk the rage of the New York trip. That had been a big mistake. Duncan had charmed Edna and Harry at dinner in their Manhattan town house, making small talk about business and politics, drawing Harry out with questions about the publishing world, complimenting Edna on the decor. But the Random House party the next night proved a disaster.

They walked into music and glasses clinking and the buzz of conversation and bursts of laughter. People, some of whom she hadn't seen for months, came to her cordially and enthusiastically with congratulations. She hugged and cheek-kissed and introduced Duncan.

Bennett had done it up fine. A string quartet played in the background. Waiters meandered through the crowd with trays of champagne and hors d'oeuvres. Duncan smiled, acknowledging introductions, and didn't leave her side.

After the party, they waited in the entryway with a host of other guests for the valet to bring the car.

"Wasn't the food luscious? What wonderful music. What an interesting gathering of people. I love my book people. Bennett knows how to give a party." She gushed.

Duncan stood stone silent. Their driver pulled up in the Lincoln. Duncan opened the door for her, grabbed her shoulder, and pushed her in. She gasped in surprise. What was that about?

He got in the other side of the car, and the tirade began.

"You embarrassed me, Mignon. The way you fawn over the men. It's humiliating."

She was stunned. "Harry and Bennett are colleagues and have been my friends for years. And the young editors in Harry's office are people I work with. These are all people I work with."

He turned to face her. Glowered. "You're a flirt, Mignon," he said. "It's cheap. And you drink too much. And bourbon with water is not a ladylike drink."

She moved as far away from him as she could get. She could feel her heart pounding with anger. Fear? She'd never known a cruel man. "I have been drinking bourbon all my life. And I have always had male friends. Some of my best friends are men. They're part of my writing life."

He didn't respond. They drove to Stamford in silence. After rage, the silent treatment. Duncan's preferred punishment.

"Happy New Year and happy new life," Carmen said when she called.

"Thanks for phoning. Happy New Year to you. How are you and Charles? And June?"

"Never mind about us. I want to hear about you. Are you ecstatically happy? Is he everything you dreamed?"

"I'm just fine." *Constrained by the housekeeper hovering around the corner,* she wanted to say. What was Hilma waiting to catch her in? The eavesdropping unnerved her.

But she couldn't tell Carmen the truth about her life. Maybe a letter.

How could she have made such an incredible mistake? She tried to rationalize. She'd been confused and so lonely. Duncan seemed like the kind of man she was looking for, the kind of marriage she had been missing all those years. Wrong. All of it wrong. He didn't want a partner or an intellectual companion. He wanted a docile complement.

She had dismissed her uneasiness before the wedding when he took over all the plans with such determination. *He's used to being in charge. He's intelligent and assertive. Accomplished and confident,* she had assured herself. His arrogance around her friends had been fleetingly disconcerting at the time. *He's nervous, anxious to impress these people, who are in a different world than he's known.*

Actually, he was a bully and arrogant with an ego beyond belief. She had known egotistical men, but never a cruel egotist. Alan would have been amused to know that after all her yearning for real passion, Duncan frightened her. Cold, cold eyes. Venom in his voice. the public charmer, the private abuser with powerful paws. Long sleeves hid the marks on her arms.

He didn't even like her. Whatever had attracted him in the first place besides the fact that she could introduce him to writers and publishers in New York City? He wanted to be "in the know" and acquainted with the popular writers, like a badge of distinction from his Manhattan friends.

"How is it that you don't know them?" he had asked after reading a story in *Life* magazine about Gore Vidal and Truman Capote. "*Life* calls them the 'Young Lions' in the literary world. It's your world, and you *don't know* them?"

"I have no entré to their parties when they return from Paris and grace New York City with their presence," she tried to tell him. "I've met Truman once. They are younger than the writers I know. They're out of my sphere. They don't write mysteries or romances."

Even finances became contentious. Alan and Mignon had one banking account initially, but after their first divorce, she had her own banking account, and she had lived largely on the royalties from her books and movies. Alan had never been too vain to acknowledge her need for financial independence. Sometimes her contribution to their finances had been essential. And she never felt the need to account for her spending.

Duncan commented on the money she spent on clothes though he expected her to appear in public as a jeweled accessory by his side. He didn't pay those bills but noted the envelopes from Macy's and Saks when he surveyed the mail Hilma put on the credenza in the entryway for his convenience.

"Mr. Perry prefers to go through the mail first," she had informed Mignon the first time Mignon had the audacity to take her own mail from the stack.

She had to hold onto her independence. She wrote to Harry and asked for money.

March 20, 1947
Dear Mignon,
   I am a bit uneasy about your finances, but you are in the best position to understand your needs. I will forward $10,000 today. Is there anything I can help you with?
   Warm Regards,
   Harry

She showed Duncan the letter. She wanted him to be aware of her personal assets and with her arrangements with Harry.

"Give me access to those accounts," he said reaching for the letter, towering over her. "I'll have my bank merge the accounts and your savings with mine."

"The letter is a private communication," she said, holding onto it. "And I've been managing my financial accounts for years." She garnered her courage. "The royalties from my books and my expenses for Woodsedge need to be separate from yours."

"Nothing should be separate." He laughed. "Finances aren't women's strong point. I'll relieve you of the burden." He smirked. "I'll manage all of it for you."

She stepped away from him. "I want to be in charge of it. I am perfectly able to manage it."

He gave her a thunderous look and stalked out of the room.

May 15, 1947

Dear Mignon,

I have sent your complete royalty statement and a check for $15,794,73. I hope this is what you wanted.

This does not include the royalties from *Five Passengers from Lisbon* which reviewers like and readers are buying. The timing for a setting different from your lovely old mansions with well-heeled occupants is perfect. Everyone is relieved about the end of the war but still aware of the men in their midst who fought it, and we are learning more and more about Europe during the Nazi occupation. The Red Cross ship as a setting gives them interesting information about those merciful transports, a bit of reality about the Nazis, along with the suspense and romance they expect from you.

Edna surmises from your letters that things are not easy. I am sorry. Is there anything we can do to help you? Perhaps you need a New York City vacation? You are welcome any time.

Warm Regards,

Harry

She tried to block the turmoil from her writing room. She needed to work no matter the circumstances. Life was tolerable only when she was writing. She could control the story. She could at least assure that the heroine found romance with the right man. She could use some of this real-life experience. She had written about affection and caring and gentle touch for so long, she had never imagined the kind of raw physical power that made a woman cringe and suffocated physical desire. The real-life experience though frustrated any creativity.

She began to dread hearing his car in the driveway and the front door opening. The quick, hard steps along the hallway. She couldn't help but remember how she had been warmed by Alan's arrival at the end of a day and Jericho's welcoming bark.

What had she done? How could she have been so naïve? What a romantic fog she had nurtured, believing in the unrealistic romance of her own books. Alan had told her more than once that she wanted to be a character in her own novels. "You want to be a strong in-charge woman like your Auntie characters, but pampered like your blond beauties, young and fragile, needing laudanum to calm their nerves and a doctor in attendance." She should have listened. She should have appreciated him.

She worked, plugging away at her writing to save her mind. Tried to create a story, to think about Gurney's Inn on Montauk, Long Island, and the cottage she had rented there just last year. Montauk. A good setting. She would put a beautiful old house on Montauk. A simple but spacious house with high ceilings, like the great houses of the nineteenth century. A brick house with luxuriant growth of wisteria clinging to the old bricks, walls surrounding it on three sides, shutting out the world, the sea at the back. A path would curve from the house to the Sound. Lilies, blue campanula, pink and purple lupin, and foxglove would fill the flower gardens.

Duncan wanted flowers arranged in the house every day. Lilies. The sainted Ann had loved the sweetness of lilies. For Mignon, the scent of death.

Writing and remembering Montauk and Gurney's Inn took her out of the present into her story-telling world. A terrace overlooked the Sound there. A grassy slope descended to the rocks and then to the sand at the water's edge. A sandy bathing beach and a modern boat house for the sailboat, a small yacht, and a couple motor boats for a perfect setting.

The ashtrays on her desk overflowed. She smoked half a cigarette and crushed it out. Lit another without thought. If she could get involved with her story, live in it, working out the mystery, she could survive another day. And she did. Working out sentences and finding words. Revising and rewriting. She fantasized about killing him with the revolver he kept in the drawer in the table beside his bed. Her heroines rarely used a gun though. Guns weren't her thing. But poison. Poisoning always created a good plot.

She longed for Alan's matter-of-fact calm and common sense. How tranquil their home had been compared to this tension-thick house where she monitored her conversation, wary of anything that might incite Duncan's explosions. Alan would have been surprised at her self-control. Stifling her spontaneity. Her off-the-cuff opinions.

"Mimi," he had said often. "Do you have to comment on everything? Do you have to interrupt during the news broadcast? Do you have to blurt out every notion? I missed half of what Murrow was saying."

Would Alan even believe it? Would anyone? Anything she said about Duncan would sound melodramatic. Was she melodramatic? She was beginning to doubt her own sanity.

The title of the novel would be *Another Woman's House.*

The villain, a beautiful blonde, a small-boned but perfectly formed woman with blue eyes and a kittenish, child-like appeal of innocence. All of it a facade. Her sweetness and appealing nature turn to vicious, cruel manipulation. Her face changes in an instant from smiling to piercing, cold eyes and curled lips. A furious look transforms her. She is not the person everyone sees. Alone with her in her fury, you see the venom in her stony eyes. The warmth turns to hatred. The public face is gone.

Mignon couldn't bear to think of the ramifications of another divorce. What would people say? Even friends would doubt her sanity. There would be a deluge of gossip and notoriety.

Duncan would never accept divorce. It would sully his reputation and erode that perfect persona he presented to his world. She was afraid of his reaction if she threatened divorce. He was unpredictable. She never knew when he would fly into a rage or if he would lash out with an open hand he raised and then lowered with a grimace of self-control.

She had to end this before the new year. She called Frank Barrett, her attorney and long-time friend in Stamford. "I'd like to have my marriage annulled."

"Not possible in New York," he said and explained the legalities of annulment. She was embarrassed, but desperate for advice. She told him everything.

"I'm surprised, Mignon, and very sorry. If you really are afraid of him, I suggest you leave quietly when he's in the city. Go to Woodsedge. Then I'll help you file for a divorce."

She made a plan. Alan would be proud of her not being impulsive. Mondays were especially long days for Duncan in the City. Plenty of time. She needed her typewriter, her working manuscript and paper, clothes and shoes enough for the two valises in her closet, and her leather cosmetic case. The rest could be collected later. Or a furious Duncan would probably have it sent. The day girl was busy with the laundry. Hilma could be counted on to go about her work and avoid her as usual. Or be smug and overjoyed if she discovered Mignon leaving.

Her hands shook as she pulled open drawers and took dresses off hangers, tossed clothes into valises. Her stomach roiled. How did she get to this place in what had been a decent life? The physical exertion helped. Two trips down the stairs to the back door and a waiting taxicab.

In one of her novels, the heroine would have turned and looked back. Big teardrops would have rolled down her cheeks from big blue eyes. Mignon didn't turn and look back. She didn't shed tears either. Only the heroines in her romances wept.

The next day Duncan's faithful man Raymond arrived at Woodsedge in the Lincoln Town Car. When she answered the doorbell, he greeted her, looking embarrassed. "Mr. Perry asked me to give you this personally," he said, handing her a letter. "I have your things," he added, pointing to the car in the driveway. Then he carried the boxes into the house. Everything from her closets and drawers, clothes, jewelry, even cosmetics thrown willy-nilly into boxes, no doubt by Hilma, happy to erase any trace of Mignon's short inhabitance of Mystic Brook Farm. When Raymond left, Mignon opened the letter. Duncan informed her that she would be hearing from his attorney. No need for personal communication. And that was that.

1947-48

Woodsedge

She wrote to Carmen to tell her she'd left him. Telephoned Faith to tell her she was back at Woodsedge. She escaped in work. Wrote to exhaustion.

She sent a draft copy of *Another Woman's House* to Harry. Then waited for his advice and revisions. She dedicated the novel to Harry and Edna for all their support and love that tumultuous year. The gossip had been vicious. They were by her side, supporting her.

Merry Christmas to Mignon alone at Woodsedge. A dreary holiday. Except for Faith and Gonnie, she didn't see anyone. Saturday, she listened to Milton Cross introduce the Met broadcast of *Il Trovatore*, remembering Alan's penchant for mezzo-soprano Margaret Harshaw and those winter Saturday afternoons—fireplace glowing, Alan ensconced in his chair, legs crossed, cigarette in one hand, conducting the music with the other.

When he was feeling especially successful after a long but productive day at work, he would put a recording of opera overtures or symphonies on the turntable. Beethoven's *Ninth* his favorite celebratory listen. He recognized all nine Beethoven symphonies with the opening chords. Those symphonies were the first record albums he bought when he surprised

Mignon with a Victrola for Christmas when they lived in Valentine.

The music was balm. They would look up from their chairs and smile at each other, silent, but connecting in some deep, but inexplicable way. She would forget her yearning for sex.

What did she love about him? He was obsessed with an ordered life. His methodical habits were boring, even annoying. But his calm and the quiet of their life together made writing possible and pleasurable.

"Phone him," Faith said. "He's aware of your separation from Duncan."

When her marriage to Duncan was the talk of New York, she had wanted Alan to know. She wanted him to know and be envious, but confessing failure was another matter. They hadn't been in touch those months of her impetuous courtship and marriage. Her loneliness superseded her pride.

"Happy New Year, Alan," she said when he answered.

"Mimi. How are you?" A smile in his voice. She felt the warmth, his concern.

"I'm at Woodsedge, as you no doubt know. Hiding from the world. Hiding from myself basically."

"I'm sorry. I truly am sorry things didn't work out the way you expected."

"I've decided to go to Reno to get a divorce. It's the six-week cure there. You may remember. And irreconcilable differences are sufficient grounds."

"Is there anything I can do to help? Should I come to Woodsedge?" He did sound concerned.

"No, but I appreciate the offer." She did wish he could come to her rescue like one of the heroes in her novels. "I have to cope with this mess alone."

"I'll be in Chicago. Phone me when you get back from Nevada. You know I care for you."

He had Aunt Nelle and Uncle Oscar, the opera in Chicago. He was absorbed in his job as he had always been. Obsessed, single-minded—she had often accused him of that. Did he miss her at all? She was incomplete without him. He could live without her. But he sounded sincere. Caring. Loving?

1948

The Flying W

The advertisement in *Vanity Fair* referred to the Flying W Ranch in Nevada as "a place to make ending a marriage easy."

"Make a reservation and get it over with," Faith said. "There is no point in trying to avoid publicity this time."

"You're right about that." Mignon was weary of the pretense and the secrecy involved in the previous divorces. "I'm not going to Arkansas to 'hide' in some 'undisclosed address' as the newspapers reported when I divorced Alan the first time. And I'm not going to stay in a shoddy hotel in Reno with the hoi polloi like the last time."

People in the publishing world in New York and the family and friends in Chicago and Lincoln would buzz with the scandal of another divorce no matter what she did.

The only grounds for divorce in New York state was adultery, and as far as Mignon knew, Duncan wasn't an adulterer. Mental cruelty and callous uncaring wouldn't count. Divorce wouldn't become final for a year after filing in New York. Nevada law granted divorce with the simple irreconcilable differences in six weeks, and she was desperate to rid herself of him.

The dude ranch divorce havens—nineteen of them in the Reno area—were supposedly ideal for avoiding notoriety and publicity. *That* was a fiction. Even Eleanor Roosevelt, visiting for some reason—Franklin was dead so not divorce—called the Flying W "a luxury dude ranch" in one of her magazine columns. Barbara Stanwyck had just left. Doris Day had been there a couple months before. Rita Hayworth bragged about divorcing Aly Khan at a dude ranch. All of this reported in gossip columns. Louella Parsons was especially keen on exposing the latest news about the movie stars in her monthly *Cosmopolitan* column. She called Reno "the city of broken vows."

What does one wear to a dude ranch? *Vogue* had recently published a story titled "Dude Ranch Chic." Boots, a western hat, a neck scarf, and denim shirt with pearl buttons. Maybe a leather skirt and jacket. Trousers with a matching jacket. Skirts, either touching top of the boot or just below the knee. Might as well play the part.

Number one dude wrangler, Bill McGee, met Mignon when she stepped off the staircase of the United Airlines flight from New York. He was what she expected in a cowboy—six feet tall, broad-shouldered, wearing Levi jeans and boots, a Stetson pushed back from his forehead to make the most of his broad smile, beautiful teeth, twinkling brown eyes.

"Mrs. Perry," he said, as he took her red makeup case with one hand and held out his other to shake. "Welcome to Nevada." With his hand on her arm, he guided her across the tarmac to the gate and through the small airport to a black limousine at curbside.

"It's about an hour and a half drive," he said as he pulled onto the highway.

It didn't require a response. Tired from the plane trip, emotionally drained from the hectic preceding days, she gazed out the window. The landscape on the sixty-mile drive to the ranch was as desolate and as lulling as the Sand Hills of Nebraska. A lone saguaro cactus appeared on the desert now and then instead of a cottonwood. An interesting setting for a novel, though this was one place in her travels she would not be tempted to use in her fantasy world. Besides, Faith got here first and featured the place in her *Temporary Address: Reno.*

Bill spoke with a deep, slow drawl the entire hour and a half. "I hope you like horses. A typical day at the ranch is horseback riding in the morning, with cowboy escorts, of course. After lunch you can make a trip to town for shopping—or a visit to your lawyer." He laughed. "Cocktails at 5 o'clock, dinner at 7:00, and then, if you like, a car will take you to a casino in Reno or Carson City. You can gamble and dance. Lots of camaraderie with the other ladies. Handsome, young cowboy escorts to keep you company."

The soothing monologue dispersed all the tension of packing and leaving Woodsedge for New York City, taxiing to the airport with the din of honking horns and the traffic, and then the long flight across country. It all just seeped away.

Finally, in the distance she saw lights breaking the deep dark that had descended on the desert. The ranch house had multiple wings with large windows lighting the night. An oasis.

McGee pulled into the driveway, got out, came around, and opened the rear door for her. He took the leather bags out of the trunk, escorted her to the door of the ranch house, and handed her the makeup case. A young cowboy met them at the door, loaded the luggage on a rack, and led Mignon down the hallway to her suite. She glanced into the living room as they passed. A slumber party atmosphere. A gaggle of women in colorful silk lounging pajamas draping themselves over the velvet cushions of sofas, drinks and cigarettes in hand, apparently home from their evening at the casinos.

An enormous bed piled high with red and gold satin pillows dominated her bedroom. If she wearied of socializing, she could retreat to this lavish apartment with a bathtub the size of a small pool and—aha—a separate dressing room with full-length mirror and a walk-in closet.

She slept. The first deep sleep in weeks. Relief. An other-worldly place. Far from real life. She woke early and donned jeans and boots for the scheduled trail riding.

Horseback riding. She felt excited with the anticipation. The solid feel of the horse beneath her and the wind in her hair again. She thought about Father and their riding together those many years ago in Nebraska —young, carefree, Daddy's girl. And Mother. Horrified by Mignon's flaunting of all conventions. Embarrassed by the two divorces and now the scandalous divorce ranch. Their phone conversation hadn't been pleasant.

"Oh, my goodness, Mignon," she had said when Mignon told her. "Not another divorce. There must be some way you can make this marriage work. Less than a year! You've given it less than a year."

Mignon had no doubt Father would have supported her with his "you have to do what you have to do" philosophy. He would have been happy that she had sense enough to get out of the marriage to Duncan as soon as she did.

The amused and tolerant cowboys were waiting patiently to introduce the chattering, giddy city women to horses and to riding. One cowboy for each rider.

"Mrs. Perry, I'm your companion for the day — Roger Allen." He shook her hand.

"Whew," he said with a broad smile, as she checked and readjusted the stirrups to accommodate her short legs. "A veteran." She was rusty, but she was experienced.

She mounted easily without Roger's help and grabbed the reins.

"Let's go then." Her cowboy moved ahead of her, and they left the others behind.

She hadn't been on a horse since Monterey five years before, but it was her father she could hear: "Mimi, sit up straight. Relax. Don't pinch with your knees. Let your legs hang down from the hip. You're tense. Let your arms swing. Let your shoulders work like a hinge."

She'd been so immersed in city life, she had forgotten the exhilaration of riding, the pure joy of galloping through the countryside, moving in concert with a beautiful animal.

"I'll definitely see to it that you're my assignment in the weeks ahead," Roger assured her as she dismounted at the end of the morning.

Lunch introduced intriguing companions. Mignon took an empty chair and sat down at a table without realizing that the stunning, dark-haired beauty next to her was Hedy Lamarr.

"My third vacation here." LaMarr laughed, waving her cigarette in a pearl holder. "Shedding husbands has become a habit."

Hedy Lamarr. Married to an arms dealer in Austria. Purportedly entertaining Hitler in their castle. The subterfuge and skill escaping. Now Hollywood stardom. This was just another drama in her life. She played the role effortlessly, spontaneously—smiling. So unlike Mignon. Guilt-ridden. Incapable of rejecting or escaping her Methodist Nebraska background. Her mother hovering like a specter with admonitions about the sanctity of marriage. But Mignon Edwards the writer hovered too. Observing the scene while she lived it. The Muse always awake.

"I am so glad I found this place," the woman sitting on the other side of Mignon gushed. "What fun. What freedom. I am so tired of the wagging tongues and the moral police at home.

"And you!" She pointed her finger. "*You* are the woman Fanny Butcher described as 'chic and charming' in her *Chicago Trib* 'Literary Spotlight.' Tell us how a Nebraska girl learns to shop for designer clothes." She babbled. "Fanny says you are a dashing figure on Park Avenue. And what about sharing a hairdresser with the Duchess of Windsor? Do you ever see her?"

Is that who she was? Fashion symbol? Park Avenue socialite with Nebraska clinging to her? What about Writer? Wife?

Emmy Wood, owner of the Flying W, appeared at the door and saved her from responding. "I'm leaving for Reno at 2 o'clock. You should meet with your attorney this afternoon, Mignon, get the process going. Anyone else need to see their attorney or want to shop?"

They stubbed their cigarettes out and got up from the table in one coordinated movement, like a dance troupe. Separated in gabbing groups. Off to play.

In the late afternoon, they gathered for cocktails. Dressed to the nines. The usual women's competition thrived here as it did everywhere. Who was wearing what designer? Whose jewels were fake? Who had the most lavishly embroidered shirt, the most elaborate Western attire? Women dressed for each other as much as to entice the admiration of men. Here, it was the handsome young men hired to mill around and join them at the bar or table.

They ate in an elegant dining room, velvet drapes, brocade upholstered chairs, the food prepared by a French chef, served by waiters in black ties and starched white shirts, each course paired with an appropriate wine. The conversation got louder as the meal progressed. The gaggle grew wine-giddy.

A niggling worry about the cost of this pampering invaded Mignon's fog. She should contact Harry to find out if *Another Woman's House,* her Duncan year novel, was selling.

After dinner, black limousines pulled up to the door for escorted rides to Reno or Carson City. They could choose to gamble or dance. Dance partners were plentiful. It was an entertaining place, a continuous party of sorts and definitely a diversion, bordering on a sinful diversion.

Mignon fell asleep easily after dancing for hours and drinking countless martinis, but she woke in the middle of the night. Real escape wasn't possible. How had she managed to make such a mess of her life? What did people think of her? She hated Duncan. Hated herself for swallowing his flattery. For rushing into that marriage. For her obsession with sex. She had made herself sick with longing for sex. Marriage was more than that animal coupling with Duncan. Nothing tender or loving. He was too bent on satisfying his need to care about her. Why hadn't she valued the good in her marriage to Alan? He was faithful. Loving. They respected each other. He didn't need to dominate her.

A letter from Carmen didn't gladden her heart.

> March 15, 1948
> Dear Mignon,
> I'm having a difficult time envisioning you at the Flying W. It sounds like living in a fantasy though I understand your not wanting to repeat the experience in Arkansas. The Flying W is quite the distance from New York City and Woodsedge. AND

your rather staid and sophisticated life there. I can't imagine the kind of women you describe.

The coddling of the rich and famous obviously has no bounds at these divorce ranches. No service too small to tender. It sounds liberating in a naughty sort of way. I have too many scruples and am too solidly grounded in the influences of childhood in University Place next to the Methodist Church to enjoy that kind of liberation!

I know you enjoy hobnobbing with some of the Hollywood stars, and you've always enjoyed dancing. Just don't wander too far from the proper persona your writing world knows and abandon the woman your friends love.

Love, Carmen

Thank you, Carmen, for the reminder about our upbringing. Our parents' morals and mores. And the indoctrination of Wesley Methodist. You might have just as well included the sanctity of the marriage vow and our parent's example and expectations.

Despite the circumstances, the six weeks in that bizarre and other-worldly place sped by. Routines take over everywhere. She rode horseback every morning. Galloped over the meadow and into the mountains. The exercise, mountain air, and pure pleasure healed. She joined the other divorcees for cocktails and evenings at Lake Tahoe. Enjoyed the unique experience of living with women. A throwback to sorority days. And probably as unrealistic.

Emmy pampered her guests right to the last day.

"Congratulations," she said as she accompanied Mignon down the courthouse steps in Reno. "You are free."

Mignon stepped lightly down that broad concrete stairway, the sun on her face. Relief like shedding a heavy winter coat. All of it unlike the gloom and sadness she had felt when she divorced Alan. Both times.

1948-49

Never Look Back

The one thing Mignon could control in her life was her writing. She lived in her novel as she'd often done in the past—*Never Look Back*. She was Maggie boarding a plane in London in a dark blue traveling suit and matching cloche with a red handbag, en route to New York City.

The stewardess, in her crisp summer beige uniform with perky hat, met Maggie and the other passengers at the door. "Welcome to Pan Am and thanks for flying with us." Maggie did enjoy flying and settled into her seat comfortably, relieved to be leaving London and on her way home. She became uneasy when the NO SMOKING FASTEN YOUR SEAT BELT signal flashed on and off soon after takeoff. A storm. The stewardess served dinner when the storm finally passed. After a leisurely dinner and a cigarette with a second glass of merlot, Maggie retired. The stewardess helped her into a berth, closed the heavy curtains, and wished her pleasant dreams.

That—her recent flight from Las Vegas to New York City sans the berth. Berths available only on transatlantic flights. But writers have license.

When the plane landed the next morning, Bill stood at the bottom of the ramp smiling, resplendent in a seersucker suit and a Panama hat.

"I'm glad to see you, Maggie."

Hands on the typewriter, gazing out the window, she worked at describing Bill and thought about Alan who had met her plane from Las Vegas and drove her from the airport to the Chatham. He was exactly as he had always been. Kind voice. Gentle firm hand. As serene and composed as always. What madness made her believe she needed more than that? Why hadn't it been enough? She wrote it:

He was exactly as he'd always been. She was going to cry; the kindness of his voice, the gentleness of his hand had done it. It wasn't easy to guess what he was thinking as they drove into the city from the airport. He was as serene and composed as always.

The penthouse apartment in the St. Regis was twenty-one stories up and surrounded on three sides by terraces planted with shrubbery, hedges, and enormous clay flowerpots. It had a small library, bedroom with dressing room, dining room, and wide French doors from the living room to the terrace. The apartment looked down on Fifth Avenue with a breath-taking panoramic view of New York— Radio City beyond the greens of Central Park to where the Hudson River glimmered.

She set the novel in her Chatham apartment, thought about Woodsedge and realized the enormity of what she had tossed aside. What insanity. Not just a man, but a place, a home, a community. Security. She was overwhelmed with homesickness for Woodsedge with its gracious, high-ceilinged rooms, the gardens, the lovely old driveway with its great maples making a leafy arch.

She finished, sent the novel and the draft to Carmen.

October 15, 1948

Dear Mignon,

I'm happy you're able to concentrate on your writing. Living alone and focusing on your work may be a healthy way to sort things out.

Thanks for sharing the work in progress. Escaping to the Caribbean in this new novel must be palliative. You've done your usual mastery of the setting. I can feel those hot, tropical trade winds rattling the palm trees and whispering among the rustling banana leaves. The thunder, lightning, torrential rain in the first pages certainly portend storm. Perhaps yours too—your writing, a refuge from the storm of grief and loneliness. *House of Storm* —great title.

I hear you in your heroine's words: "It was a sensible, rational kind of marriage. We were best friends. I could have been cared for and happy the rest of my life."

I always thought you and Alan were good friends. It's a firm basis for a marriage. Charles and I have always been friends. Cantankerous friends at times. It's not perfect, but it gets you through the bad times. I think you need him.

Your heroines often say, "I will be taken care of." The story often ends with the appearance of the second man, a startlingly handsome Byronic type. I would say not unlike Alan!

Thinking of you—

Carmen

Mignon sat down at her desk, gazed at the city skyline from the penthouse, then lit a cigarette, and called Alan to wish him a Happy Thanksgiving. "I miss you."

"I miss you, too."

"Miss our life." She paused. Inhaled. "Would children have made a difference?"

"You know I enjoy children. But we settled that in the beginning, Mimi. It wasn't possible. For either of us. You should accept that."

"I know. I'm thinking about your discontent. I hated your discontent. Your restless moving from one job to another, one place to another. Always discontent. Always looking for something different."

"Mimi, you didn't mind the moves those early years. You were anxious to see the world, as I recall. Couldn't wait to leave Nebraska. You traveled without me every time you needed a new setting for a novel."

"I know. I live my books. That's why I need new places, new people, new experiences."

"I made a good living with all those job changes. You even had your dream house. The house you said you could live in forever."

"I know. I know. I do love that house. Woodsedge is home."

"Love the house . . . love your work. You live in your books."

"I do live in my books. But we were supportive, weren't we? I did move with you even when I wasn't happy about it. I appreciated your encouraging my writing. That you respected it. Took it seriously."

She heard the flick of the lighter and the exhale of his cigarette. She could almost smell the smoke.

"This isn't a novel though, Mimi. You can't romanticize our life. I'll never be that man you create in your romances. But I am aware of your needs."

The inhale and the exhale again. "I can't change what I am. Nothing will change in that regard. We faced that for years."

She could see him, shirt sleeves rolled up, leaning against the wall, phone in one hand, cigarette in the other. She could see his frown. His slow smile.

"We did manage. Most of the time. My skipping from job to job. Your need to put writing first. It worked."

"I think we need each other."

The next day she sent Harry the drafts of the two novels she had worked on that summer and fall—*House of Storm* and *Never Look Back*. For years Harry had cautioned her about establishing a formula—the older woman, a spinster, aunt, or companion, who may or may not be diabolical, and the bright and beautiful young protagonist attracted or involved with two handsome men, one of them always Machiavellian, the other calm, dependable, modest but brilliant. *Engineers are unique men,* she had written in her first publication. And the stories sold.

"Even your protagonists who have spirit and independence always *need* a man," one of her critics complained. True. Even Carmen said that her male heroes always arrived to save the day. But she was comfortable with the formula. With that kind of life. And the stories sold.

Alan met her at Woodsedge. They had a quiet Christmas. Light snow fell on the pines, gently covering the sweeping lawn. No wind. A storybook Christmas Eve setting, a Norman Rockwell painting.

Bowing to Mother and Father's Kentucky heritage, they ate corn bread stuffing with the turkey, served on their wedding china, and drank champagne from the wedding Waterford. Red candles on the table for Christmas, silver candles for their twenty-fifth anniversary.

Alan dragged the ten-foot-tall Virginia Pine in from the front porch where they had deposited it after an afternoon trip to the village tree market. He struggled to set it up in the bay window, smiling as she directed from the sidelines. "It's leaning to the left. No, no, too far to the right. Move it closer to the window . . . closer."

Then she climbed the stairs to the attic and, one-by-one, carried to the living room the boxes of ornaments she had collected on their travels and hadn't opened for years. Each fragile memento wrapped in white tissue paper.

Alan brought a ladder in from the garage, and she held it to stable his climb and his reach as he attached the angel Carmen had given them for a wedding gift to the top of the tree. Then he began to wind the strings of lights from the treetop. She stood beneath him. They clipped lights, working together, winding the cords around the tree.

As he stepped down from the ladder and moved it aside, she had a flashback. "Remember that first glorious Christmas in Chicago with your Aunt Nelle and the concerts and *Die Fledermaus* on New Year's Eve."

"We have the recording." Concentrating, he methodically thumbed through the record jackets in the cabinet where he had arranged his operas alphabetically by composer when they first moved into Woodsedge nine year before. "Found it." He smiled with satisfaction, held up the colorful jacket photo of Mary Garden, took the recording out of the sleeve, and put it on the Victrola.

The Chicago Symphony's *Fledermaus* wafted through the living room, and Mignon reminisced. "Remember that awful Christmas in Valentine and the blizzard and the roads closed so we couldn't go to Lincoln for Christmas."

"Yes, and you ranted and raved. Cried with frustration about our being trapped in 'the nowhere,' even though for weeks you had been complaining and resenting Helen's elaborate plans for the family Christmas."

"Remember Christmas in Paris. Montmartre and climbing to the Basilica and the vendors with roasted chestnuts and hot cider on the streets . . . and the sidewalk cafés, open in spite of the cold, coal-burning heaters set amidst the tables."

She remembered the exhilaration of that first trip to Europe, Alan trudging along, amused with her Paris agenda and her passion to experience all of it, everything she'd ever read about. She remembered their communion of pleasure in the museums: The Louvre, Musée d'Orsay, de Montmartre, de l'Orangerie. His interest in the art, especially the sculpture, had taken her by surprise. He'd never understood her idolizing artists.

They wound strings of red and green lights around the tree, *Fledermaus* in the background, their reflections and the colored lights mirrored in the window glass and on the snow outside. Alan grasped her hand as their strings met at the front of the tree and pulled her into his arms. They waltzed to Mozart, stepping one-two-three, one-two-three, in wide sweeps across the living room, their hands and feet in sync, their bodies remembering the moves.

Woodsedge and Alan and two new novels—A New Year.

Acknowledgments

My gratitude first to June House for introducing me to Mignon Eberhart and inspiring me to write about her. Then . . .

Thanks—

—To my beloved Bards writing group, here and in heaven.

—To early readers Barbara Peterson, Marlys Guimaraes, Bonnie Wells, Ann Marie Boyle, Candace Simar, and Martha Burns.

—To Candace Simar and Camp Candace writer friends for advice and encouragement.

—To Sheila O'Conner for inspiration and for the pleasure in the learning journey.

—To Jeanne Cooney and Candace Simar for years of encouragement.

—To Sally Wills for urging me to "just do it (write a novel) and enjoy doing it."

—To Ann Marie Boyle for cheering me on with advice about all things—creative and practical.

—To Sharon Harris for superb copy editing, line editing, and proofing. For forcing me to give the dog more space and to birth the baby after the pregnancy pronouncement.

—To Tarah Wolff for the beautiful cover art and for bringing this novel to fruition.

Finally, my thanks to my Professional Engineer spouse for his advice in some obvious sections of this novel and for always having understood that a woman needs a room of her own. And thanks to our daughters for reading everything I write and shouting their support.

Rick Cypert's biography, *America's Agatha Christie: Mignon Good Eberhart Her Life and Work,* and Mignon Eberhart's novels were invaluable resources.